PRAISE FOR HANNA PARK

The prose is sensual and glittering, reveling in the romance of green Irish landscapes—home to witches and faeries—and Gaelic lilts.

— FOREWARD REVIEWS

There's something incredibly immersive about The Scald Crow, a book that throws you headfirst into its world without hesitation. It's rich, atmospheric, and filled with a distinct voice that sets it apart.

— BOOKSIRENS' READER

Hanna Park writes like she's sitting across from you at a pub, telling ghost stories between pints. Sometimes poetic, sometimes blunt, always immersive.

— LITERARY TITAN

THE SCALD CROW

A BEYOND THE FAERIE RATH NOVEL
BOOK 1

HANNA PARK

BAISONG PRESS

This novel is a work of fiction. While some characters are inspired by Irish mythology and historical figures from the 1500s, they have been adapted and fictionalized for the purposes of storytelling. Any historical references have been interpreted creatively, and this book is not intended to be a factual or scholarly representation of history or mythology.

All characters, events, and settings are either purely fictional or used fictitiously. Any resemblance to actual persons, living or dead, is entirely coincidental.

The Scald Crow

Copyright © 2025 by Hanna Park

All rights reserved.

Cover Art by *Niki White* www.nikiawhiteart.com

Visit Hanna Park at www.hannapark.ca

Baisong Press, Box 291, Port Carling, ON P0B1J0

First Edition, 2025

Digital ISBN, 978-1-0689975-0-1

Paperback ISBN, 978-1-0689975-3-2

Paperback Large Print ISBN, 978-1-0689975-6-3

Hardcover ISBN, 978-1-0689975-9-4

Published in Canada

to those who believe

1

Ireland is a mystical place where Faerie belief lives. *Na Daoine Maithe*—the Good People, the Other Crowd, Them––referred to with reverence and fear.

Calla

"I'm sorry, lass. There's nothing I can do. The rental company wants the vehicle back to Dublin." The tow truck driver gazed toward me through warm blue eyes, my broken rental car hanging from the tow bar of his mud-splattered truck.

"Dublin? But I'm going to Ardara." How could I have known the flock of black-faced sheep dotting the sloping green hills would scatter across the road the exact moment I reached for my cold cup of double-double dark roast coffee? I grappled with the steering wheel, twisting hard left and away from those deep, endearing eyeballs. Submerged axle-deep in the boglands? Well, I didn't expect that.

The car had bounced off the road, flew over the ditch, and lurched to a hard stop, deploying the airbag and knocking me senseless. I wrestled with the airbag, stabbing it with my handy dandy utility knife—something every woman should always carry.

"I'll run ye over to Donegal town, but I can no go to Ardara." The man scratched his forehead with grease-stained fingers. "There's a wee fair about today. Ach, but you'd need your wits about ye, lass. 'Tis a sharp crowd."

"A fair? No. I can't go to a fair, not like this." I extended my muck-stained hands. "Look at me. I can't believe this happened." I planted my hands on both sides of my face, dragging my fingers down my cheeks and spreading more muck.

"Aye. Aye." He turned to his flip phone, punching numbers with a fat finger. "Don't worry, lass. I'm after a mucker going your way."

"A mucker?" He didn't answer my question. He chatted into his phone, nodding his head with every pause while I relived my moment of despair.

The open window had offered the only means of escape. I scrambled head-first, fell flat on my face, and kissed a chorus of heather and heath. The peat gurgled its welcome, wrapping me in a wet blanket of earth and sea, wool, and wet dog. Slime oozed between my fingers. Yellow bees buzzed around my head.

The nice man spoke into his phone with a quick Irish lilt. I couldn't understand a word he said.

"To be sure, to be sure." He ended his call and then smiled. "It's sorted, lass. Oisin will come around the bend at any moment. He'd be happy to give you a wee lift. Aye, that he would. That he would." He nodded.

Shadowed thoughts filled my mind.

Would the water-breathing lung suck me into its depths, inhale the nutrients from my body, leaving my remains pickled for the next millennium? Or could the groaning mass be a portal into the underworld, a threshold between this world and the next?

"Oh-sheen?" My situation slammed me in the face. Somehow, the wrinkles on the tow truck driver's face lent some credibility to his character. But now my future lay in the hands of a man called Oh-Sheen.

"Aye, Oisin O'Donnell. Talk the hind legs off a donkey, that one. Those were likely his sheep after running ye from the road. Ach, nothing to be scundered about, lass. 'Twas an odd wind this morning likely unsettled the wee beasts." He lifted his nose, taking stock of the blowing currents.

"An odd wind? Okay. How will I know this Oisin fellow?" Hugging my backpack to my chest, I watched the man, my very only best friend in all of Ireland, climb into the cab of his tow truck.

The bog had determined my fate and spat me out. Knee-deep in the resinous heathland, I plucked one platform sneaker after another from the muck, launched myself forward, clung to the slippery bank, and discussed the rest of my life with the bees.

My thoughts scattered with the goddamn sheep.

"He'll be driving a tractor hauling a clatter of turf. You can't miss him. Now you stay put, lass. And he'll likely find you." He leaned out the window, then pulled away, leaving me in the middle of the road, wondering what in the world 'turf' could be.

The sheep, every single one of them, grazed away, oblivious to my predicament.

"Okay," I said into the cloud of exhaust, peering after my broken rental vehicle. I wondered how long I should wait. By my calculations, Ardara was another hour away by car. The wind intensified, whistling over each blade of grass. I planted my hand on my head, saving my ball cap just in time.

I looked in every direction, searching the glacial landscape for any sign of life. White cotton balls danced on long stems. Mats of heather blanketed the rolling slopes. Who'd have thought a watercourse of muck would flow beneath those vibrant banks? I swallowed hard, appreciating that dangerous beauty for the first time.

I walked back and forth, pacing from one side of the road to the other. No tractor. No trailer. No Oisin. I dropped my backpack onto the pavement.

The clouds shifted, blocking the midday sun. The sheep lost interest and wandered far and away, one by one. Two magpies jumped onto the road—one for sorrow, two for joy. I repeated the familiar nursery rhyme in my head. The curious birds pecked the earth, swiveling their pretty heads in every direction.

A fast-moving vehicle loomed larger by the

second. Hope flirted with my heart when the engine screeched, protesting the driver's heavy foot. I glanced toward the gurgling bog, unable to commit to another mud bath.

Tires whirred, grinding the pavement. The car's rear end swerved sideways, and the driver emerged from the sporty car.

My mouth dried. My heart fluttered. I looked up and up again at the long drink of water. Formed from the crags of Iron Age rock, the man embodied the essence of an ancient Celt.

"Would ye be the wee lass in distress?" His voice painted images of misty glens and shadowed lakes, cloud-capped mountains, and rolling green hills—Ireland, the Emerald Isle, a land of a thousand hellos, or something like that.

Dear God, I hoped that wasn't true. I had banked on some anonymity here—a land where no one knew who I was or what I was––the strange girl who saw things others didn't. *I have a gift. I call it a curse.*

"Are you Oisin?" I realized he wasn't driving a tractor or hauling a load of turf. His attire suggested someone else. Tan cargo pants, snugged tight over thick hips, complemented the khaki-colored combat boots. My gaze followed each button of his matching button-down shirt. Hard muscle shaped the canvas fabric and kept it wrinkle-free. He exuded a rugged charm belonging to the wilderness or a desert storm. He seemed a man not to be underestimated.

"No. I'm Colm. Colm O'Donnell. Oisin's my brother. It sounds like ye got into a bit of trouble." He lifted his eyebrows, his blue eyes catching me in the riptide of a turquoise sea.

"I did. Yes. Well, thanks. You, Colm O'Donnell, are a lifesaver." I lifted my shoulders and preened like a delicate little dandelion.

"You're a bit wet." Pink waves flooded his face--the moment etched itself forever into my mind until my realization of my situation crashed down on me again. I could look. I couldn't touch.

"I lost control of the car. Crashed into the bog." I plucked a loose twig from my sleeve, scrunching my nose at the rising stench.

"Aye, are ye all right then?" He towered over me, ravishing me with more than his scent.

"I'm fine." I gazed into those eyes. Oh yeah, that man could easily rob me of my soul.

"I'm sorry, luv, but have we met before?" He blinked once, then twice, his head tilted perfectly so. Copper pennies fell from the sky, framing his long face, full lips, and square jaw.

"No. You don't know me." My mouth dried,

and a vibration settled deep in my soul. I wondered whether he had been there forever.

"Aren't you the girl on the telly? You are, you're Calla Sweet." His knowing gaze set me back on my heels.

"Excuse me? How did you know?" My mouth dropped open, my gaze zeroing in on the big Irish lad standing in the middle of the clear blue sky.

"Look, it is you." He fact-checked his phone's browser and then offered his screen—my face smiled back.

"Well, yes." I pinched the bridge of my nose. How long could I play that charade? I was not that girl, not anymore. I had loved my job. Frontline anchor on a major television network, in line for advancement, my future golden. But then, after a few too many pops at the last office party—kaboom. Cat out of the bag, secrets revealed. It was bad enough when they believed my affliction was a simple case of Tourette's. *Breathe, Calla. Let. It. Go. It's a new day. It's a new life. That's a song, isn't it?*

"Are ye sure you're all right, luv?" He peered at me, his gaze inviting conversation.

"Oh yeah, just great. How about you?" I bobbed my head up and down, forcing a smile.

"My day just got immeasurably better." He extended his hand, a long, smooth hand with neat fingernails trimmed into perfect ovals.

I stared at his boots, noting the intricate ladder lacing finished with a neat bow. Not a speck of mud anywhere.

"I can't. I'm sorry. I don't do that anymore." There's no way I'd shake his hand—not now, not ever, uh-uh, no way. I bit down on the inside of my mouth, taking one giant step backward.

"You don't do what?" He seemed oblivious to my discomfort, ushering me toward the passenger seat with a sweep of his big hand.

I avoided answering his question.

"Are you sure about this? Do you have a towel or something?" I gestured toward my disastrous state: my bog-soaked sneakers, my denim street coat, and the dripping brown stench in them.

"Not to worry. It's a rental." He smiled through those shining baby blues and climbed in behind the wheel of the compact car.

"A rental?" I slithered into the bucket seat, setting my backpack on the floor. I inhaled his scent—all sunshine, lollipops, and hot chocolate swirling in minty froth.

That life-changing moment, when disaster struck, floated through my mind.

"We wish you the best of luck in your future en-

deavors. You showed such promise, dear. We are sorry things didn't work out."

"Excuse me?"

"Budget cuts, dear. Your position has been terminated."

I couldn't sugar-coat that, no matter how hard I had tried. I chewed my lower lip, quelling the heat gathering beneath my eyelids. I would not cry. It was only a job—it was all I had.

I left my career behind and trudged out the door. A cardboard box packed with my laptop, my coffee mug, and the photo of my adopted family— the chances of finding another position in the broadcasting industry were slim to none. People talked. They didn't whisper. They shouted it for the world to hear. Snide comments between friends—not friends, not anymore. And word traveled fast, Calla Sweet, the crazy girl. She's trouble. She's troubled. That's what they thought. And I take all the blame. I could not deny it. I said things, blurting out the obscenest prophecies at the most inopportune times. At first, people found it funny, but then it morphed into something ugly. I made them afraid. That's what I did.

"The sheep scared ye off the road, did they?" His voice danced with my heart while my mind searched for answers I couldn't find.

I wouldn't recognize a solution if it smacked me in the nose. Let's be honest. My life was a fucked-up mess I was running from. *Keep your mouth shut, Calla Sweet—my mantra from now on.* I'd learned my lesson well, to coin the phrase.

"You could say. This is a rental, huh? Are you visiting Ireland?" I twined my fingers together, reminding myself again. I could look. I couldn't touch.

"Aye, for another week. A wee vacation, visiting the family." The deep tenor of his voice held my attention.

"You live in Canada, I take it?" I presumed from his comments and his immediate recognition of my smiling face. I shifted in my seat, sending whiffs of bog stench throughout the vehicle.

"Nova Scotia for the past seven years." One lustrous curl fell onto his brow. Copper highlights, auburn lowlights. Just wow.

"Hmm." I removed my ball cap, unleashing the Kraken. Untamed and wild. Some would say unruly. My hair always had and always would live a life of its own.

"Well, let's get on then. Where are you staying?" He gunned the motor, his eyes shimmering.

Who has eyes so blue? I shook off the enchantment. The sooner I arrived at my destination, the better.

"The Black Horse Pub. Do you know it?" My destination rolled off my tongue. Since when had I become one of those friendly people?

"Aye." He rested his left hand on the stick shift —no jewelry. "My family lives close by. My brother owns the bakery in Ardara. You'll have to try the sticky buns. Tell him I sent you." He dropped the gearshift into overdrive, rocketing the little car to the moon.

"Your family?" My stomach fluttered and then groaned. When had I last eaten? When was the last time I sat that close to a man?

He smelled so good. Clean laundry and spearmint. Every time he smiled, his teeth sparkled. The insanity of my situation dawned on me. Twenty-nine years old and still a virgin. How pathetic.

"A big Irish family. Seven boys, Hugh Jr. and Tadgh are identical twins, and the rest are Irish twins. All of us were born within five years of each other." The crooked grin on his face told a happy tale.

"Must have been wild." I gathered my hair behind my head, twisting the black mass over one shoulder. "Having such a big family? Especially on the holidays." I swallowed the lump in my throat and opened the passenger window, inviting the swirling wind.

"Aye. I don't often get back." His rough tone caught me off guard. His eyes changed from soft blue to icy glaciers, signaling the end of the conversation.

In an instant, I realized how unapproachable he had become. There was something dark and almost terrifying in the set of his jaw. I shifted to the edge of my seat, distancing myself from him. What kind of fool would get into a car with a stranger?

"Do you have a family of your own?" I dug deeper despite the shiver running down my spine.

"No, lass. Love has never found me." The dark force lifted, and light returned to his eyes, the demon releasing him from its grip. "Have ye been to my wee country before?" His facial muscles relaxed, and he smiled, oblivious to my horror.

"No, I'm holding the V-card on that one." I looked out the window at waves upon waves of wildflowers, at undulating hills and rocky outcrops, the wind buffeting my face. My stomach flipped sideways, and a familiar warmth surrounded me, raising my heartbeat into a pounding echo only I could hear.

The sun moved, and the world dimmed. The haar crept over the fields, the sea fog coming for me alone. My mind had left my body, the connection to the other side absolute, opaque, and somewhat obscured. A crow, all-seeing and all-knowing, flew through the half-light over mountain and sea, following its path. I had closed my eyes and focused on the one part remaining the same—my pounding heart.

My therapist called it disassociation, a disconnect between my mind and the world around me, a needed escape from reality. Nope, not what that was—that was a full-on, out-of-body experience, and the most profound sense of foreboding came with it. I had learned not to fight the sensations. Clenching my hands into fists didn't help. The scourge swallowed me every time.

The fog lifted, leaving behind dew-laden blades of grass dusted with diamond jewels. I pinned my lips together, breathed through my nose, and let the tide wash away. That was the way of it—waking up to a brand-new day with a sad, sad secret. Those otherworldly sensations had been mine forever. What they meant or why they happened remained a mystery.

He hummed a melodic tune, unaware of my absence. Whatever ghosts he lived with were his alone. I had my problems to deal with. I glanced at his watch—thirty minutes left of the joy ride to paradise. I calmed my racing heart and reminded myself to be friendly. What could it hurt?

"What do you do for yourself, Colm? Tinker? Tailor? Soldier? Spy? Sheep farmer?" I gave him the biggest smile in the whole fucking world.

"I have a tree farm in Nova Scotia." Shadows flickered in those baby blues.

Something didn't sit right. The way he dressed, for one. I pressed for more.

"You don't look like a tree farmer." I raised my eyebrows, staring him down. His smirk raised another red flag, one of many I had ignored on this journey. "What kind of tree farmer wears combat boots?"

"I was once with the *Sciathán Fianóglach an Airm*." He spoke the Irish language with a smooth lilt. His charming demeanor would captivate any other woman. "It means the Army Ranger Wing, a special unit within the Irish Army." He veered right, missing a pothole in the road.

"You said 'once.' Why did you leave?" I regretted my question. Expressing interest could only lead to complications I was unprepared for.

"I found myself at odds. It was better to make a change." He tilted his head, his voice so soft I craned to hear. "And now, I own a wee farm in Nova Scotia."

"You're serious? You farm trees?" A nurturing horticulturist? A spear-throwing warrior or an axe-wielding combatant, given his Viking size frame.

"Aye." He refused to meet my gaze, but the smile on his lips confirmed my suspicions.

"Are you a dangerous man, Colm O'Donnell?" I studied him, looking for a reaction. He gave nothing away.

"No, *mo grhá*." He cut left at the upcoming roundabout. The welcoming sign showed a castle and read Donegal, Historic Town.

"I hope you don't mind. I need to make a stop." Colm braked the car and pulled off the road into an automotive parts depot. Behind a high chain-link fence, the metal roof of an industrial building showed.

"I don't mind." I settled deeper into the seat.

He climbed from the car, his long strides taking him across the parking lot. Moments later, he returned, carrying a small cardboard box.

"Would you like a coffee or perhaps tea? The toilet?" He placed his hands on the car door, leaned in, and killed it with a brash smile.

"I'm fine, but thanks." I couldn't imagine stripping out of and back into my soiled undergarments. I wanted a hot shower and a bar of soap.

He returned to his seat, filling the vehicle with homey goodness even my bog-soaked stench couldn't squash.

He shifted gears and followed the slow-moving traffic along the river's winding banks. I hung my head out the window, following the flight of a great egret swooping low over the gentle banks.

"One of many fairs in Ireland." He nodded toward the intersection, a cobblestone diamond bordered by three merging lanes of traffic, where a gathering was underway.

Medieval tents, with flags billowing atop pointed spires, gave the market fair a pagan atmosphere. The salty sea breeze mingled with the lilt of so many voices.

"Aye, ye best have your wits about ye. 'Tis a sharp crowd." I grinned, giving my best imitation of my very only best friend in all of Ireland.

"Not bad." He locked eyes with me, his smile warm and welcoming.

I looked away, my gaze following a clown on stilts juggling red balls high into the air. A woman gestured wildly toward a fishmonger, filleting a large fish with a bloodied knife while his helper scooped blue-shelled mussels into clear plastic bags.

"Donegal Castle up ahead." His melodic lilt was a constant distraction, capturing more than my gaze.

"A real castle?" My desires wandered with the winding road. I wondered what it would be like to play in the castle dungeons with a man like him. I kept that thought to myself.

"There's not much left of O'Donnell's castle—the trip staircase, the ground floor. But the restoration keeps many of the original features." His rumbling voice caressed my heart.

I stayed there a moment too long.

"A relative, I take it?" We sat in backed-up traffic, the stone walls of Donegal Castle looming ahead.

"It's complicated, but yes. From way, way back." His eyes filled with shadows, and his grip tightened on the steering wheel. The car inched forward, passing dimly lit pubs overflowing with patrons. Cafe tables sat opposite lace-covered windows—restaurants served all-day breakfasts, scones, and tea. Shop windows stared back, showcasing everything leprechaun and everything green. A Gypsy woman sat on a three-legged stool on the wide sidewalk, working a little girl's hair into delicate braids.

"You're lucky." I envied him. Grounded in this land, his lineage ran deep from one century to the next. "I have no one," I murmured under my breath. My ancestry remained a mystery, one I hoped to discover. My adoptive parents' faces flashed before my eyes. I missed them. They were all I had.

"Are ye hungry? Would you like to stop?" The hearty aroma of braised stew and the comfort of crispy beer-battered fish and chips floated through the open window.

"Maybe a rain check, huh?" I plucked the stretchy spandex, showing off the brown stain climbing the length of my leggings. Microbes of E. coli crawled over my skin. I gazed at the muck beneath my fingernails.

"You're traveling alone, *mo grhá*? No partner? No husband?" His glance expressed more than a passing interest.

I hesitated, unwilling to divulge my current status. If he looked, my secrets were there for all to see, but why would he bother?

"So, what do you do for fun, Colm? When you're not busy chopping down trees?" I chuckled under my breath.

"There's more to tree farming than that." The slight muscle tick in his jaw told me all I needed to know.

"Do you go to the pub? The gym. The squash courts? Do they play squash in Nova Scotia, Colm?" He had no intention of sharing the truth with me. And why would I care? I couldn't be with him, even if I wanted to.

"Have you heard of Hurling? Ireland's national sport?" He pressed the brake pedal, nosing into traffic—backed up in all directions.

"Oh my, God. Look at that." My breath hitched.

Plumed in ostrich feathers and draped in purple, two jet-black Friesians pulled a funeral hearse. The two powerfully muscled horses drew the death carriage along the cobblestoned street, carrying a flag-covered coffin on its last journey. The horses took my breath away, and the driver gave me pause—attired in black livery, his expression sober beneath his black top hat. The spoked wheels turned, marking the passage of time—for all of us.

I stared through the glass windows at the faces shrouded in sorrow. One carriage after another, followed by those walking. They sang hymns and recited prayers.

A woman turned away, hiding her child's face

from the funeral procession. Shopkeepers closed their doors and pulled down the shades.

My heart tightened, and my mouth dried as I comprehended the sight before me.

"Welcome to Ireland. We celebrate life, death, and everything in between." Colm inched the vehicle forward, keeping a sympathetic distance.

Keening cries chased the stately cortege. I looked overhead, discerning nothing. That soughing breath belonged to me.

"Calla?" Colm threw me a sidelong glance.

"I'm fine," I murmured. I closed my eyes, fighting the impending fog and the encompassing warmth threatening my sanity.

"You seemed far away. Is everything all right?" His voice lingered, filling the gaps in my mind with rough edges.

"Hurling, huh? Is that like cricket?" My voice caught in my throat. I focused my thoughts and drilled down on one thing only—shutting down the murmuring voice.

"Similar, but a faster game." He turned north at the castle keep, leaving Donegal town behind. The road tunneled through hedges of glorious blooms, lacy caps of purple, mop heads of pink. We passed white cottages roofed in thatch, each with tidy front yards.

"Do you play?" I knew a thing or two about the game. My favorite movie in all the world—*The Grand Seduction*. Is that what this was?

COLM

She tilted her head toward me, her gaze thoughtful.

Without a doubt, she was out of my league. How often had I turned the television to channel 549, hoping to glimpse Calla Sweet's newscast, and then clicked the remote, selecting a high-definition channel where I could appreciate her every nuance? The shimmer in her eyes. The curve of her lips.

How long had I been obsessed with her? I dismissed that thought. Obsession was for the crazed. I settled on star-struck, a more apt description of my infatuation.

Admiring her from behind the television screen was one thing, but meeting the captivating woman face-to-face proved another story. I tightened my grip on the steering wheel, dousing the flames of desire with hard denial.

I snuck a sideways glance.

Willowy, tall for a woman. Her skin glowed,

almost ethereal. She sat straight-backed, a shining black mane flowing over her shoulders. Even bathed in mud, she was more than beautiful. My heart coiled in my chest, yearning for her smile, for her gaze to reach mine. Beneath those wild locks lay a woman teeming with intelligence, a formidable adversary, more than a prize worth winning.

The car's front end dipped, hitting a pothole. She didn't notice.

I ran through the scenarios and found none worth considering. The sooner I rid myself of this pretty package, the better. Beautiful women spelled trouble. Nothing but trouble.

"Not much anymore. There's a big match every festival day. Ardara versus Glenties. It's a big event for Ardara." I tried to deny her hold on my heart and failed.

"Festival day?" She lifted her eyelashes, gazing through those famous dove-grey eyes.

"Aye, the Irish Calendar: quarter days, cross-quarter days. Bealtaine is the next one." I considered the days remaining and my flight schedule.

"Hmm, maybe." She stared me down but didn't commit. There was a definite reluctance in her gaze. Reading people was a way of life, but trusting my instincts kept me alive.

"What brings you across the pond? To Ireland?" I shifted gears and glanced her way. She looked down whenever she smiled. If someone caused the rare beauty pain, we should string them up and flay their skin from their bones. Rage ate away at my gut, every bone in my body ready to defend her from harm.

"Aren't you the curious one? You know what they say...curiosity killed the cat." She clenched her fingers, then released them. "I inherited a property outside of town from a relative I didn't know I had."

"Here in Ireland?" I couldn't hide my surprise. I had so many questions. I sensed she would shut me down if I pushed too hard.

She reminded me of a hummingbird––her movements were quick yet fluid. The melodic hum of her voice awakened every nerve in my icy heart. My sweating palms made holding the steering wheel difficult. Those physical reactions were unfamiliar to me. Long ago moments flashed through my mind, happy times when love mattered. Life changed me into something else, someone I didn't recognize.

"Abracadabra, right? It's one of those Faerie tale kinds of things. What brings you back to Ireland?" She shifted in the bucket seat. She crossed her legs, then uncrossed them.

Her every action spelled trouble.

"The ould one turned seventy last week. My father," I said, answering her curious gaze. "Tell me, who was your relative? If you don't mind me asking?"

My fingers itched to tame that glossy mane, to smooth the cowlick swirling the crown of her head. Her high cheekbones, elegant jawline, and pointed chin were testaments to the remarkable features of a people who once called Ireland their own—a people who prized physical strength and revered intelligence—an ancient civilization that battled for our homelands. Those memories had long since faded into the mists of time.

"Dermot Sweet of the Glengesh Pass, an older man who passed last year." She shrugged, lifting her palm in explanation.

"Hmm, I can't say I've heard of a Dermot Sweet, but I could ask around." My pulse hammered, and cold sweat collected beneath my collar. From the way her lips curved up, I had the distinct impression she found me amusing. And too pushy. I opened my mouth to say something but decided against it.

"Why?" Her piercing gaze read me like a book.

"We have the same last name. Maybe he's my biological father. It is odd, though." She surprised me by sharing more. "Here's a clue. I was born in Ireland and then adopted. There's no record of my birth. I arrived in Canada with a name—already labeled. Calla Rioghain Sweet." She moistened her bottom lip with the tip of her tongue.

"So, you're an Irish lass." I turned my gaze back to the winding road.

"Technically speaking." She gazed out the passenger window, lost in the rolling hills.

I wanted those soft eyes to melt into mine.

"Makes sense." I nodded, multiple scenarios buzzing in my head.

"What do you mean?" She rewarded me with another version of Calla Sweet—the look she would flash toward the television cameras. Her face revealed a myriad of emotions, reminding me of a storm cell swirling through winter clouds. There was a presence about her, something dark, something magical. The mystery intrigued me.

"You look Irish. Pale skin. Black hair. Ree-en is an Irish name. And your adoptive parents had no other information?" I tapped the steering wheel, my hunger rising. I told myself I was not one of those crazed stalkers star personalities protected themselves against.

"They died last year in a house fire. The records were burned." Her voice didn't waver. Her poker face hid all emotion.

"My condolences." The need to comfort her overwhelmed me. Indecision filled my mind, and doubt filled my heart. Her plight called to the hero in me, if one ever existed.

"Thank you," she whispered, her gaze meeting mine.

"And you left Canada? Just like that? I'm badgering, aren't I?" I accepted one thing. She could out-stare me any day of the week.

"There's nothing left for me there. I lost my job." She shrugged, yet her bottom lip quivered. "I got fired."

"Fired? From the network?" I gaped at her. I tuned in, captivated by her candid humor and her empathy. How often did she report tragedy after tragedy, with tears falling from her eyes? "Good evening, this is Calla Sweet on location." Her throaty voice flying through my surround sound system would stop me in my tracks. She mesmerized the world. What army of eejits fired a girl like her? "You were grand, Calla. I'm so sorry."

"Yeah, well, thanks, but I'm fine. It was a job. Besides, it's time for a fresh start." She swept her tongue across her lower lip.

"That's quite a start, moving to another continent, a place you've never been. All on your own." Making conversation with her came easily. I admitted, not one of my strong suits.

"Yes, well...no reason to stay is a reason to go." She pressed her lips together and then looked away.

"Well said." I gripped the wheel, hoping she would return to me.

"Hmm, thanks. I read that somewhere." Her voice faded, lost in the wind's sigh.

My blood chilled. The terror filled my mind as it so often had. Ciarán, my brother, the youngest O'Donnell, disappeared from the world of the living seven years ago. I found it impossible to let him go, to let his memory rest in peace.

My superior officer questioned my stability. I could not deny the charge. But did I need to leave? They offered help. Help, I refused. I sought solace in a bottle. I became someone else. I walked away from everyone and everything I loved.

"Hey? Are you okay? Do you want me to drive?" Her voice brought me back from the dead.

I straightened my whitened knuckles, my stomach turning, Ciarán's face flashing before my eyes with each bend in the road. The O'Donnells embraced the supernatural as an integral part of our lives.

"The past haunts me sometimes." I focused on her lush mouth, the crystals flickering in her deep-set eyes, and her translucent skin, highlighted by delicate blue veining. Calm flowed over me and through me. I stared, unbelieving.

My thoughts twisted, and I battled my conscience—right from wrong, good from evil. Did I even know the difference?

"I know what that's like." She didn't smile. Instead, she gazed into the thick foliage, green sails whipping by. "Tell me, Colm O'Donnell. What do you dream of?"

"That's a funny question." I pressed the brakes, anticipating the next switchback.

"Not really." She twined her hands behind her head. "Most people spend their lives searching for something."

"Here we are. This is Ardara." I punched the accelerator, following the banks of the Owentocker River.

The town showed itself, one slate roof after another rising in the distance.

"Oh, it's so pretty." She gazed up the big hill.

The center diamond, a cobblestoned gathering place, separated two intersecting roads into three distinct paths. Pubs, restaurants, and woolen shops galore lined the main street.

"There's my brother's place. Hugh Jr.—Doctor Hugh." I motioned toward the white stucco house on the corner.

"A doctor?" She noted the location of the walk-in clinic.

"Aye. Hugh can cure all that ails ye. Made the folks proud, that he did." Guilt stabbed my heart. *"Why did I leave the force? Why did I run?"* I questioned my decisions for the first time in a long time. Life could have remained simple.

"Do you like being a tree farmer, Colm O'Donnell? You seem, I don't know, so much more." Her curious gaze stopped my heart for the second time. I created a mental image of my home. Sheltered by the mountain's slope deep within the Cape Breton Highlands sat a log cabin built with my own hands. It was a quiet life and one I had become accustomed to.

"Are you a clairvoyant, Calla Sweet? Are you reading my mind?" I chuckled, unable to shake the mind-bending sensation akin to a bow screeching across the taut strings of a fiddle. I sighed inwardly, refusing to acknowledge her question or answer it. Lies became easier with time. I left the military with a specialized skill set, highly trained as a sharpshooter. Those who required my services knew where to find me. If they offered forgiveness, would I be deserving? I thought not.

She blinked, releasing me from her scrutiny.

"Here we are. The Black Horse." I pointed toward the stone building rising two floors high, the steep roof lined with slate. I drove beyond the pub, pulling into the next available parking space.

"Thanks. Can I reimburse you for the gas?" She searched her backpack and pulled out a glittering pink change purse.

"No need, luv." I jumped from the vehicle, weaving through car bumpers. I clasped the passenger door handle just in time.

"Colm O'Donnell. Good day to you, lad. You'll be needing a trim soon enough." A familiar voice summoned me—Joseph, the bald barber, jutted his chin in my direction, concluding that a haircut was due.

"Likely so, Joseph, likely so." I gave the man a quick smile while confronting the certainty of my situation. She was more than dangerous. She was an affliction. My mind stewed, gnashing at options. She owed me a raincheck, and I intended to collect.

She swung her long legs onto the pavement. Her gaze found Joseph and then flickered toward me. She took a long step, avoiding the puddle, but lurched forward and tripped on the broken curb.

"Jaysus, watch yourself." I grasped her elbow, lifting her upward.

Lightning bolts flowed through me, and Hell's breath took mine. The aura surrounding her changed from day to night.

"You're too late." Her eyes blazed, and shadows rippled across her face. She snatched her arm away.

"Too late for what? Calla?" The dark halo dissipated, replaced by the slamming of car doors and the honking of horns. Joseph said something about Wednesday at five o'clock.

She lifted her eyelashes, revealing my reflection rippling in the dark, glassy water. Without a backward glance, she turned and walked away, leaving me gasping for air and drowning in a sea of salty tears.

2

alla
I turned from him and sprinted down the street, vaguely aware of people staring. But they weren't people; they were nothing more than twisted shapes and pulsating waves of color. Enticed by the pinwheel's hypnotic haze, I sank deeper into the vortex. My perception skewed and spun out of control. I clutched my backpack and kept moving, distancing myself from his intense gaze.

I knew what I saw. Colm's father died a peaceful death in his living room—quick and painless, his favorite show blaring on the television. There was no point in telling him. What would that accomplish?

I escaped through the next available doorway and found myself in the local apothecary. I moved through the aisle until I could go no further. The young girl, dressed in a white shop coat, approached. "Can I help you, miss?"

"I'm not sure." I scanned the colorful display. Condoms of every size stared at me. Large. Standard. Snug. Latex. Polyurethane. Lambskin. Natural. Organic. Fair Trade. Vegan. Ridged. Flavored. Studded?

Snug and cozy worked for me. A girl could always wish, couldn't she? Beside the condoms, there was a vibrant display of ancestry kits. *Go figure.* Discover your heritage, they said. Learn about your ancestors, they said. Find new family relations. Why had I not considered that before?

"How does it work?" I held the DNA kit, turned the box over, and scanned the directions.

"It's quite easy. Your saliva goes into the tube, and you send it in." She studied me with rising interest.

"That's it?" I nibbled the inside of my lip, considering the pros and cons. Did I want my DNA out in the big wide world? What if there were more like me?

"Aye. Would you like those, miss?" Her singsong voice encouraged me to take the plunge.

"Okay, sure. Can I do this right now?" I ripped open the box and dumped out the contents.

"Of course. That's the collection tube and the return envelope. We can post it from here." She motioned at the stacked pile of outgoing mail.

"You can? Okay." I held the tube to my mouth and then spit, gob drooling from my lower lip.

"I did this myself." She gave me a tissue. "I found cousins I never knew I had."

ACCORDING to the etching above the doorway, the Black Horse Pub and Inn, a patchy array of uneven rubble stone, was established in 1866. Double-hung windows fitted with green muntin bars adorned the Inn's face. Flower boxes bursting with pink and purple pansies sat on every sill. English Ivy clung to the rough stones, creeping in all directions.

A girl wearing a yellow rain slicker, a black checkered miniskirt, and red rubber boots balanced on a rickety ladder. She leaned into the rough stones and, with one hand, twisted a lightbulb into a hanging lantern.

The skies opened, throwing liquid sunshine

upon the earth, slashing the pavement and over-flowing the gutters with water.

Rain poured down my face, washing away the last mud splatters. I raised my arms, welcoming the cleansing shower, laughter bubbling inside me. I smiled for the first time since ruining Colm O'Donnell's day.

And then the rain stopped. Sunshine splashed diamond glitter over the black pavement. A rainbow arched over the horizon: bold yellow, pink, and blue bands. I took in the flock of seagulls perched on the ridge of each rooftop. Their enthusiastic screeching filled my heart with an odd sense of happiness.

"Hello, are you Calla?" She clambered down from the ladder, her raincoat glistening with rain-drops. Water fell in streams through her auburn curls. She showed no signs of being perturbed by the sudden downpour.

"Yes. I am. I have a reservation." I covered my eyes, blinded by the sparkling pavement.

"I'm Saoirse. It's me you've been speaking with when you call. It's a fair day, isn't it?" She spoke in lively beats.

"Sursha? Yes, it's nice to meet you. Is it always like this? Sunshine and rainbows?" I looked down the empty sidewalk, searching for a sign of the tall copper-haired Celt.

"Aye, it's a grand wee country. Come in. Come in. How was your flight?" She brushed her hands across her short skirt, her gaze following mine.

"The flight went well, but the drive was problematic. I almost hit a flock of sheep." I bit my lip, picturing the black-faced sheep that caused my predicament.

"Nasty beasts. They own the road." She peered at me through shining amber eyes. "Why are you covered in mud?"

"Well, I had a small accident. I drove off the road and into the bog." I twirled a muddy tendril of hair behind my ear. "Colm O'Donnell drove me into town."

"Oh, bad luck to you." Her smile didn't reach her eyes.

"Do you know him?" The question popped out of my mouth.

"This is a small town, and the ceilings are low." She smirked.

I lifted my eyebrows, and she explained the innuendo.

"Not much happens in this town that's not talked about." She laughed. "The O'Donnell clan is well known here."

I wallowed in guilt—the big Irish clan would soon grieve one of their own.

"Look at ye, poor thing. Are ye all right? Are ye hurt?" She sang with concern, surveying me, searching for signs of damage.

"I desperately need a shower." I opened my coat, showing the mud stains the rain hadn't washed away.

"Aye, and likely a spot of tea?" She smiled. "One thing we have is hot water."

"Both sound great. Thank you. It's been a long day." I fell into step behind her.

"Good day, Pádraig. How are you this fine morning?" She gestured toward the burly fellow crossing the intersection.

I stared at his copper hair, the dark frames perched on a strong nose, his square chin. My grin faltered, and I struggled to stand upright.

"Same as yesterday and the day before." His voice boomed from across the street.

I appreciated his style—the boxy jacket layered over a cable-knit sweater, fitted trousers, and glossy loafers. Not a tree farmer.

"Did Orlaith call in the order? We're running low on just about everything." She sang back.

"Four o'clock, luv. No worries." He headed for the stone bridge, which spanned a flowing river.

I scanned each storefront. The Fat Bastard bakery sat halfway up the big hill. My heart sank watching the bubbly personality stride in the other direction.

"That's Pádraig. He's the baker in town. His scones are magic. Once you try them, you'll be hooked." She searched the roadway.

"Paa-drig? Is he Colm's brother?" I rested my palm on my forehead—thinking of him hurt my head.

"Yes, there are many O'Donnells." Her smile wavered but then returned.

Two—and three-story commercial buildings, roofed in slate and painted in muted shades of pink, blue, and green, lined the busy street of Ardara. Smoke curled from each chimney, emitting an earthy aroma I recognized: bog. The bog served as more than a distraction. It provided a heat source. It was an industry.

A rumbling engine distracted me from my revelation. A red farmer's tractor pulled an open trailer stacked high with white bags filled with dark lumps of turf. A black and white dog bounced to and fro in the tractor's cab.

She waved at the dark-haired driver.

My intuition answered my question—the O'-Donnells were integral to the community.

"Well, thank goodness you found us. What an adventure. You must be starved." She bounced along in front of the tractor.

"Thanks. I am." I stepped sideways, avoiding a puddle.

I followed her beyond the pub's entrance through the archway in the stone wall. A long breezeway led to an interior courtyard. I hugged my arms around my chest, unprepared for the cold kiss swirling within. The quiet space breathed peace. The sky seemed so distant. Looking up, I followed a catwalk around the perimeter of the stone building.

"Wow. This is amazing." I motioned to the upper railings fashioned after sprawling tree branches and the narrow staircase climbing upward. I ran my fingers over a perfect leaf, a budding bloom.

"Thanks, I created them." She shrugged, then rubbed her forehead.

"You made this? Here?" I asked, admiring the intricate craftsmanship.

"I enjoy working with my hands." She motioned toward a blue door, peeking through the hungry vines. "That's my workshop. Sculptures are my favorite, but I do all kinds of things. Fancy gates. Candle holders. I do commission work."

"Ooh, can I see?" I dropped my backpack onto a wrought-iron table in the courtyard's center. The twisted legs resembled the gnarled roots of an oak tree. "Wow. This is amazing."

"You want to?" Her eyes danced with flecks of amber light.

I expected a dark space, but to my surprise, white walls glowed with fluorescent light. A tiled floor shone beneath my feet and hosted everything a metal worker could need: a forge, a press, a welder's mask, a vise, gadgets, and tools for fabricating iron. Sprawled across an oversized desk were sketches of the most intricate designs I had ever seen.

"These are exquisite." I traced one with my finger, a lover's arch, a simple design of intertwined leaves.

"Thanks. This is where you'll find me when I'm not in the pub." Her words held notes of sadness.

"Are you managing the place on your own?" I recalled our numerous phone conversations. She had answered my calls day and night.

A stabbing pain pierced my brain, a wave of nausea threatening my vision. I threw my hand to my forehead, stilling the pulsing sensation.

"Yes and no. I have Orlaith, thank goodness.

We're one of the few pubs serving food. Well, until eight p.m. After that, all hell breaks loose." She looked at the ceiling. "You've arrived at a quiet time. Most of the touristy shops are closed. They won't open till after the long weekend. Some will open for Bealtaine."

"Bealtaine? How do you celebrate? There aren't many Celtic celebrations where I'm from." My thoughts traveled to the hurling game Colm invited me to. Visions of him pounding through grass and mud in athletic shorts and a tight-fitting T-shirt danced through my mind.

"We celebrate all the pagan holidays—loads of craic. People take caravans out to the dunes. We have a bonfire on the strand. We love feast days. You'll have to come." She studied me.

"The strand? Umm, okay, sure." My heart raced. What did I agree to? And why was everyone so friendly? I exhaled, releasing the tension in my shoulders. Stretching my wings, so they said. Was that my new mantra? God knew I needed one. I stared wistfully at the balcony. Behind those red doors were hotel rooms with a bed, a bathroom, and, hopefully, hot water.

"We don't see many folks this time of year. What brings you to Ardara?" She glanced at me with curious eyes.

I had the distinct impression she considered my visit strange.

"I've inherited a property not far from here." I chewed on the tip of my fingernail, wondering the same thing myself.

"You're not just visiting, are you? You're moving here?" Her forehead puckered into three distinct lines.

"Yes, I'm the sole beneficiary of Mr. Dermot Sweet's estate. It seems we're related somehow. I have an appointment in a couple of days with the lawyer." What was I thinking? Moving away from the only home I'd ever known.

"Sweet? Calla Sweet. Jesus feckin' Christ. No way. I didn't put it together." She planted her hands on her hips.

"You knew him?" I asked in a quick voice. Who were you, Dermot Sweet? And, for that matter, who was I?

One constant remained. My ability to see another's death followed me here and raised its ugly head at the first opportunity. Colm's confusion would by now have turned to grief.

"Dermot tipped the bottle from time to time. He was a nice man, though. He supplied the pub with honey." She smiled.

"Honey? He was a beekeeper?" I held my

breath, feeding my delusions with happy thoughts.

"Aye. He was very particular about his hives. It was like they were a part of him. I guess you could say he spoke to the bees. I do miss him, though. He made me smile." She closed the lights and locked the door.

"I have no idea why he left his property to me. The lawyer had no idea." I shook my head sideways. "It's all very mysterious."

"Well, I love a good mystery! Listen, you won't need to buy a car. Dermot collected vintage cars and old trucks. You'll be the proud owner of some prize-winning relics." She led me to the staircase, rising to the second floor.

"Oh, cool." The steel rungs rattled as I followed her along the catwalk.

"You're in the Garden Suite," she said, handing me the key. "Your stay comes with dinner daily, which we serve between five and eight p.m. For breakfast, I would suggest the East End Cafe. They serve a superb Irish breakfast."

"Great, thanks." I ran my thumb over the rectangular slab of driftwood emblazoned with a black horse. "Do you have any other guests?" I glanced at the welcome mats positioned before each door.

"No, not right now. Come down when you're ready. Orlaith just cooked up a big pot of cockles. You won't leave hungry, I promise you." She laughed and walked away.

"Cockles?" I tilted my head at the unfamiliar word.

"Saltwater clams. We gather them when the tide is low. Oh, do you have any food allergies?" She peered over her shoulder.

"No," I said, feeling glad. Saoirse wore her heart on her sleeve, and I would hate to disappoint.

SAOIRSE

My mood lifted, and relief buoyed my spirits. My new guest, Calla Sweet, seemed unassuming and easy to talk to. She had an aura surrounding her—a dark energy. I wondered if she would be friends with someone like me.

What were the chances an O'Donnell would rescue her? And Colm O'Donnell, at that. His stony face glared at me at his brother's wake. Seven long years ago, the love of my life, Ciarán O'Donnell, of the O'Donnell clan, disappeared without a trace. They said time would heal the pain. But for me, time stood still. The day Ciarán disappeared, Saoirse Dunne died.

"Be on with you, Saoirse. You need some secrets of your own." I talked to myself, freely engaging with the earthly spirits. I noticed one lonely beer keg standing outside the pub's back door. "Who put this here?" I huffed with displeasure, shoving the keg to one side, the metal rim scraping the paver stones, screeching in my ears. "Where are you, Ciarán?" Saying his name brought a brief respite to the pain. The Otherworld. Summerland. How often did I argue one side over the other? I dwelled on his absence every day. Sometimes, when I looked in the mirror, he stared back, and his sweet tenor voice rang out, "Saoirse, I'm here." I closed my hands over my ears, shutting out the voices.

The door slammed, leaving me disoriented. Dust motes lingered in the half-light, leading me through the storage room and into the main hall. The lover's alcove, a stone archway nestled into the side wall where lovers held hands and promised the night away. Envy filled my being every damn time.

The dust motes gathered shape, the apparition taking a ghostly form. When its cold hand touched mine, darkness choked the light, and the floor rose to greet me. I threw myself into the alcove, gripping the bench seat with whitened knuckles. "Breathe. Breathe. You've seen this before." I lit the stubby candle from last night's lover's rendezvous. Closing my eyes, I visualized my connection to the soil beneath the stones. I slowed each breath, and one by one, my thoughts cleared.

I smoothed my palms over the oak table, whispering silent words. "Within me, strength abides. Guide me through life's changing tides." I focused on the reservoir of strength hiding from me. I left that place and found another. My quiet place. My happy place. I stared at the glassy water at a cloud-covered mountain, where one solitary sunbeam peeked through thick clouds. The light enveloped me in a protective aura of inner strength, sending me a message. "I am enough. I am enough." I resided in the quiet moment, stating my intention clearly. My heartbeat slowed, and warmth radiated from within. I thanked the goddess for sharing her strength and assisting me once again.

"Is that you, Saoirse?" Orlaith's voice startled me, taking me away from Ciarán.

Dear Goddess, he's all I thought of.

Because you wouldn't let him go. Face the facts, girl. He's gone. He's dead. Dead. Dead. Dead.

I pictured all the horrible ways Ciarán could have died. Left to rot in the boglands? Thrown from a cliff into the sea?

No. No. No. Not dead. Not dead. He ran from the promises he made. You pushed him too hard. He didn't love you. No one loves you. You're a stupid, stupid girl, and now you're alone.

My mind crowded with unwanted thoughts.

"Saoirse? Did you remember the potatoes?" Orlaith stirred the stockpot with a long wooden spoon, and the aroma of her world-famous chowder wafted through the kitchen.

"There's some right there, Orla. In the cupboard." I opened the lower pantry, heaving the bag from underneath. "Do you want me to peel?"

"Dear gods, luv. Did you see a ghost? You're fair pale, dearie." She beamed over the steaming pot.

"I did, Orlaith. You know this place is haunted." I pinned my lips together, attempting to hide my smile.

" 'Twas it the wee girl? I swear she's an odd one, the poor thing." She tsked.

"No, not this time. It was a man. Hunched over with bugged-out eyes." I chuckled despite myself.

"Be off with you now. Is the new guest settled in?" She dabbed her eyes with her apron.

"I think so. The poor thing crashed into the

bog. The car's banjaxed. Ach, I hope the cistern doesn't act up again. I promised her lots of hot water." I reached for the water jug, filled a tall glass, and handed it to Orla.

"The bog? Oh my. How did she get here, then?" She looked up, her face flushed pink.

"Colm O'Donnell drove her into town." I bent over the sink, skinning the potatoes and tossing each one into a large stockpot filled with cold water.

"Did he? Now, there's a man who would look good on ye. That he would." She pursed her lips.

"Orlaith, please. Don't start." I gathered the peelings and threw them into the composting bin.

"He's returned home to find a proper wife. It's plain to see." She clucked her tongue.

"Oh dear, I forgot to show her where the laundry machines are." I gazed at the dishes piled high in the sink.

"Is this the jumper ye made?" She picked at the sleeve of my sweater. "Ye have a talent for everything, luv. Look at the time. Those lads should be arriving any minute now."

"What, lads?" I squared my shoulders.

"Wee Jimmy's bringing Niall to see the place. A wonderful fiddle player, Niall, is. Be off with you, and I'll tidy up. Where are the potatoes, dearie?

Ach, now, would you look right there? All peeled and ready to boil." She lifted the heavy pot, placing it on the hob.

"What are we serving tonight, Orlaith? Should I drop by the market?" I surveyed the scene. Orlaith, my chief cook, came to me from a competing hotelier. They gave her the boot because her memory failed once too many times. For me, she was a forgetful godsend and the best cook in the parish. When funds allowed, I would hire another person to help make life easier. But until then, my alarm clock rang every morning at five a.m. My scarred fingers were evidence enough of my lack of skill with a kitchen knife.

"I'll get out of your way, Orlaith." I walked into the storeroom, closing the wooden door behind me. Why did I feel like crying? I was one of the lucky ones. How many women owned their establishments? Okay, Da helped me—for the bank. But every penny I'd saved went into refurbishing this old building and returning its former glamor.

I looked into the mirror, and Ciarán's face stared back, unchanged and so lovely. Shiny blond locks framed his manly face. His image blurred. Or maybe those were tears in my eyes. I placed my palm on the mirror—yearning to walk through the looking glass and be with him. How many spells had I cast attempting to bring him back? Or called upon the power of the coven? If Ciarán were dead, he would have answered. I refused to give up hope. I refused to believe he was dead. The signs spelled another power much greater than a handful of Irish witches.

CALLA

The shower was great, but soaking in the tub was heaven, touched with sunshine. I breathed in fragrant blueberry bath salts, stretched my aching muscles, and inspected my pruned-up toes. I washed my hair three times, rinsing away the lingering stench of bog.

I towel-dried my unruly locks and stood before the foggy mirror, reliving each moment since my arrival. Not three hours into my journey. Three hours. I played through the sequence of events. He opened the car door. His delicious scent was intoxicating. So close. Too close. I stumbled, and he reached for me, saving me from a fall. "Watch out. Watch out." His voice had echoed in that melodic lilt. That was all it took. My world went black, and I belted out the words of the doom-bringer. Colm's face, eyes wide open and filled with shock.

I could hire a driver and catch the next flight to Canada. But why? There was nothing left for me there.

I gazed through the windowpanes onto the street below. A man sat on a wooden bench, leaning on a walking stick. A woman pushed a stroller down the sidewalk. A long-eared dog sat outside a butcher shop, wagging its tail as customers went in and out. I weighed the risks. The chances of seeing Colm were low, and he would soon leave, back to Canada, where he belonged. I would stay, he would go, and my secret would remain safe. *Keep your mouth shut, Calla Sweet.*

I talked myself into believing. What choice did I have?

Calla Sweet, the frequent flyer, knew a thing or two about traveling—carry-on only, which in my case meant a well-worn backpack. My limited clothing consisted of one pair of jeans, two pairs of black leggings, two cashmere sweaters, five black thongs, two lacy brassieres, and one emerald green clingy dress, vacuum sealed in plastic—just in case. Of what? I didn't know.

I admired the simple furnishings and white-washed walls. A gilt-framed photograph of a black horse standing in a grassy field hung on one wall. I studied the horse's fine confirmation, wondering who he once belonged to.

"Where are you going to wear this?" I asked out loud, shaking out the ankle-length dress. The velvet was soft on my fingers, and the muted green was easy on my eyes. I hung it inside an ornately carved wardrobe beside my sweaters, one black and one gray. I leaned inside, breathing in the aromatic scent of cedar. If I climbed inside, would I be transported to another world? The possibility sounded divine.

I suppressed a yawn, padding barefoot across the hard-wearing carpet. The bed featured a blue-striped duvet and coordinating pillow shams. An accent pillow showcased an embroidery of the same black horse. I gazed longingly at the bed but refused to lie down or sit.

I switched off the lights and exited my room. I hesitated, Colm O'Donnell's face flashing in my mind, my steps rattling the steel staircase, taking me into the quiet courtyard. I passed Saoirse's workshop and hesitated inside the covered breezeway, shoving the what-ifs aside and glancing left and right, tracking the line of traffic down the intersecting streets. A woman stood in the diamond, gazing at an ivory statue of a musician playing a violin. The chip truck had a long line of customers. I turned and moved along the sidewalk, driven by a strong gust of wind. A four-legged creature, a long-haired, gigantic beast with a shaggy head, brushed past me. I watched the dog continue his journey beyond the steepled church. I stood outside the Wild Horse for what I didn't know, but I spent five minutes gazing at the eye-catching posters pasted inside the paned windows.

A honking truck and brakes squealing shook me from my reverie, and I placed my hand on the cast iron latch and shoved the heavy door.

The pub was everything I imagined an Irish pub should be: low ceilings, wood beams blackened by wood smoke and aged by time, lanterns emitting a soft yellow light, the quintessential red carpet flowing from one cavernous room to another, and embers glowing red in the hearth of a rough stone fireplace.

I strained my ears, hearing Saoirse's muffled voice. I inhaled sharply when a panel in the wall swung open, revealing a hidden door leading into a back kitchen.

"Aye, then, Aye. We should go." A woman with ruddy cheeks and silvery hair carried a stainless-steel pot in gloved hands, the steam fogging her spectacles.

"Jolene can look after the place. Oh, there you

are. Good." Saoirse turned her head. "Orlaith, this is Calla, our guest from Canada. She's here for three days."

"Hello," I murmured, resting my hands on the brass rail. My stomach bounced with nerves. I settled onto the bar stool and gazed into their welcoming faces.

Orlaith smiled and placed a steaming bowl of chowder before me.

"This is incredible." I allowed the rich, creamy broth to wash over my tongue, savoring the salty-sweet flavors loaded with meaty globes.

"I'm after a scone for you, lass. Now, you hold on." Orlaith's face creased with smile lines. She lifted a glass lid from a cake stand stacked with fluffy scones.

"Hey, have you ever been to an Irish wake?" Saoirse caught me off guard.

"A wake? No, I haven't." My stomach heaved like the waves of a storm-tossed sea.

"Ach. 'Tis great craic. Lots of chit-chat. Buckets of fun. Well, not so much for the poor bugger who died." Orlaith swept her hands over the full skirt of a white and blue flowered frock cinched tight at the waist.

"If you don't have plans for tomorrow, you

should come with Orla and me." Saoirse wiped the bar top with a white cloth.

"But I don't know the people." My throat closed. I stared from one to the other.

"Oh, but you do. You know Colm. He drove you into town?" Her eyes widened.

"Colm?" I shrank back from the counter.

"No. No. Colm's father. He passed on this afternoon. Watching the telly, isn't that right, Orlaith?" She shook her head in sympathy. "It's the talk of the town. So unexpected."

"What better way to meet everyone? This is Ireland after all––'tis expected," Orlaith said, leaving no room for argument.

I opened my mouth to speak but decided against it.

"How is it for you, luv?" Orlaith nodded at my empty bowl.

"The soup was amazing. Thank you so much." I said, hoping against all hope that they would forget the invitation by tomorrow.

"Aye, look at that. It's lovely to see a girl with an appetite." Orlaith sent a sharp glance to Saoirse. "Another bowl, luv?"

"Orlaith." She made a face at the older woman, scrunching her lips and arching her brows.

"Thank you. That would be great. I can't believe how hungry I am." I watched her ladle soup in a fresh bowl and set it before me. The bottomless pit I called my stomach gurgled appreciatively.

"Where are you heading, miss, once you leave us?" The wrinkles around her mouth fanned into a smile.

"Calla's moving into the old Sweet place," Saoirse told her. "Maybe we'll get our honey supplier back, yeah? There's a business opportunity there, Calla if you're not afraid of bees." Her gaze returned to me.

"The Sweet Place?" Orlaith spun around. Her mouth dropped open, and fear flashed through her eyes, magnified threefold by her thick prescription glasses. She clasped her hands in prayer, her complexion greyed, and her knees gave out.

Saoirse lunged forward, but it was too late.

I jumped out of my seat as Orlaith fell backward, landing face-up on the hard stone floor.

"Orlaith? Orlaith?" Saoirse knelt beside Orlaith, holding the older woman's hands between hers.

And just like that, I forgot the no-touch rule. I flew behind the counter, crowded the narrow aisle, and rested two fingers on Orlaith's racing pulse.

Fractured light pierced my mind, and I saw what Orlaith saw.

White clouds, perfectly formed puffs of fluffy cotton, dot a baby blue sky. Nestled into the craggy side of the mountain slope, a straw-thatched shieling made from rubble stone and bonded with clay chinking. The low drone of bees buzzing from wildflower to wildflower sings in the mid-morning air. The sweet smell of a summer's afternoon fills my senses.

A donkey cart approaches, its spoked wheels creaking along the uphill path. The driver, a kind-faced man, urges the long-eared donkey forward.

"Ériu, we have to go. You must hurry." Orlaith rests her hand on Ériu's upper arm, but the girl named Ériu seems unaware. She gazes at something only she can see. She remains motionless, her thoughts elsewhere.

"Aye, Aye. 'Tis fine, Orlaith, 'tis fine." Her cherry-red lips barely move. She raises her golden head, her blue eyes reflecting a turbulent storm. She holds a sprig of yellow daisies adorned with delicate white alyssum and sprays of lavender tied with a blue satin ribbon.

"Whenever you're ready, luv." The driver tips his straw hat.

"Aye, we should be on then." Ériu lifts the floating lace of her wedding dress, revealing a sky-blue underlay. She places her slippered foot on the iron step of the donkey cart and lifts herself into the bench seat. Or-

laith scrambles behind her, gathering the ruffled train of Ériu's dress.

"There now. There now." She fusses with the lavender crown entwined in Ériu's golden locks.

The driver clicks his tongue to encourage the donkey while the two women, hand in hand, giggle as the cart bounces down the mountain trail.

The donkey abruptly stops when a curly-horned black ram darts onto the dirt path.

"Whoa." The driver's calm voice steadies the enraged donkey.

"Put this on, Ériu. I almost forgot." The excitement in Orlaith's voice is contagious. She dangles a silver bracelet with a horseshoe embedded with tiny sapphires, sunlight glimmering from the delicate links. "For good luck."

She fails to notice Ériu's stricken look or how her rosy cheeks pale to ash.

"Ach, now. Don't fret. Don't fret." Orlaith gripped my wrist, her eyes locked with mine.

"It's okay. Just breathe," I murmured, sending calm to the elderly woman.

Her breathing slowed—and her rosy complexion returned.

"Are you okay? Should I call the doctor?" Saoirse hooked her arm around Orlaith's waist and lifted her into a sitting position, placing her palm on her forehead.

"Ach, no. Help me up, lass. Help me up. These old bones aren't as spry as they once were." She leaned forward, blue veins pulsing in her neck. Using our outstretched arms for support, she rose onto her feet. "Oh, dearie me, look at this mess."

"Why don't you take the rest of the day off? I can manage." Saoirse cupped Orlaith's elbow, leading her toward a round table within the fireplace's warm embrace.

I couldn't forget what I saw. Orlaith's memory of a golden-haired woman named Ériu sent chills racing down my spine.

I SPENT what was left of the day browsing the nearby shops and filling my guts with greasy grub from what the locals called a chipper. I could have curled beneath the cozy duvet and slept till morning, but resisted the urge. Instead, I found myself inside Saoirse's pub, grabbing snippets of conversation wrapped in a thick Irish dialect, words unknown to me, like punter and chancer—howya and hoor.

Men and women shouldered up to the bar. Locals crowded the round tables. Laughter cackled from one room to another. Newcomers received a hearty slap on the shoulder from friends in common. I weaved through the crowd and slid onto an empty barstool.

Beyond the imposing stone walls, a chilling death rattle shook every window. Sharp knocks echoed from the arched doorway, but no one entered. The wind howled, sucking the happiness from the room. I stared into the emptiness, entranced by an unknown phantom.

Saoirse waved, drawing my attention away from the darkness. I staved off the imagined horrors by clutching the cuffs of my new sweater, the thick ivory wool comforting my soul. I curled my toes inside my brand-new sneakers and willed those visions back into the hellscape from which they came.

In the corner of the bar stood a man cloaked in the most interesting costume, the deep purple hood shrouding most of his face. He spoke to no one, and no one talked to him. His gaze found mine, but then he turned his head. His burly features struck a chord in the core of my being. The set of his jaw reminded me of someone else.

"Hey! You made it!" She threw me a bright smile. "What would you fancy?"

"White wine, please." I matched her enthusiasm, reminding myself that the night was young and I should pace myself.

"Chardonnay or a Pinot Grigio?" Saoirse's shiny hair was pulled into a knot, the fly-away pieces framing her heart-shaped face.

"Chardonnay, please." I scanned the tables, looking for him. Colm's return to his tree farm would not happen soon enough for me.

"Watch yourself. It's a dodgy crowd." She giggled and turned away, returning with a generous pour of fragrant white.

"You look pretty tonight. I love your sweater." I complimented as she slid a coaster emblazoned with the Black Horse logo across the bar top.

"I wouldn't know what to do." She set the glass on the coaster, her gaze moving between me and the waiting patrons.

"What do you mean?" I studied her wistful expression.

"Look around. They're feckin drooling over you." Saoirse grinned, her eyes sparkling.

"New girl syndrome." I shrugged off the compliment.

"Welcome. Welcome. We have a request from the chancer holding up the bar this evening." The fiddler, a bearded man with flashing eyes, plucked a few strings. The banjo player followed up, strumming a few chords.

I turned toward the band, drawn to the mysterious notes of a harmonica.

Barstools scraped the stone floor, glasses clanking the tabletops.

I lifted my chin, scanning the sea of faces. The conversation swelled, and then the place erupted into a familiar song everyone sang.

Across the bar, a patron drummed his fingertips on the counter, demanding Saoirse's attention.

I couldn't help but notice the quiet one hidden in the shadows, his faceless stare never leaving Saoirse.

3

C*olm*

Death comes to us all. No amount of whisky could dull such pain. A wreath ribboned with black crepe hung from the front door of the O'Donnell family home and served as a somber reminder of where the patriarch of the O'Donnell clan had lived. My thoughts returned to yesterday, to the girl with the dove-grey eyes. She left me floundering in confusion, twisting my mind with her tortured words.

"You're too late," she whispered, then ran, leaving the impression that something horrible had happened.

My ringing cell phone confirmed Calla's prophecy, Mam's voice on the other end. Calm.

Soothing. "Colm, you need to come home. You're da's dead."

The moments blurred, daylight fading into blue twilight. Nightfall offered no respite. The coming dawn shaded the sky with pink hues, promising a new day—yesterday. Was it only yesterday?

My father's giant frame filled the pine coffin, lying east to west against the far wall of the big room, an ivory pillow nestled under his balding head. I pressed my fingers on the lapel of his chocolate brown suit, the fashionable houndstooth pattern, all the rage twenty years before. A string of rosary beads, compliments of Mam, were twined between his gnarled fingers.

The bowl of salt sitting on his chest would chase the evil spirits away. His shoes—the soles worn, the leather polished, waited to take him into the next world. Calm surrounded him. His thoughtful composure followed him even into death.

"Sorry for your trouble, mate." A rumbling voice filled with sympathy reverberated throughout the room.

"Paddy, thanks for coming." I grabbed my old-school chum's hand, my heart lifting in recognition. How long had it been since I returned home? Too many years.

"If there's anything I can do for the family, for your mam, you'll let me know?" He turned, lighting one of the many clay pipes dipped in beer and filled with a twist of tobacco. "Lord ha' mercy." He inhaled a long puff and passed through the death room, his words lingering on trailing fingers of smoke—meant to keep the evils at bay.

Voices murmured as old friends, extended family, and those who knew him wandered from room to room, filling Clonmara with life.

Candles flickered at either end of my father's coffin, signifying the light in the next world. Aunt Polly, Da's last remaining sibling, watched the melting wax––should a silent shroud appear, death would visit again.

We followed the old traditions—the curtains drawn lest the demons enter. The mirrors—gateways to the otherworld—faced the walls lest my father's spirit should take a wrong turn.

"Colm, how are you, hon? I'm sorry about your da." A sweet soprano voice turned my head.

"Susan." The hole in my heart shrank with every hello, every hug, and every story shared.

"It's bad luck to him, forgive me for saying.

How's your mam?" Her quiet voice expressed sympathy.

"Not so good... It came as a shock." I nodded, clasping her hand.

My father died a healthy man, the chance to confess his sins stolen from him. At my mother's bequest, a sin-eater was called upon, an ancient custom forgotten by most. In a ceremony witnessed by few, the man consumed a simple meal passed over my father's corpse. Washing it down with a mug of ale, he offered his prayer, "I give easement and rest now to thee, dear man. Come not down the lanes or in our meadows. And for thy peace, I pawn my soul. Amen." The sin-eater's gravelly voice haunted my mind. Where would his soul land when the reaper came?

"Sorry for your trouble, mate."

"Colm, you remember Sam? From school?" Breda, my first cousin on my mother's side, raised her white eyebrows, fixing her coal-black eyes on mine. Not one for formality, Breda wore a denim jacket over a pine-green jumpsuit paired with white sneakers. She rested her hand on my upper arm. *She worries about my soul.*

"Sam, it's been a long time. Thanks for coming."

"God bless all in this house." He clasped my hand.

We stayed the long hours of the night to guard my father's soul—to ensure his passage to the other side. Eamon, my father's most loyal friend and my mentor, held vigil into the wee hours, telling tales, lifting our spirits, and nodding off in the corner armchair, snoring like the old bulldog he was.

When the dawn rose on the third day, my brothers and I would carry the casket down the street and up the hill to the little church where the priest would say mass. The next day, we would say our last goodbyes.

"Good sleep be with him," another murmured.

Seats filled and emptied. Neighbors and friends shared stories of the ould one, little things said—all those memories added to the clamor of death. People talked about closure, something I never understood.

The hands on the old mantle clock stopped at 11:35 a.m.—the moment my father passed, so no one asked the dreaded question. One open window directly above the casket allowed his spirit to leave.

It was what he would have wanted.

My parents raised seven boys in a cottage by

the sea, christened Clonmara on their wedding day.

I left the reception, my throat dry. Casual conversation was not my strong suit. I preferred to observe, favoring quiet solitude, but that's not the way of the Irish. I entered the kitchen, a family-sized room painted canary yellow, nodding toward the ladies sitting at the long dining table, most I recognized. I rummaged through the upper cupboard for a water glass.

Mam gazed at me with worried eyes. She wore the widow's costume, a high-collared black dress she had worn seven years before for the youngest O'Donnell. When the hope of Ciarán's return died, they organized a wake in place of funeral rites or a church mass. Hundreds came from all around to offer their sympathies for the lost son.

"How are you, Colm? How's the weather in Canada? I hear it's fair cold." Aunt Polly stood at the end of the L-shaped counter, her elbow bent, mashing yellow yolks with the tines of a fork. She sent a concerned look toward a younger woman with pink hair and purple glasses, introduced earlier as Aoife, another newcomer, who placed three tarot cards face up.

"Aye, it is, Auntie." I read each inquisitive stare. None dared ask, "Why did you leave Colm? Why did you leave your parents grieving not one son but two?" I waited for the stream of water to run cold.

Everyone loved Ciarán, the seventh of seven sons, but I loved him most. We were inseparable, Irish twins born eleven months apart.

Aunt Polly filled a piping bag with her mashed egg mixture, the tip of her tongue resting on her lower lip.

Oonagh, our closest neighbor on this lonely road, turned from the refrigerator and set a plate of hard-boiled egg halves on the checkered counter. The pungent aroma filled the room: deviled eggs with a touch of curry—Da's favorite appetizer. Aunt Polly didn't acknowledge her help.

"Colm, a sandwich?" Mam prodded, her voice gentle.

"I'm good, Mam." I chugged back the glass of water. Da's death brought back the loss for all of us. Ciarán was the baby in the family, but he was my doppelgänger. I sensed his presence, especially in that time of sorrow.

"Right there, Polly. That one is half empty." Oonagh crowded Aunt Polly, inspecting her work.

"How long has it been, Colm? Colleen's wedding, it was." Auntie set her piping bag on the counter, untied her polka-dot apron, and handed it to Oonagh with a flourish.

"It's nice to see you, Auntie." I placed my hands on Mam's shoulders and gently squeezed them. Auntie looked as I remembered, her glossy black hair pulled into a tight bun, bird-like eyes appraising everything and everyone.

"Ladies?" Aunt Polly expertly popped the cork of a bottle of sparkling white wine, filled my mother's glass, and then topped off each lady's glass. She turned toward Aoife and, with the bottle at a precarious tilt, splashed wine across the table.

"Oh, no," Aoife gasped, sweeping her tarot cards away from the fast-moving puddle.

"Sorry, luv. I don't know how that got away from me." She righted the bottle, holding it close to her chest.

I dove in with a stack of napkins, sopping up the mess.

"You need to eat, luv." Mam's voice drowned out Aunt Polly's giggle.

"I'm good, Mam." I threw the sodden napkins into the overflowing garbage, lifted the bag from the can, tied it off, and placed it on the back porch.

"It's a tough puck, luv, losing your da, but we'll get through." Mam's mind seemed clear. She spoke to me and those in the room. They nodded in agreement, all ready to help at a moment's notice.

"Clodagh, let's try again. Give them a good shuffle." Aoife handed the tarot deck to the elderly lady. I recognized Clodagh from Padraig's shop. She worked weekends during the busy season.

I set a plastic bag in the garbage bin, checked the seal, and sidestepped toward the sink, avoiding Auntie on her way to the refrigerator. I washed my hands, inhaling the fragrant scent of lilac soap.

"Colm, luv, have a sandwich." Mam handed me a china plate, waving her hand over platters of sweet pickles and ham sandwiches in front of an empty chair—Da's chair. I studied my mother— her eyes were red. Had I cried? No, I had not allowed myself that emotional release.

"Mam, why are we using the good china? Paper plates would do." I shook my head at the pile of plates ready for the dishwasher.

"Tell us again about the *Bean-Sidhe*, Clodagh. Did you see her?" Oonagh paused from her paprika shaker, surveying the egg platter with a sharp nod.

"Aye, gave me a fright. It did. Wailing, like fingernails screeching down a blackboard. And the wind rattling the windowpanes at the same time. I thought we were in for a storm." She relived the horror, her face paling.

I half listened to the bantering hens, my stomach rumbling as I filled my plate.

"Clara saw her the night Roger died. She thought the dog was dying. Aye, she did. Father Donald told her it 'twas nothing but the wind." Aoife laid three cards face up again, oblivious to Polly's pointed stare.

"It was just like they say. Hunched over the bank of the river with nothing over her shoulders but a ragged grey cloak, the wee thing sat there, combing her hair with the most beautiful silver comb. I was afraid to look at her. She lifted her head. It was her eyes—fiery red from all that keening." Clodagh nodded her head up and down, her lips tight.

I glanced at Mam. She failed to mention her account of the *Bean Sidhe*.

"What do you think, Aoife? Is it a good time to travel?" She clasped her hands together, her eyes hopeful.

I leaned against the door, chewing on a gherkin pickle. The tarot reader offered fortune-telling in the tiniest building on the main street, a mere ten feet wide and two stories high. She seemed comfortable among the elderly ladies, perhaps too relaxed.

"Colm? Storey's coming home." Auntie's face brightened as she spoke of her only son. "Aye. He tells me there's a big announcement coming. It's about time, aye? Your uncle and I are so hoping that the boy settles down. Dearie me, if we're not getting any younger." Auntie trotted to the refrigerator, retrieving the bottle of wine.

"A wedding, Polly?" Clodagh smiled, her eyes lighting up.

"Aye, it can't come soon enough for my liking." Polly set the bottle down.

Aoife flinched.

"Will ye be booking the hall, Polly? Does Father Mike know?" Mam's eyes were bright.

"Don't I wish. Don't I wish. I'll be back in a wee moment, ladies." Auntie left the kitchen, mumbling something about melting candle wax.

"Will ye have a drop of comfort, laddie?" Eamon leaned his hefty frame on his shillelagh, his good hand grasping the knobby-horned walking stick. He cut a dashing figure in a tailored tweed jacket and tapered trousers the color of a misty morning, with a white cotton shirt casually unbuttoned at the collar.

"Aye." I nodded to the ladies and followed Eamon down the long hallway.

"I'll be missing your da. Taken too soon. He was." A blanket of silence lay before us. His mention of my father raised a well of emotion I had yet to deal with.

"Aye." I stared at the ham sandwich on my plate. I didn't trust my voice.

"We go back a long way, Colm. A long way." He waved the thorny stick toward the nieces and nephews. They clattered away, screeching like the river banshee the woman called Clodagh spoke of.

"We do, Eamon." I shifted in my boots, squaring my shoulders.

"I'll be calling on you, laddie. Soon enough." He peered over his spectacles, his rheumy eyes flashing quicksilver, his soft voice contradicting his tough exterior. "Come, let's sit a while."

He turned and walked into a parlor filled with overstuffed couches. The haze of tobacco smoke didn't dissuade him.

"How are you doing, Eamon?" The wing chair groaned under my weight. I set my plate on the coffee table, my thoughts lingering on his comment. This was an odd time for Eamon to mention an assignment. I studied the lines etched into his brow. The older man had my attention.

"Ach, no worse than usual." He poured whisky into two glass tumblers. The brown spots spreading over the back of his hands reminded me Eamon's twilight years were waning.

I scratched my head, wondering where the years had gone.

"About time you joined us, bro." Hugh Jr. tipped his head, raising his glass. "To Hugh Xavier O'Donnell. May his soul rest in peace."

We threw back the whisky and slammed down the glasses. Others lifted their glasses in reverence, filling the space with resounding echoes of sympathy.

"Such a hardy soul he was." Eamon removed his glasses and wiped his eyes with the back of his hand. "I'll miss him."

"As we will." I topped up Eamon's glass and my own, fortified by the Irish and my brother's companionship.

"I could use your hands, Colm. If you're around? The north field." Oisin helped himself to four ham sandwiches.

"Aye." I nodded. Stacking hay on a hot, sunny day soothed the soul.

"What are you doing?" Ten months younger than Pádraig, Cillian planted his tattooed hands on the table's edge. He came from away, living in Paris for the last three years.

"What?" I glanced up from the food left on my plate—one ham sandwich, four pickles, and one strawberry—the bread slices piled on the side.

"Pádraig will lose his shite. He sees you decimating his prized sourdough." Cillian turned, showing off the rose tattoo on the shaved side of his head.

"The mohawk suits you." I lifted my chin, acknowledging the edgy hairstyle and the bold shade of blue that set him apart from most Ardara men. I grabbed the mustard and squirted each open face.

"Jaysus, what is it? What is it now?" Pádraig, the eldest O'Donnell, rounded the corner. He dropped a platter overflowing with sandwiches onto the table.

"Nothing," I murmured. I liked to avoid trouble.

"Is it bad? What's wrong with it?" He lunged toward my plate, lifting each abandoned crust toward his spectacle-covered eyes.

My brother lived for baking. His shop, The Fat Bastard, was renowned for fresh baked goods, butter tarts, sticky buns, and Pádraig's famed sourdough bread.

"I'm watching my weight." I dug into the last crustless sandwich, smearing mustard on my chin.

"Your weight? Do you have any idea what goes into this?" He gestured with his hands, his voice rising.

"It's the best I've ever had." I grinned. I remembered a much younger Pádraig, his fire-engine red curly hair dusted in flour, his hands deep in dough, and our dear departed Nana supervising the delicate procedure.

"Be careful, bro. Dough is a starchy subject in these parts." Cillian twined his fingers together, waiting for the spectacle to begin.

"Another tat, bro?" I grabbed Cillian's wrist, inspecting the bracelet inked around his forearm. "It's time you started your own business, yeah?"

"Have you seen Tadgh?" Hugh Jr. searched the crowded tables for his identical twin.

"He's sweet on the new girl." Oisin rose from the table, returning with a soon-to-be-emptied bottle of Irish.

"Haven't seen him all morning. Why?" I swallowed the last bite.

"The starters fecked on my car." Hugh Jr. glanced at his watch.

"What new girl?" Cillian wolfed down the remaining crusts on my plate. He looked like he could use the calories.

"Slainte." Hugh Jr. lifted his glass, throwing the golden elixir back. The brothers followed suit.

"Well, who wouldn't be? She's a stunner." Pádraig chuckled.

"He means built like a brick house." Oisin grinned, motioning with his hands.

I walked from table to table, gathering empty plates into a tall stack while scanning the faces of each O'Donnell brother. One missing—but not forgotten. The shadows moved, and I saw Ciarán's face. Where are you, Ciarán? The answer was hidden from me. I left the sitting room, my hands full.

Breda stood beside my father's roll-top desk in the foyer, her fingers busy refilling clay pipes with tobacco. She worked away, seemingly oblivious to my presence. When the wind rattled the window-panes, she looked up. The door flew open, bringing Saoirse, the witch, followed by Tadgh and his hairy brute of a dog, Kevin.

"Thanks for coming, Saoirse. It means so much." Breda held Saoirse's pale hands and kissed her cheek. "I love the dress." She stepped back, keeping her at arm's length, admiring a black long-sleeved dress swirled with blood-red vines, the color of Saoirse's curly hair.

I stood there, waiting for what would happen next. Saoirse's gaze met mine.

"How are you, Kevin?" Breda crooned to the furry wolfhound.

"What about me, Breda?" Tadgh pulled our cousin into his thick arms, pecking her cheek.

Their voices mingled, and I lost the run of myself, my thoughts delving through old files and yellowed pen strokes, notes taken seven long years ago—evidence shelved as useless. Saoirse's face flushed under my scrutiny, her smile frozen in place. Did the Garda miss something? Did I miss something?

"Bloody hell, Kevin." I gasped as the wolfhound clattered past, knocking my knees from under me. I cursed the dog and myself when Mam's Blue Willow china flew from my hands and shattered onto the hard floor.

Breda threw me a stony glare, her black eyes flashing. She grabbed Saoirse's arm and navigated through the broken pieces of china. Mam's voice rang out, welcoming her as one of our own.

CIARÁN

Voices rang out from another part of the house, the library, or perhaps the drawing room. Pádraig's lilting tenor rose above everyone else's, bringing a smile and erasing the sadness weighing down my soul. I would have given anything to join them.

If only.

I left the shadows and approached my father's casket. I rested my fingers on his great shoulders—the shoulders I would ride upon as a child. I would not see him again, not in that realm or the other. His soul journeyed elsewhere and would not return. I pressed my lips against his forehead and whispered my last goodbye: *"Codladh sámh*, Da. Sleep well."

"I've never thought of it that way before. To think of them sleeping. A peaceful, dreamy sleep." Her voice broke the everlasting silence I had endured for the past seven years. I looked up, drawn to the glow in her eyes. Her entrance into the room appeared ghostlike, just like mine.

"This is my fault. So much of this is my fault." I admonished, admitting my guilt, which felt freeing. I looked at my father. He was just as dead to them as I was. It was better that way. The family deserved peace.

"Don't think that." Full of warmth, her words flowed into me, reminding me of what I once was—flesh and bone, not the shade I was now.

"Who are you?" I studied her, unsure of her standing within the Faerie realm. It was unlike them to follow me. I had, after all, earned the privilege of moving freely within the mortal plane concealed beneath the enchantment they had imposed upon me.

"Calla, Calla Sweet. I'm sorry for your loss." She bent her head in sympathy. Her eyes were familiar, the same as Themselves. They were luminous, reflecting all the light in the world.

"How interesting." I rubbed my chin, lost in the possibilities. A Faerie girl living in the mortal realm? Was that what she was? My experience with Faeries told me one thing—beware.

"Excuse me?" Curiosity flickered in those uncommon eyes.

"I saw you at the pub last night." I studied her, debating the pros and cons of sharing my soul with a being such as her. To ask anything of Them came with inherent risks.

"Yes, I remember. Do you know Saoirse?" She lowered her eyelashes, her gaze calculating. So like Them.

I stood my ground—now was not the time to falter.

"Yes, I know, Saoirse."

The icy breath of winter brushed my face, the chill paralyzing. Suspicions confirmed. Magic emanated from her—Faerie magic. I exhaled through my nose, allowing my limbs to lengthen and my joints to relax. There were no wards against her kind. I had learned long ago to submit.

I opened my mind and gave her what she sought—the truth. After so many years, I had nothing to hide. I allowed my thoughts to drift, showing her Saoirse lying in my arms, her hair flowing over her shoulders. She was mine, and I was hers. There would never be another. I lived in those lost moments. They were all I had left.

Saoirse and I had a future—'had' being the operative word. I bear the blame. Could I change the past and undo that moment? For them to know I lived? What horrors would it put them through? Maybe she would help, if not for me, then for Saoirse.

"Not without divine intervention," I murmured under my breath—seven years lost because of my arrogance.

The icy hand released me, replaced by the

sounds and smells of my father's house. My knees buckled.

"What's that?" She tilted her head and touched the casket's edge with her fingers, drawing the shadows to her. I watched as they clung to her, becoming part of her. I realized one thing. She was neither of the mortal realm nor entirely of the other.

The clouds shifted, and an imperceptible mist crept through the open window and slithered across the floor. My return to the Other Realm drew near. There was a time when I believed escape could be achieved.

I joined the dance, leaving my beautiful Saoirse behind. I walked across the realms of my own volition without thinking about the repercussions. Any fool knew the consequences of mixing with the Faerie folk. I trusted those I thought were friends, arrogant in my confidence. I learned too late who and what they truly were.

"Have you ever made a poor decision?" I debated asking that strange being for what? Redemption?

"Yeah...lots." She laughed. "Have you spoken to them? I mean, most things can be fixed, one way or the other. Tit for tat, if you know what I mean." She spoke in melodic, enchanting tones.

I pitied the mortal who fell under her spell.

"No. It goes way beyond." I pressed my hands flat against the wall.

I glanced for the last time at my father, finding solace in one truth. His spirit had found its way to a better place. I could only hope for the same grace.

"I'm sorry to hear that." Her angel voice channeled darkness into light. My heart leaped, filled with an emotion I had for so long refused to entertain.

She was not like Them. She was something more.

COLM

A gentle breeze carried a voice, enchanting my mind and transporting me to a place where shadows dwelled. Next to my father's casket stood the woman of my dreams. Her black mane swept into an intricate Celtic knot. An oversized black sweater of the finest weave hugged her upper thighs, and black tights clung to well-formed legs. I stared too long at the sparkling white running shoes, replaying the moment we met. She had worn white shoes then, although they were barely recognizable.

The brass wall sconces cast a golden light, illuminating her from behind and forming a halo around her silhouette. She reminded me of a dark angel. Her mouth intrigued me—how her bottom lip pouted beyond her upper lip. Her mere presence exuded mystery.

"They say they live within you. Right here." She lifted her hand, catching a pocket of air. "I like to believe their spirits are never far." She looked away, her smile touching every corner of the room.

I had no intention of seeking her out, but now the improbable seemed possible. There she was, standing before me. I smiled, wondering if she often talked to herself.

My skin prickled beneath the starched dress shirt. The suit jacket I wore seemed suddenly too tight. I cleared my throat.

"Hello, Calla." My voice cracked. Was it only yesterday I had driven her into town? Lack of sleep, combined with grief-laden guilt, left my thoughts muddled. Or perhaps it was the whisky. I stared, bleary-eyed, only half myself.

"Colm, I'm sorry. Sorry for your loss. How are you?" Her voice washed over me. Soothing. Sultry.

I didn't know what to make of that subtle gesture. But then a smile lit up her eyes.

"I've been better. Why are you here?" The murmuring voices faded, and I heard the quiet for the first time since my father passed.

"Saoirse brought me. I hope I'm not intruding?" The pieces fell into place. Saoirse owned the Black Horse Pub and brought Calla to my father's wake.

"No, of course not. This is Ireland, after all." I smiled, and my heart flared with happiness. I had no idea how to approach that emotion. This was not the time or place to feel it, yet there it was. I wanted to reach out, wrap her in my arms, and never let go.

I lifted my gaze toward the open window. A salt breeze carried a cold north wind. The curtains fluttered, and the candles flickered. A deep sense of foreboding crawled under my skin, causing me to pause. I looked at Calla, who appeared unaffected by the change in temperature.

"I'd like to pay you. For yesterday. For the gas?" She searched through her handbag, pulling out twenty euros. She extended her arm, handing me the bill.

"What? No. That's unnecessary." Darkness spread along the floor as a hooded crow alighted on the window sill. I held my breath, struck by the bird's imposing size. The crow bobbed its black head, showing off its black-feathered throat and gray-tufted chest.

"Kraa. Kraa." The bird squawked, commanding the room with its call. Intelligent eyes inspected Calla alone. The crow ruffled its striking plumage, unfurled its glossy black wings, and soared into the overcast sky.

"What was that?" Calla jumped back, her gaze following the crow's flight.

"A 'hoodie,' otherwise known as the scald crow. They're uncommon in these parts, especially this time of year." I scratched my head, wondering if the visit conveyed a dark message. "The locals would say the 'hoodie' visits when death is near."

"Death? You mean an omen of death?" The color faded from her cheeks, her gaze darting around the room.

"That's what they say." I saw myself reflected in her dove-grey eyes. My mind fought with conflicting emotions. The woman presented a distraction I didn't need, yet I wanted her. I felt helpless against her charms.

"Colm." She spoke my name the way a lover might. She trailed her fingers over mine.

My throat closed. My hands shook. How had I

gotten by her side? I couldn't remember moving across the room, but she was before me, her fragrance seeping into my pores—moonlight and black orchids. My awareness of her heightened, and I leaned into her touch.

An icy breath whispered, demanding I follow. I turned toward her, wondering if anyone else had felt the cooling breeze, but I couldn't tear my gaze away.

"Calla? Where are we going?" The situation struck me as strange, but I didn't know why.

She moved through the mourning crowd on the wings of a bird. None looked her way, or mine, for that matter. We were in a time draft of our own making, and everything and everyone had ceased to exist. The air between us compressed, the four walls closed in, and a blur of light enveloped us. I could almost touch it, but the shimmering silver bands remained out of reach. Her long strides took her beyond the clapboard house, beyond the horse paddock, through long meadow grass and carpets of wild thyme. The ocean roared, throwing frothy streamers into the sky and crashing one after another onto the rocky shore.

She didn't answer my question, just teased me with a backward glance. She halted beneath the budding branches of an ancient oak tree.

"I want you, Colm." I sensed trepidation in her voice, laced with fear, but then she plunged her hands forward and rested her palms against my chest.

Desire ripped my heart into two distinct pieces. Both belonged to her.

The ground shook, and the branches cracked and splintered overhead. The ocean became a roaring whirlpool. Heat tore through me—her heat. I became one with her essence, drifting through a wonderland of frozen lakes and smoky forests. Aromatic pine, touched with winter's frost, shielded us from harm.

Her eyes widened, and yet she said nothing.

Whatever that was, I was utterly powerless against it. I surrendered to the otherworldliness of the situation, questioning nothing. My heart pounded in my chest.

"Kiss me." She curled her fingers into my shirt, closing the gap between us.

I threaded my fingers through those silken locks and drew my thumbs along the delicate curve of her jaw.

A soft moan reverberated in her throat. She tugged me closer and nibbled my bottom lip, tentatively at first.

Rational thought left me when her lips

scorched mine—when she swept her tongue inside my mouth and explored wildly. When she dug her fingers into my hair, seizing the kiss and making it her own, I circled my arms around her, pulling her into a hard embrace. I had dreamed of this moment.

A soft breeze slipped over and around us, melting the winter snow and awakening the earth to the coming spring. I saw something that took my breath away—a goddess, wrapped in a delicate gown of gossamer silk threaded with stardust, sat astride a milk-white stallion. Woven into her lustrous ebony locks—a thorny crown of hawthorn blossoms. Radiance surrounded her.

Heat surged through my limbs. Hunger fed my soul. Bealtaine—the night when the majestic white stag chased the white doe, marking the sacred ritual: the union of the spring goddess and the horned god. Seed scattered, fertilizing the land. Faeries danced. She was the hunted, and I was the hunter, pursuing the sovereign queen on this Bealtaine eve. Her sighs fractured my heart into jagged shards. My cock throbbed for this woman.

"Thank you." A sob rose in her throat. She looked over her shoulder and then back at me, her face wet with tears.

"What's wrong, *mo ghrá*?" Her distress slammed through me. I pressed kisses along her delicate cheekbones. Her flesh was icy cold.

"Nothing. Everything is fine. Just fine." She tucked against me, burying her head beneath my chin.

"Colm? You make a better door than a window. Move." Breda prodded my shoulder. Her onyx orbs threw darts straight through me.

I wavered, lost in the eerie. Wisps of light floated through bloodshot skies. Whispers called to me, and a voice sang—Calla's melodic voice. The tingling sensations subsided, and the room came into focus.

Calla stood ten feet away, clenching my father's casket, her peaked nipples teasing her cashmere sweater, her lips swollen from our kiss. Her eyes, those dove grey eyes, shimmered with silver light.

Cold sweat gathered beneath my shirt's collar. The white stag and the white doe did not exist in Ireland. Those were mythical creatures of the Otherworld. And yet, I could not unsee the vision of the goddess following the moon through the quiet greenwood.

She scraped her teeth lightly over her bottom lip and repositioned, crossing her arms over her breasts. A wisp of hair fell over her face, one I so desperately wanted to touch.

"Calla?" My bewildered voice was a quiet echo. I tried to make sense of what had just happened and could not. The vivid details of our encounter faded into the stark reality of the moment.

Her gaze shifted toward a stray sunbeam illuminating the carpeted floor. The lights dimmed, and the candles flickered. The gloom surrounding my father's body transformed into a glowing ball of light, a radiant starburst hovering over his chest before disappearing.

"Your da, Colm. He's on his way to Summerland. Did you feel the divine power? It was his energy, his soul. What kept him so long, I wonder? What was he waiting for?" Saoirse clasped her hands together, her brown eyes charged with gold flecks. When she squeezed Breda's forearm, the candles cornering the casket flickered and extinguished completely, shrouding the room in dim light.

"Bloody hell." Breda's face paled, her gaze darting toward me.

I moved past Calla, intending to light the candles at each corner of my father's casket. The wicks sputtered, refusing to ignite.

Breda gaped at me.

I backed away from the casket, my breath curling in the air.

"Oh, and you'll never guess, Calla's singing with Niall at the burial. Wait till you hear her voice. It's with the angels." Saoirse tossed her head, oblivious to the force floating around the room.

"Yes, there's always a song in my head." Calla shrugged. Her soft, honeyed voice slithered through my mind and crept under my skin. She was the devil in disguise.

"That's unnecessary." I paced from one end of the room to the other, turning on table lamps. I dismissed the offer with a wave, my tone harsher than intended.

"Colm." Breda raised her white eyebrows, disapproval written on her pale face.

I had experienced something similar once before, during a training exercise meant to allow recruits to experience firsthand the torturous effects of mind-bending drugs. The simulation was nothing compared to my walk through the Otherworld with Calla Sweet. I steeled my mind against the enemy force. But she was not the enemy. Complex logic replaced the fantasy I had held moments before. I accepted my initial reading of her. She was from a different time. But what phenomenon was she? Time travel was too fantastical. I dismissed the theory of reincarnation. And what of the prophecy she spoke? She whispered I was too late. How did she know my father had died? The hairs on my nape rose, and my ears roared.

The complexity intrigued me. I was familiar with dead souls and ghostly spirits, but this was entirely different. That was something the old ones spoke of.

I strategized my next move. The more time I spent with her, the more I discovered. I acknowledged the thrill of that realization. I left my musings, concluding my thoughts: why would I refuse if the most beautiful woman in the world offered to sing at my father's burial?

"Excuse us, ladies. Calla and I need to talk." I took one step forward, offering my elbow.

"We do?" Calla showed no interest in joining me. Perhaps seeking forgiveness rather than permission was not the right approach.

"You do?" Breda's mouth hung open.

"Yes, we do." I curtailed my enthusiasm. One thought raised its ugly head: resisting her charms wouldn't be easy. She was an affliction.

Calla shrugged and, without a glance in my direction, sashayed down the hallway.

I hung back, admiring the view—round bottom, shapely thighs, legs that went on forever.

"So, what is it, sweet cheeks? What's on your mind?" She faced me, planting one hand on her hip.

I found her precocious manner amusing.

"You clean up nice." I offered my hand, hoping to guide her into a quiet corner, away from prying eyes.

"Hey! Stay in your own lane." She turned sideways against the wall, avoiding all contact, yet her gaze remained fixed on mine. Her eyes shifted, changing from dove grey to silver and then back again.

The distance between us hummed, and my world became a muffled place where I could neither speak nor move.

"What? What are you?" My heart throbbed in sync with hers.

"What's wrong, cupcake? Lost in the sunshine?" Her voice caressed my mind, sweet like cotton candy.

"Are you a witch?" My stomach dropped to the floor, and my ears popped. For the second time today, I felt alive.

"A witch? Hmm, I don't think so." She smirked, and my heart quaked.

"I didn't expect to see you." Free from her enchantment, I extended my fingers and bent each knuckle. I gazed at the soft skin beneath her jaw. "Or kiss you."

"Not ever?" The hum left her fresh scent in its wake. She took one step forward, trailing the tip of one red fingernail along the edge of my jaw through two days of bristled scruff. "A new look, huh? Brings out the sparkle in your eyes. I like it."

"Explain the vision." Her touch sent heat arrowing in all directions. What I would give to be somewhere else, with that woman—my heart's desire. I would willingly admit she held the advantage.

"What vision?" She smirked, tilting her face and pouting those lips.

There were too many people—too many eyes and ears within proximity.

"Hmm. You got it bad, huh?" She turned to leave, and the loss consumed me.

Emptiness—a sensation I hadn't felt in such a long time—made my bones ache.

"Wait, we need to talk." My mouth went dry, and that familiar hum returned, but the energy differed. My heart skipped erratically, the blood coursing through my veins energized.

"Looky here, lucky charm. I'm not lookin' for a

new bestie." She smiled knowingly. When she moved, the aura surrounding her shimmered.

Was I the only one who could see it?

"Hey, a conversation. Give me that." I offered my palms up in apology, hoping to gain her trust. Everything I thought I knew, I didn't.

"I'm sorry about your father. Truly. It's an awful thing. I know how painful it can be." Her voice dropped one seductive octave. Calla Sweet, the girl on channel 549 who cried for the world, stared into my soul.

"It was a shock." I grasped the wall with one hand. "Looks like you're fitting right in."

"Saoirse has been good to me." Her gaze held me hostage.

I had the distinct impression she tested me.

"And Niall?" I mentioned the fiddle player, regret coating my tongue immediately.

"Niall? Are you jealous, Colm O'Donnell?" Her eyes danced with merriment.

"I'm concerned, that's all. You're new here." I considered her question. Maybe I was. "So you sing? You're a singer? I didn't know that." I attempted to change the subject. I wanted more than anything to relive that dream.

"Where is this going, Colm?" She placed her

index finger on her chin and widened her eyes in animated wonder.

I wondered the same thing.

"Listen, I'm sorry for my outburst earlier. It was uncalled for. I'm glad you're here." I looked into her shadowy eyes, and again, my ears popped.

"You are?" She tilted her head, lifting the corners of her lips into a curious smile.

"I didn't think I'd see you again." My confidence grew, and my psyche responded to her opalescent vibrations, luring sensations I had never experienced before meeting her.

"Hmm." She crossed her arms and then exhaled. "Hey, which brother did I meet?"

"Sorry?" I asked, taken aback by her question. I dared not look too long into her eyes.

"In the room with your da. I spoke to one of your brothers. I didn't get his name." She tilted her face, her gaze questioning.

"Perhaps you were speaking with my father's ghost. Da always had to have the last word." I shrugged, unsure of where our conversation headed.

"No, he called your father, da. I heard him. Tall. Blond. You couldn't miss him." She convinced me of one thing. She believed what she said.

"There was no one there, Calla." I relived the moment—my father lying peacefully, his hands clasped together. Her voice echoed in my mind, speaking in comforting tones to someone.

"He walked away when you showed up. I've seen him before. I saw him at the Black Horse just last night." She searched for answers, her brows creasing.

"Hmm." I considered the probabilities. She could be a medium who spoke to spirits, but what of the other day? "You're too late," she had said. I prevented her fall but caused her physical pain. I recalled the fear running through her eyes. My blood ran cold, and I looked at her in a different light.

I offered my hand, testing her reaction. I expected her to walk away, and she did. I followed her down the dim hallway.

"What business do we have? What do you want?" She turned on her heel and leaned forward slightly, commanding my respect.

"I didn't think you would be here." I stalled for time. She was not a witch or a spirit medium. No, she was something else entirely.

"And yet here I am." She clapped her hands together, waking me from the trance.

"I wanted to...well, once things settle down, could I show you around town? Help you get sorted in your new place?" I steadied myself. I questioned my assumptions. Could I be that far off base?

"My new place? You're not much of a player, are you? Look, you're a nice guy, Colm. Maybe even the full package." She moistened her lower lip and then smiled.

She was, in a word––captivating. Yet, I was already aware of this. She possessed a dangerous allure, mesmerizing my thoughts with a whim.

"I'm a nice guy." It would be so easy to lose myself in those starry eyes. I wondered where she would take me. The possibility filled my mind with unease.

"You'll see me at the burial. If you're okay with that?" Her voice soared with her rising eyebrows.

If I listened, I heard tinkling bells. That's what Saoirse meant when she said Calla sang with the angels. The Angels or the Other Crowd?

"Yes, the day after tomorrow. Of course. Look, I'm sorry. I don't know what I thought. I'm glad you're making friends." My perception changed. Her kind were vengeful beings and not to be trusted.

"You're glad I'm making friends? You're funny, Colm." She backed away but came to a hard stop in the middle of the hall.

I followed her gaze to the family portrait hanging on the wall–the last time we were all to-gether, on the winter solstice seven years ago.

"There he is." She pointed to the third brother from the left.

"That's Ciarán." My brother stared back from beyond a thin pane of glass, unsmiling—some-thing I had never noticed before.

"Yeah? Well, that's the guy." Her voice dropped to a haunting whisper.

"That's not possible. Ciarán's gone, and he's been gone a long time." The hairs on my neck rose when Ciarán whispered, "Brother."

"Oh, he's not gone. I spoke to him. I saw him." Calla shook her head. Her voice conveyed honesty. She believed.

"He is, Calla." I disregarded her sincerity and ignored her words. A stabbing pain struck my frontal lobe, debilitating my mind. I retreated into the dark, suffocating hole where I had existed for the last seven years.

In the military, a well-known maxim empha-sized the importance of teamwork, loyalty, and dedication to the mission: "Never leave a man behind." That maxim represented an unbreakable bond of trust and commitment. Ciarán had been my mission, and I had failed him. I let him down when he needed me most, and guilt weighed heavily on my conscience.

"You're not listening." She batted my hand and walked away, leaving me staring after her, unable to respond.

Her words played in my mind like a broken record. "He's not gone."

I turned and slammed my hand against the wall. Plaster fragments fell to the floor, and the pictures swayed. Had I been blind? Had I accepted my brother's fate too readily? The shadows whispered, and her words sank in. Ciarán lived.

"You drive, Colm. I'm fair knackered." Breda tossed me the keys to her car, a baby blue convertible coupe.

I inspected the vehicle, noting the worn tires, polished chrome, and the damaged right fender mirror.

"You sure?" I pushed the driver's seat back. "Where are we going?"

"Martin's, in Killybegs." She snapped her seat-belt into place and settled into the bucket seat.

"A long way for a loaf of bread, Breda. What will Pádraig say?" I nosed the low-slung two-seater through the many parked cars and down the laneway.

"Well, it's nice to see things haven't changed." She shifted sideways, fixing me with a sharp gaze.

"Hmm?" I veered left, avoiding a deep pothole.

"Look at you...a regular pork chop on steroids. Looks like you haven't missed too many meals. Hey? Are you listening to me?" She huffed.

"Aye." I chuckled for no reason.

"Why are you laughing?" She shook her head, exhaling exasperation.

"No reason." I glanced at my favorite cousin.

"Hmph. I've been going to the gym with Saoirse. Ciarán's Saoirse? You know you were rude to her. You weren't very nice." She admonished me the way a mother talks to a child.

I flinched at the mention of Ciarán's name. In one fleeting blink of an eye, I saw Calla's face—the shock, the denial, the acceptance.

Still, I found myself torn between two opposing forces—wanting to believe and the inherent skepticism lurking within me—the ability to question when others rushed forth had saved my life more than once.

"What was with the ball of flame Saoirse tossed out there? Magic dust from her last seance?" I muttered, unwilling to fully commit to what I saw. The glowing essence floating over my father's casket proved the Otherworld exists. I couldn't deny it.

"After growing up Irish, you don't believe?" She gazed with wide eyes, her voice haunted.

"Has she not found someone? I thought by now." I chose another topic, my mind racing from one far-fetched reality to another.

"Still wears his ring. Did you know she owns a pub?" Breda stared out the side window, her lips pinned in a straight line. "Her da went in on it. Helped her out, aye? Turned it right around. Trad nights. Cheap Tuesdays. At least she has that."

The long bonnet dipped, and Breda flinched.

"Nice." I shifted gears, dropping into overdrive and punching the accelerator.

"I know you and your da... You know, he was looking forward to your visit. It's too soon for him to leave." Her voice trembled.

"Oisin will help Mam with the farm. And I'm here now." Did I say that? Was that what I wanted?

"Oisin? He has enough on his plate." She leaned back in the seat, lifting her shoulders.

"Aye." I shifted gears, Calla's silvery voice echoing in my mind.

I could rationalize her psychic abilities—seers were commonplace in Ireland—but the aura surrounding her was beyond rationalization. Unknowingly or not, she had wielded magic, holding my hardened soul in her hand. She transported me to another place, where she kissed me. I sorted through each moment—the wonder in her eyes, the passion. My thoughts drifted, and I wondered where she was now.

"What about you? Are you still, you know? Talking to the air? Seeing things?" She poked my arm and then grinned.

"That was Ciarán, not me." I glanced her way. She knew Ciarán had the sight, could see and talk to the Other Crowd. I would keep my suspicions from Breda a while longer. Accusing Ardara's latest resident of being otherworldly would get me locked up. But if what Calla said was true.

"Jaysus feckin' Christ, Colm, watch out. You almost hit that car." Breda jumped in her seat.

"Relax. He's got brakes." I smiled, taking full advantage of her good nature.

"Don't tell me to relax. I've ten payments left.

Don't you feckin' smash it." She scolded me, her voice undulating with every curve in the road.

I tapped the horn twice and waved, passing a slow-moving farm tractor.

"Jaysus, is your foot stuck on the feckin' accelerator?" She threw her hand onto the dashboard.

"Shush." I grinned when the car slid on the wet pavement.

"Don't shush me, you bastard." She swept the white strands away from her face. I recalled the day her hair changed from lustrous black to ghostly white. Struck down by Scarlet Fever at twelve years of age, she hung onto life by a thin thread, the effects lingering long after. I have often considered the time she spent in the world of the dead and the toll she must have paid. Once, I asked the question. She responded to my concern with a cold, dark stare.

"You need to drive this thing, Breda. Blow the carbon out. When did you turn into such a Nervous Nancy?" I punched the gas for good measure, fishtailing the back end.

"There's nothing wrong with me. You, Colm O'Donnell, are the problem." Her face paled.

"Hmm." I pondered Breda's statement.

Rush-filled fields thick with mud stretched in

every direction. Dark clouds drifted across the stark skies. A cold chill seeped into my bones.

"Well, I'm glad you're back. You should stay." She scrunched her nose and then laughed. "Jaysus, I've missed you."

"I have a life of my own, Breda." Somehow, returning didn't hold the thrill it had a day ago.

"Are you thick in the head? Can't you see, we love you? Why don't you buy that fishing boat you always wanted?" Her voice rose, her eyes filled with hope.

"Ciarán's dream." I tapped my fingers on the steering wheel, my mind conjuring up images of the past, of the summer day a long time ago. What a find it had been—a broken-down rowboat washed up by the seas. Of ten-year-old Ciarán, sweat pouring down his brow, affixing a pole-wood mast to the middle beam, and Breda, her pale hair falling into her eyes, painting the prow a vibrant royal blue. Breda—always part of every memory.

"The two of you had such grand plans. Stop this, Colm." She stared me down.

"Stop what?" I tilted my head toward her, seeking clarity.

"Blaming yourself for Ciarán. You did all you could. So did your da...How long are you going to keep punishing yourself, then?" She peered at me, her brows drawn tight.

"I've missed you too, Breda." I smiled.

We left the main highway, snaking through lush green fields, the landscape rolling with every bend in the road. We passed through small villages and remote lookouts—so many shades of green—bloodied with so much pain.

Everything remained the same, yet everything had changed. Breda had been right about one thing: it was time for me to stop running.

4

Calla

"Hey, thanks for driving me. I appreciate it." I marveled at Saoirse's driving skills. Her chin barely skimmed the top of the steering wheel, yet she chased every twist and turn the narrow road presented. Faster. Faster. Each bend inspired awe. From the grassy mountains towering high into the clouds to the pretty cottages nestled into the lush landscape. Just wow.

"I don't mind. It's not far, anyway. Do you have what you need?" She hit the wipers, clearing the drizzle from the windshield.

"I think so, thanks to you." I hugged a wicker basket filled with goodies from the Black Horse

Pub: a container of Orlaith's famous chowder, cockles packed separately, with specific instructions to add the tiny delicacies at the very last moment, sheaves of fresh baked Wheaton bread, and a block of fragrant white cheddar.

"See the place with the slate roof? That's Niall and Bonnie." She motioned with her lifting chin.

"Oh, okay." We zoomed past a white stucco cottage at the bottom of a green slope. Niall and his wife Bonnie were friends from the pub. The moment was etched in my mind—the crowd silenced when I joined the singalong. *"Where did you learn that song? It's Elven. It's with the angels,"* they said. They welcomed me, sealing my fate. They knew my name and where I lived. A thousand hellos before the night ended. I could only imagine what tomorrow would bring. What would happen when they found out the truth? There were no secrets in Ardara town.

"Dermot's place is just around the next bend." She took her foot off the gas, allowing the roadster to coast down the next hill.

"Saoirse, listen. I want to apologize––about the wake. I didn't mean to...to rush you out." Colm's face came back to me, not broken, not confused. No, he looked right through me, his jaw set in a hard line, his gaze burning with hunger and something far more dangerous.

That moment eclipsed all others. I had wandered into the land of lust, and dear gods, he walked with me—in sync, in time. I kissed the man in a meadow, under a tree, or did he kiss me? And now, my dreams were filled with him. They seemed so real.

My pulse raced. My mind was a switch that wouldn't shut off. Too much had happened, too much to take back. The pressing question was my connection with Colm O'Donnell and our shared visions. Sexy. Hot. Visions. I clamped my lips tight, refusing to acknowledge the heat. If I closed my eyes, the wind would sing, the clouds would unfurl, and I would be lost. It was more than an out-of-body experience.

And then there was the man only I could see—his brother, Ciarán. I spoke to him, and he answered, his blue eyes wide with awe. I thought nothing of it at the time. He gave me the distinct impression he wanted to share something significant. I tried again to delve deep, but my mind resisted, thrusting me backward and rejecting my efforts—an impenetrable wall I could not breach. My connection with Colm felt different; it was as if Ciarán belonged somewhere else.

I shook my head, meeting Saoirse's confused gaze.

"Huh? Don't be silly. You arrive in Ireland, and on your second day, a crazy barkeep drags you off to a wake. You hadn't even settled in yet. Think about it." Her voice, layered with melancholy, lingered in my mind.

I studied her. Since leaving the wake, Saoirse seemed in a world of her own. I blamed my early flight from the O'Donnell residence just as the festivities were about to begin.

"No, it's okay. It was enlightening." I visualized Colm's brother, remembering how his lips moved and his chest rose beneath his crisp white shirt. I had the distinct impression he wanted to tell me something, but then he disappeared like the mist on a foggy day, leaving behind a faint scent of rosewater.

And what of Colm? He spoke to me. Or did Ciarán whisper in my ear? I couldn't get him out of my head. *That's a song? Isn't it?*

"Breda and me. We go way back. Well, the whole family. I know them all quite well." She tilted her head in my direction. "Can I tell you something?"

"Of course." I held her gaze, hoping she would

share her secrets. Maybe, just maybe, I should go first.

"I was happy to leave." She looked away, her shoulders quaking slightly.

I stared down a narrow road flanked by steep green slopes.

"There are just so many memories. That place. That house. I'm sorry, I'm blathering." She gripped the steering wheel tighter, speeding through the winding pass, the tires drumming on the slick pavement. She shared nothing else. The question of why drummed in my mind, yet I had no right to pry. She had her secrets, and I had mine.

"Are you all right, Saoirse?" What would one touch tell me? I knew so little about my 'gift' that I feared experimenting. I should have embraced it all those years ago and learned from it instead of running away. I struggled to process the encounter with Orlaith. Witnessing someone's memories had never happened before. I shivered despite the cozy sweater I wore.

"I'm fine. I didn't sleep much." She smiled, giving me a darting glance.

"No? Is something bothering you?" I pushed my problems aside.

Saoirse. Sweet and kind, and oh so sad—

Saoirse. I studied the dark cast beneath her eyes and her sharp cheekbones.

"It's nothing, Calla. It's fine. Oh, blast, hold on." She slammed the brakes. The tires screeched, and the car came to a burning stop. "Brilliant. Just brilliant."

"Oh, look at the sheep." I spread my lips into a smile. The round eyes of so many black-faced sheep stared back.

Since arriving in Ireland, my abilities morphed into something else. I had wandered away from the present three times, and those were not simple daydreams. I saw shadows where none existed. I heard voices. I seemed stuck in another place and time and couldn't find my way back. And what of Orlaith...I pinned my bottom lip beneath my teeth, considering my future with these people.

"Is Niall bringing you to the burial?" She punched the accelerator when the last sheep meandered into the long grass.

"Yes." How did I get embroiled in the landscape so quickly? How soon before they discovered my menacing charms?

"If anything changes, let me know. Okay? See the hedges? They mark the boundaries of Dermot's croft." She pointed her chin toward the boundary stones climbing the mountain slope, disappearing into a cloud-filled sky.

"It's quite a hill." I followed her gaze.

"Here we are. This is Dermot's. Um, sorry. This is your place." Saoirse pulled onto the shoulder of the road, the car's wheels swishing through the tall grass along the road's edge.

"Oh geez. This is it?" Two monolithic stone piers, one pointed upward and the other cut flat, stood at the entrance of Dermot Sweet's estate, and between them loomed a rusted iron gate.

"Halfway to heaven, that's what Dermot called it. They say the Faeries dance on the flat one." Saoirse nodded toward the stone pillar on the right. She left the car idling at the gated entrance.

I stared into the dark maw of a long grassy laneway shrouded by a canopy of trees, unable to ignore the prickling sensations coursing over me. "Faeries?" I raised my eyebrows, allowing her to explain.

"Do you know about the Other Crowd?" Her confident and matter-of-fact tone caught me off-guard.

"Well, yes. Sort of." I nodded, reflecting on the Celtic Myth and Fairytale class I had taken at university, recalling ancient tales of the Fir Bolg, Fomorians, and the Tuatha Dé Danaan.

"Be careful not to offend them. They can be sensitive to intruders." Her concerned gaze confirmed my suspicions—Faerie belief remained alive and well in that part of Ireland.

"Sensitive?" I wondered how the Faeries could be offended by little old me.

"I'm sure you'll be fine. Dermot lived here for years. He never spoke of Them." She shrugged, but her shadowed gaze caused me some concern.

"Okay." I giggled. "Would you like to come in? Maybe do a Faerie sweep with me?" I jingled half a dozen odd-shaped keys, hoping I wouldn't have to walk down that long, dark laneway alone.

"No, I'm sorry. I have to get back. Is that okay?" Her eyes begged forgiveness. "But I'll see you tomorrow."

"No worries." I climbed from the car, glancing at the flat-topped stone post, wondering what creatures danced by the moon's light. I half intended to see for myself.

"If you need anything, anything at all, call me." She leaned out the window, her worried expression causing my stomach to clench.

"Thanks." I waved, watching her drive away. I swallowed my fright, squashing the disturbing Other Crowd thoughts. What were these mystical beings? Saw-toothed, crazed beings whirling evil spells? Or teeny-weeny pixie's making dreams come true? I chose the latter.

I fumbled with the keys, trying each one in the old lock. A ratchety click told me I'd found success. I hung the lock on a crosser and hauled on the gate, straining at the rusted hinges. I gazed at my hands and grimaced at the rusty residue.

"Come on. Open sesame." I dug my heels into the mud, yanking until the hinges freed, dragging the gate across the long grass while talking myself into the unthinkable—leaving the gate wide open in the feathery grass.

I slung my backpack onto my shoulder, carrying the basket, and left the main road behind. I ventured deeper into the laneway, into the forest of tall trees. A green canopy dappled with sunlight gave birth to a thick underbrush dancing with bluebells and a filmy carpet of green ferns. A warm tang wafted on gentle currents, freeing the earth from winter's icy grip.

My awareness heightened. An unearthly chill crept along the ground. I relaxed my shoulders, breathing through my nose.

A trio of blackbirds burst through the underbrush, soaring low over the forest floor and weaving through the standing trees. I took a moment to appreciate their graceful flight. The tinkling sound of rushing water replaced the flutter of wings.

I gazed in wonder at the sight before me. Water tumbled over gentle waterfalls, lingering in shallow pools before searching for the sea. A fairy tale bridge, rounded stones stacked in another age, crossed the stream. Carved by ancient hands, speared stones, broken and moss-covered, told a story of their own. I placed my hand almost tentatively on one particularly gruesome spike. White lights danced behind my eyelids as I stumbled, thrown backward by a powerful force. I steadied myself and ran across the bridge, escaping those old stones.

"*Tá tú abhaile*, a Rioghain." A voice rang out in sweet, dulcet tones, and I understood the meaning. You're home, Rioghain.

"Who's there?" I hugged the basket, peering into the silent forest, scanning the nearby stand of birch trees for any signs of life. I turned my head, fear holding my feet still. The question—who would call me by my middle name? I had only ever shared that tidbit with one person.

I picked up my pace and followed the beam of light penetrating the woodland while airing my suspicions with the buzzing bees. They followed me everywhere, their hum convincing me that I imagined the welcoming voice. I listed the external elements at play: the rushing water tinkling over the exposed rocks, the wind whistling through the trees, and those damn birds. I would save those gruesome spikes for another day.

"What the..." A big-eyed bird shot straight out of the ground, then zipped in a bat-like fashion between the trees, croaking like a frog in heat. I jumped backward, falling flat in the soft spring mud. I lost sight of him in the underbrush, his tawny feathers camouflaging him perfectly.

"First, sheep. Now a bird," I sighed. At least I had saved the wicker basket from sailing through the underbrush. I swept leafy debris from my jeans and hiked up the basket. What else could the Emerald Isle have in store?

Colm's face appeared before me, snatching away the peace. When I thought of him, I lost my breath. I placed my fingers on my lips, remembering his velvet touch. I kissed him, and he kissed me back. How did it happen? How did his thoughts blend with mine? There was a moment where he took control, and I let him. I pushed the memory away. What good was remembering? Being with him or anyone else remained an impossible dream.

I lengthened my stride, leaving the wilds of

that enchanted wood behind. The scalloped ridge of a thatched roof showed itself. The tendrils of smoke curling into the sky from the snub-nosed chimney struck me as odd. Did the lawyer mention a caretaker?

The cottage appeared the same as all the cottages on the Glengesh Pass—rectangular and no more than one room wide, with sash windows haphazardly placed across the front wall. The sled-red painted door matched the trim around the windows. A bicycle leaned against the front wall, adding to the charming ambiance.

The cottage surrounded by neatly trimmed grass and tidy cobblestones was expected. But the border of calla lilies? Was that a mere coincidence? I lingered in the courtyard, gazing from the cottage to the barn to the garage.

Saoirse's musings were correct. Dermot Sweet owned three vehicles, a modest portfolio of stocks and bonds, and the property—a small holding located halfway along the Glengesh Pass ten minutes between Ardara and Glencolmcille—and from what I understood, two hundred head of black-faced sheep. What did I know about sheep?

I dropped the basket and backpack onto the cobblestones and explored the garage. The hinges creaked, revealing a tidy space, a workbench, and shelves lined with glass jars filled to the brim with nuts and bolts, and screws of different sizes.

I ran my index finger along the fender of a candy apple red full-size pickup truck. I concentrated. Nothing.

I discovered the key fob, vehicle registration certificate, and the insurance documents laid out for one purpose. The logbook displayed my name printed in bold block letters.

Who was this man?

A car draped in a beige tarp awaited discovery. I pulled the cover over the long hood of a classic dark green coupe. Chrome accents gleamed while a wildcat leaped from the hood. The steering wheel and stick shift were located on the left.

"Holy mother of God." I imagined unleashing that beauty on those winding roads.

I returned to the cottage, my mind reeling. Why would this man leave me with everything he owned in the world?

I rested my hand on the half door and nearly jumped out of my skin when a tiny wren flew into my face, flapping her wings and chirping murderous thoughts.

"All right. All right." At that point, nothing surprised me. I pursed my lips and whistled birdsong to appease my avian assassin. The wren watched me with unblinking black eyes.

I turned the skeleton key in a rusty lock, leaned into the door, and found myself standing on the uneven flagstones of a small hallway. A diamond-shaped, leaded-glass spy hole cut into the inside wall allowed me to peer into the reception room beyond. The room was a quiet shade of green, furnished with an overstuffed couch flanked by two end tables topped with matching Tiffany lamps; the stained glass dragonflies seemed to dance.

Stationed on a low table, a chess board, the carved pieces poised in play. My thoughts skipped around the table. Mr. Sweet and I had something in common, after all.

My gaze followed the timbered walls and high rafters, captivated by the beautifully draped plaid hanging over the second-floor railing. The vaulted ceiling created a warm, airy atmosphere.

Bookshelves lined each side of the fireplace where turf glowed, the breathing embers reminding me of a red-tipped cigar, the sweet-smelling aroma exuding a pleasant, earthy bouquet. The chimney's two keeping holes held a clay pipe and a dusty ball of yellow yarn. I removed each item from their hiding holes and examined them. I lifted a silver candlestick from the mantel, inhaling the remains of a beeswax candle.

My gaze turned to a gilt-framed portrait of a man and a woman standing side by side. The man wore a flat cap, a tweed jacket, a white shirt, and a tie. But the woman held my attention. It was the golden-haired girl from Orla's memory. Her blue eyes smiled, and the hem of her lacy dress wafted in a gentle breeze. I fought a wave of dizziness. The tick-tock of a grandfather clock comforted me.

Sidestepping the woman's penetrating gaze, I entered the adjacent bedroom and plopped onto the bed, admiring the four turned posts crowned with intricately carved acorn caps. Through the lace curtains, ancient mountains reached into the sky. I smoothed my hands over the soft chenille bedspread, stretched out, and closed my eyes—a new mattress, a must-have. Should I shop online or support the local town's economy? I checked my cell signal, realizing there was none.

I raced to the bathroom, a wave of nausea threatening. When had I last eaten? Yesterday—it was yesterday. I had skipped breakfast to meet with the lawyer, sign the last of the papers, and collect the keys. I turned on the cold water and splashed it on my face. I spun around, noticing how well-stocked the bathroom appeared, with thick yellow towels piled on one shelf and slabs of soap wrapped in wax paper on another. A rope with a plastic dolphin hung from the ceiling. I pulled it, and water flowed into the corner shower stall.

Not so rustic, Saoirse. I chuckled to myself.

I followed the yellow linoleum into the back kitchen, where layers of blue paint coated a horizontal plank wall. A footed oak cabinet reached the ceiling, its open shelves showcasing an array of blue and white crockery, round plates and chipped platters, a spice rack, and a full bottle of Irish whisky.

I paused at the back door, glancing around the small alcove that was just big enough for someone to remove their boots. A canvas work shirt hung on a hook, and a gnarly-looking walking stick leaned in the corner. I held the work shirt to my nose, breathing in the sweet scent of hay mixed with a faint hint of honey. My heart stopped when I swung open the top half of the back door.

That was Ireland: a herd of black-faced sheep scattered across the steep slope, each swathed with a splash of red paint—and the clouds—living, breathing, misty formations drifting across a gray sky, while a waterfall trickled through a gash in the mountainside.

A distressed bleat shattered the silence—one of my flock was distressed. Jolting into action, I grabbed the walking stick for a weapon and raced out the back door, intending to protect the poor little lamb from what? The big bad wolf?

The skies broke, blinding me with a ray of sunshine. I looked both ways, only to find that the distressed sheep had vanished.

Perched atop the cedar rail fence was a little man wearing a green felt hat, a loose white shirt beneath a brown wool vest fitted to his miniature frame, short navy pants, and dark stockings. He jumped to his feet, his buckled leather brogues landing silently. His bucket hat barely touched the top rail.

My mouth hung open.

"Séamus welcomes you, Miss Rioghain, to Seldom Inn." He tipped his downy head, his blousy arm sweeping his felt hat in a wide arc. His pert lips lifted into a smile.

"Excuse me? Who are you? And how did you get here?" I dared not look away. The storybook man stared back, his dark eyes radiating warmth.

"Séamus lends a hand from time to time. Séamus hopes the croft is satisfactory?" He planted his thumbs in the pockets of his short pants.

His voice held the same dulcet tones I heard in the forest.

"Seldom Inn?" Trying not to smile seemed impossible.

"Mr. Dermot was seldom in. The croft is aptly named." He gestured toward a barnboard sign with the exact words painted red.

How did I not see the sign before?

"Séamus has long waited to meet you, Miss Rioghain." His words voiced more than a mild curiosity.

"No one mentioned you to me." I loosened my grip on the walking stick, satisfied he meant no harm. "And how do you know my name?"

"I would be a friend, Miss Rioghain." He dipped his chin, placing his hands on his finely threaded vest.

I studied the little man with renewed interest.

"A friend?" His peculiar speaking and strange clothes left me confused.

"Rioghain is your true name, given by your mother." His mahogany brows pinched together, his eyes translucent pools.

I saw myself, dressed in swaddling clothes, cradled in a golden basket.

"My mother?" The air left my lungs, and I

struggled to stay upright. I hoped he couldn't see my confusion.

"Your father wishes to meet you. Would you come with?" His eyes softened as he extended his hand. I gazed into his shimmering orbs, which reflected the majestic spires of a stone castle surrounded by dense woodland and lush green fields.

"Excuse me?" But that revelation was just too much. I clenched the horn of the walking stick, impaling my palm with a protruding thorn. The wind rolled over the meadow, and the blades of grass sang. "Meet my father?" The thorn pierced deeper.

Sunbeams rained down from the sky.

Heavy boots crunching over the gravel walkway intruded on my conversation with the strange little man. I released Séamus from my gaze and turned toward the disruption.

"Good day, Calla." Colm stood in the garden path, swatting honeybees with both hands. Dark half-moons clung to his eyes, and days' growth of stubble shadowed his chin. He wore cargo pants and a novelty T-shirt, which seemed out of place. He stepped away from the lilac bush and grinned sheepishly.

"Colm? What are you doing here? How did you

find me?" Whirling away, I gazed beyond the cedar fence into the face of a long-eared donkey. His mahogany coat glimmered in the sunlight, his blond mane as wild as the landscape. The donkey lowered his head, pulling up tender shoots of green grass.

"It wasn't difficult. Only one Dermot Sweet lived in Ardara." His voice faded in and out.

I heard only half of what he said.

"Is this about the burial tomorrow?" I turned toward him. A deep ache struck my belly, followed closely by the urge to touch the scruff scribed to his angled jaw.

"No. This is about Ciarán." The air stilled, and the smile left his face. He looked as haunted as I felt.

"Nice shirt." I lowered my gaze, and a giggle bubbled up in my throat. The pixie twirled her wand, leaving magical dust on the front of the black T-shirt.

What happened at the wake was an anomaly. Jet lag. Delirium. I could taste him—still feel the soft brush of his lips, his corded muscles beneath my fingertips. I conjured up a million scenarios that could never happen. Letting my guard down was one of them.

"A gift from Breda, my cousin? You met her at

the wake." He sliced me in half with a sharp glance.

"What are you doing here?" I curled my fingers over my palm, seeing the crimson line running down my wrist for the first time.

"What happened to your hand?" He drew closer, expecting I would seek comfort. His voice soothed but did nothing to quiet my rampant desires.

What did the therapist say? Something about running and adrenaline. Scratch the itch. Calm the mind.

"It's just a scratch." I kept him at bay with the thorny staff. "What do you want?" I spent last night alone, consumed in a haze of lust—visions of Colm O'Donnell dancing from one peaked nipple to the other.

"You said you spoke to Ciarán." He said each word carefully, slowly enunciating as if he knew how close I stood to the edge.

"And you didn't believe me." I should send him on his way. I glanced toward the donkey, happily munching on tufts of grass.

"I have questions." His commanding voice jolted me into the present.

Ciarán—the only reason Colm was here. He

was not interested in me. His agenda was selfish and personal.

I gazed into those baby blues. Quelling my infatuation seemed an impossible task.

"About the man in the photo?" I refused to name him. That would make it real. Seeing ghosts, talking to imaginary little men. But what of the golden-haired woman in the picture frame—her eyes followed me everywhere. I swept my fingers through my hair, dislodging a stray honeybee. The bee hummed and then flew away.

"What did he say to you?" He reached out, taking the walking stick from me and winding his fingers around the blackthorn staff.

The wind shifted, and the mountain cast shadows across the farmyard. The blood in my veins chilled, moving through my body like a melting iceberg. My mind numbed, and all those worries I held onto disappeared as if they had never existed.

"What?" I rested my hand over his and waited for the moment I stayed too long—the moment all hell would break loose, but I saw nothing, felt nothing: no death, no memories. I gazed over the flatland between the mountain and the forest, at the mist folding over the rocky outcrops, engulfing the yellow flowering gorse—no sign of Séamus, no donkey, lots of sheep.

My fingers strayed over his second knuckle and then his first. I licked my lips, waiting for the tsunami to strike. Instead, the sky dropped, becoming one with the mist, enveloping the valley in a ghostly haze.

"Tell me what you want, luv." Colm traced the bloody seam marking my palm with the pad of his wide thumb.

His nearness filled me with so much heat that my mind shattered.

"I need to know." My voice became a low moan as I leaned into him and became part of him.

"What do you want to know?" The groan in his throat fed my hunger. His arms embraced me, his hands sliding lower, pressing into my lower back.

"Everything." I pulled at his lower lip and swept my tongue against his. I was only vaguely aware of his chin scraping mine.

"Aye." He smoothed and warmed my skin, cupping my breasts and tweaking each taut nub with a circling thumb.

Every nerve ending I possessed ignited. Embers burst into fiery flames.

"Let me please you." His voice filled with passion, his face mirroring my need. He ran his big hand between my shoulder blades, and the air cracked.

"I want you, Colm." Heat pooled between my thighs. He made my blood burn. I dug my fingers into sculpted pecs and hung on for dear life.

"Calla, was it Ciarán? Was it my brother you spoke with?" His rumbling voice brought me back into the here and now. He stood in the courtyard, one hand clasping my shoulder, the other holding my walking stick. "You mentioned you saw him at the pub? The Black Horse. And then again at the wake. You had a conversation with my brother."

The pixie on his T-shirt tossed glitter into my eyes, tearing me away from the beautiful dream. I could no longer deny the obvious. I was the problem, unable to carry on a normal conversation with a man without zoning out and losing myself in the land of lust.

"Look, just forget it, okay?" My throat closed, and my voice left me. I turned away, watching the fog bank retreat into the honeycombed crevices in the mountain's face. A moment ago, his hands made love to me.

Hallucinations were one thing, but that was something entirely different. He seemed utterly unaware I had kissed him. Dear gods, what was wrong with me?

"We searched for years. Followed every clue. The *Bean Feasa* was called upon to cast her spells. Nothing helped. It was like Ciarán had walked off the face of the earth." His voice cracked.

I wanted to throw my hands over my ears. Why was he sharing his pain with me?

"Look, I'm sorry about your brother." Rays of light beamed from the sky, setting every blade of grass on fire. I threw my hands to my face and rubbed my eyes.

"Calla, are you all right?" He gripped my shoulders, squeezing gently. His eyes showed concern.

"You need to leave." My stomach heaved. Bile rose in my throat. I backed away from his embrace.

"Calla, please, Calla. Is he with the Good People?" His soft voice caressed my soul as if I even had one.

"The Good People? Is that a cult?" I gave him a sly smile. He needed to walk away before I did something I might regret. Tomorrow would come soon enough.

"Ciarán could see Them. He had the sight. He may have left willingly. But why? Why would he do that?" He spoke in a monotone, lost to his demons, giving me a glimpse of the real Colm O'-Donnell—a broken man obsessed with loss.

Were we so different?

"I'm not who you think I am." The adrenaline that had rushed through my body moments before dissipated, leaving me weak-kneed and so tired.

"What did he say, Calla? What did Ciarán say?" He cradled my elbow—the same hand that had inflamed my desires and made me feel.

I leaned into him, waiting for the ghastly vision to show itself. It would come, and it would go again.

Lightning struck the skies as three horsemen, red-haired and red-faced, frocked in crimson raiment, galloped head-to-head straight at me. As black as night and crazed with bloodlust, their three mighty steeds kicked up the earth, fiery flames shooting from their dead eyes. Banished from their home, the three horsemen rode between worlds, never veering or changing course. No, they would thunder through me, their ghostly spirits leaving me broken inside. Their message held a warning.

If only I knew what it meant.

"What did he say, Calla? What did Ciarán say?" His face contorted with pain.

I couldn't unsee it.

"You need to leave." My heart raced. My mouth

dried. I couldn't help him. I was not that person, and I didn't want to be.

"Calla, please." His cajoling voice turned pleading. His eyes tortured.

My unbridled lust for Colm was one thing. Visions I could handle, but I refused to be a medium between worlds. I did not sign up for that.

"I can't help you." I pressed my hands into his chest, holding him away. I could touch him—at least I had that.

He turned away, his rigid jaw telling me our discussion was far from over.

I gazed at my shaking hands, unable to process what had happened. I closed my eyes and calmed my mind. When I opened them, I noticed a sparkling sequin stuck in the folds of my sweater.

Saoirse

I turned my back on him, avoiding eye contact as I walked across the red carpet. The fireplace beckoned. I stirred the coals with the iron poker and added another briquette, stepping back as the embers popped. My ears pricked at every rustle of his clothing and every squeak of the barstool. He shouldn't be here.

I blamed myself for what had happened those years ago—a love spell meant to bond Ciarán's love to mine instead sent him into the land of the dead: the wrong moon, the wrong crystals, my inexperience. I mistook the signs, and the power of my spell took off like a mad cat, spitting energy in all the wrong directions. And because of my mistake, the black forces took my love away.

The way his hair fell across his brow reminded me of Ciarán.

"I'm surprised to see you, Colm." I watched him back, my lips freezing into a tight smile.

Even then, I couldn't control my reaction to Colm O'Donnell. A cutting edge lurked beneath the surface, concealed by his welcoming smile. I likened it to a grenade about to explode.

"You don't mind, do you?" He rested his palms on the counter, his gaze piercing.

Like I had any choice, now, if he caused a disturbance, that would be another matter. And yet, I doubted anyone would question him, being who he was and all. More than likely, I'd be blamed. More gossip. More side-eye glances. And what of it? I told myself I didn't care. I studied him with the same hard glare. He had left the force. He held no official title. He was just Ciarán's brother.

"Mind? No, why would I mind? It's open-mike

later if you'd care to join in." I nodded toward the corner where speakers and microphones sat waiting. The pub should crawl within the hour with patrons—the calm before the storm.

"Me? Sing? Jaysus no. The place looks good, Saoirse." He played with the bristles on his chin.

Somehow, I didn't feel like smiling. The arrogant prick had dragged me over the coals too many times.

If they knew the truth, I would be burned at the stake.

"Thanks." I wiped the counter with a bar cloth, rubbing one water ring after another. If I rubbed hard enough and concentrated on all my energies, could I make Colm O'Donnell disappear?

"I'm not a copper here, Saoirse. I have no jurisdiction in these parts, not anymore." His voice held a slight tremor, piquing my interest.

"Will ye have a pint, Colm?" I ran my hands down the sides of my black jumper. I saw no issue profiting from his visit.

"Whisky. The good stuff." He tilted his head toward the premium bottles on the high shelf and slid twenty euros toward me.

"Whatever you say." I poured a generous measure into a glass, relishing fragrant notes of smoky peat and subtle hints of seaweed. I left the bottle on the counter.

"What cauldron was this brewed in?" He sniffed the aged whisky but studied me.

The O'Donnell's gaze could scorch the earth.

I leaned on the bar rail. I had learned one thing—killing with kindness didn't hold water with an O'Donnell. I'd rather throw salt in the wound and be done with it.

"The distillery up the road? Brings back the local traditions some." I met his steely gaze. He could read the label, couldn't he?

"Aye, I thought you might be building love potions again." His lips twitched, and he almost smiled.

I threw him a stony glare. His comment didn't deserve a reply. It would take one incantation to rid myself of that arrogant bastard.

What Calla saw in him, I'd never understand. Yet she had mentioned his name more than once, a hint of longing lingering in her voice. Sure, he was handsome. The O'Donnell men were drop-dead gorgeous, and every one of them was single. How they managed bachelor status in such a small town was beyond me.

I sighed, turning from him lest he see the tears

welling in my eyes. He noticed everything, the cheeky sod.

It would have been different if Ciarán hadn't disappeared. We belonged to one another. The Claddagh ring on my left hand served as a daily reminder. The emerald set in the gold band exuded warmth, some days more than others.

"It's the bottle. It's so you." He lifted the handcrafted bottle from the bar top, smoothing his thumb over the long gooseneck—still, his focus didn't waver.

"What are you implying?" His insinuation struck deep, but I held fast, refusing to take the bait.

"You're not on trial, Saoirse. Ireland hasn't burned a witch since 1698, and even then, they strangled the poor unfortunate first." He chuckled, but the smile did not touch his lips.

"I can't believe you. Where do you get off?" I lashed into him, my temper flaring. What I did with my time was none of his business.

"Sit awhile. Confer with the devil. Please." His eyes widened, and he smirked.

Unlike Ciarán, Colm O'Donnell was always strange, not one to smile. When Colm left for away, I breathed a sigh of relief.

"I don't mix business with pleasure." I took the bottle from him and placed it back on the shelf.

"And this is business?" He stared into the swirling amber, then returned the glass to the paper coaster.

"We're not friends. Never have been. Can't see starting now." My voice sounded bitter even to my ears. He was Ciarán's brother, after all.

I stilled my mind, repeating the Wiccan's Rede, the one I had chosen to live by...harm no one, do unto others.

"I have questions." He laid his palms on the bar top.

His tone made my hair stand on end.

"Should I call my lawyer?" I said with a sarcastic tone. Why did I let him get under my skin?

"Friendly questions." The lines etched on his face revealed how deeply disturbed he was.

"Why are you dragging this up? Why now?" I scoured his expression for a clue, setting my mind into battle-ready mode.

"There's been a development." He drew his thumb and index finger over his jaw.

His words fired my imagination. He had been deployed overseas when Ciarán disappeared. Upon his return, he took matters into his own hands, initiating a search scouring all of Donegal County and then some. It was not pretty.

"A development? What does that mean?" I braced myself, using his dark energy as my own.

"The night Ciarán disappeared. What do you remember?" He lifted his chin, his tone accusing.

"It was a bad moon." Yet the pain in his eyes shone brighter than mine. I took comfort in that.

"A bad moon?" His eyes shadowed in the dim light.

"It was Samhain. Ciarán was being 'Ciarán.'" Samhain—the night when the veil thins, November's Eve, when ghosts and spirits wander Middle Earth free to roam, to cause havoc and mayhem within the mortal realm.

"Continue." He pressed his lips into a tight line, hiding behind his haughty demeanor.

I held my tongue. Whatever daemons the O'-Donnell boys had commiserated with on Samhain night wasn't my concern. I decided to play his game.

"We were at Stuart's Halloween party. I was helping Treasa in the kitchen. He went outside to smoke. He never came back." I looked down, staring at the glittering emerald. My thoughts raced with possibilities.

"You said Stuart owed Ciarán money." He ran his thumb over the lip of his glass, his gaze steady.

"I did? Yes...I guess. It's been a long time." I crossed my arms, reserving my strength.

"If I remember correctly, you left town right after. You were swanning about the country for a long time. Where did you go?" He supped his whisky, staring through those O'Donnell eyelashes.

"Where did I go? I had nothing left." I hissed, then chastised myself for losing my temper. I would not let him win.

"Hmm. I'm curious about your new friend, Calla Sweet." He smoothed his fingers over the bar rail, his voice cajoling.

I busied myself with beer glasses, lining them up in a neat row, and watched his reflection in the mirror. The purple smudges under his eyes stood out. "What about her? She's nice. I like her."

"You brought her to the wake." His tone accused me of so much more.

"Yes, I did, and she's singing at the burial. But you know that already." I reminded him of the arrangements made.

"Does she know who Ciarán was to you?" His gaze narrowed.

I flinched at his use of the past tense.

"No, she doesn't. I don't talk about Ciarán much. I'm trying to move on with my life. You should try it." The conversation brought the pain back threefold. I wished he would leave, yet I hung on to every mention of Ciarán's name.

"She spoke to someone. At the wake. But the room was empty...except for Da." He looked into the shadows, his face haunted.

I noticed how affected he was and considered giving Breda a ring. Instead, I slid onto the stool beside him.

"Who was she speaking to?" I found this conversation intriguing. I had some knowledge about channeling energy and making contact with spirits. Could Calla possess supernatural abilities? I pictured the darkness enveloping her and believed it to be true.

"I thought Da's ghost was having the last word. But...when she saw the family portrait, she pointed Ciarán out. Do you know what that means?" He played with his napkin, rolling it between his fingers.

"No...tell me, Colm. What does it mean?" I knew exactly what it meant.

"She's one of Them, Saoirse. One of the '*Na Daoine Maithe*.'" His Adam's apple bobbed in his throat.

I straightened, drawn to the urgency in his voice.

"The Good People? That's a big stretch. She arrived on a jet plane, and you drove her into Ardara. You do remember? She didn't come through the mist. I know she's beautiful, and her eyes. Well, yes, I can see what you mean." I grinned like a loon, considering the possibilities. I believed in the Otherworld, in the old gods.

"You know Ciarán had the sight. He was known to knock around with them." His rough voice brimmed with suspicion.

"Aye." I tilted my chin, fascinated.

"How many *scéalaith* have told tales of mortals taken by Faerie beings? Mortal women married off to Faerie Kings? And what of Ciarán? Did he go willingly into the fray, or was he forced to?" He rubbed the back of his neck, his discomfort apparent.

I stared at him. Why had he suffered me moments ago if he wanted to talk about Faeries? Colm O'Donnell did not do small talk. No, he had something else in mind the entire time.

"You think the Other Crowd took Ciarán?" The band circling my finger warmed, and in an instant, I knew the truth. Did I dare believe that Ciarán lived and thrived in the Otherworld? If Calla could see and truly speak to him, could she get him back? Colm's voice hammered inside my head. I picked up the last part of his conversation.

"He may have gone willingly for the craic. He knew Them. He was familiar to Them. I know how this sounds." He looked away, his gaze melting into the turf fire.

I stewed in his misery, then shared Ciarán's conversation from that fateful eve.

"He said the Faeries were dancing, that the holly bushes were full of them." Sweet angel notes played in my ears as I relived that night.

Pop music blares from the open doorway, casting a warm, golden glow into the night. Cars are parked along the laneway, spilling down the narrow road. The Samhain celebration is in full swing.

"Did you lock the doors?" I glance at Ciarán's car as if we had anything worth stealing.

"The doors are locked." He clicks the key fob, the headlights blinking red.

"We won't stay too late, okay? Promise?" I lift my long black skirt, sidestepping the puddles pooling on the gravel road.

"We won't stay long." He lifts his hands, pulling my pointed witch hat over my ears.

"Stop it." I pushed him away, giggling.

He chuckles, his hooded cloak concealing his smile.

The purple satin cascades to his feet, glimmering in the moonlight, while the misshaped silver stars sparkle.

I look into a night of changing colors, my mind filling with unease. The sky grumbles, and a lightning bolt strikes fire, lighting up the branches of one lonely tree.

I jump into his arms, taking comfort in his strength.

"May I have this dance, m'lady?" His breath tickles my ear—his laughter infectious.

He was my wizard, and I was his witch.

"She saw him. Here in the pub, but she spoke to him during the wake. Had a full-on conversation." A muscle ticked in his jaw.

"Calla said that?" How many times had I felt his presence? I dreamt of so many things, but I sometimes wondered who held the reins.

"She didn't tell you?" He ran his thumb along the underside of his jaw.

I looked at Colm, really looked at him.

"Why would she tell me?" My heart exploded in my chest.

Ciarán. Not dead. Not dead. Warmth touched my face. The air stirred even then.

"Hmm. I would have thought." The words fell from his lips too quickly.

"If what you say is true...and I'm not saying, I

believe you. Calla's a clairvoyant, at one with the earth's magnetic force. It doesn't mean Ciarán is with the Faeries." I wanted to believe, and yet I refused his theory. I needed time to think. If Calla was what he said, then the divine lived within her. But could she walk between worlds? I intended to find out.

"So you agree there's something about her? Something...different?" He threaded his fingers through his hair.

"Magic flows in these hills, Colm. Powerful magic." I snapped my fingers at him, making him start. I laughed, chuckling, happy, giddy laughter. It felt good to have the upper hand for once.

The hinges creaked, and the door opened, bringing bright light into the shadows.

"Good day to ye, Saoirse." Niall, a lean man with a kind face, carried his fiddle. A clatter of young musicians prepared for a session out accompanied him. I gazed into the smiling faces and glanced at the clock's face, realizing the day was passing.

"Understand me, Saoirse. This isn't over." Colm set his tumbler on the counter.

"You can't bring back the dead, Colm. Believe me. I've tried." Those words, I spoke truthfully. As an Irish Witch, I honored the dead and prayed to the goddess on the powerful sabbats that Ciarán might show himself. But maybe he had, just not in the ways I'd hoped.

The musicians sparked it up, knocking out a familiar tune. Niall glided his bow over his fiddle, filling the long hall with a medley of notes. The door burst open, and the damn broke, flooding the foyer with a rabble of happy faces.

"Howzit, goin,' Saoirse. Ya'all right?" The local constabulary rambled in one after the other, hollering their greetings.

"Not so bad, Colleen. How's it going, Paddy?" Glancing over my shoulder, I noticed Colm's empty stool. I caught a glimpse of the door closing behind him. "Sorry, ladies," I murmured to the angels and then threw back what remained of his whisky. Heat coursed through my body for the first time in a long while.

5

─────────

C*alla*

It was a soft day for burial. A breeze moved the warm, almost humid air. White clouds scattered across a deep blue sky. I wished I were not wearing the green velvet dress. Although it clung to every curve, the linen would have been a better choice, the flowy one with the tiered skirt and satin buttons. But the dress was in a box, crossing the Atlantic Ocean.

I inspected my face in the fold-down mirror of his eight-person, quasar-blue family van and dabbed my lipstick. My pale skin and hollowed-out eyes told the tale of a life that had already fallen apart. How could it get any worse?

Before, when life was grand, I would sing at

weddings, funerals, and bar mitzvahs. Ballads and sad songs made my heart sing. Making people cry was what I did best. Meeting Niall and landing that gig was a godsend.

"Are you ready, luv?" Niall adjusted his navy tie, his expression serious. He epitomized professionalism in his tailored navy suit, pressed white shirt, and shining loafers.

"Almost." I pinned the holly crown into my hair. I had found the necessary accouterments for a charming headpiece: holly twined with ivy and white-petaled anemones just this morning. I had looked through those lace curtains into the wandering mist until I could stand it no longer. I slipped into Dermot Sweet's rubber boots, claimed his plaid work coat as my own, and walked along the stone boundary walls with the sheep staring on, scanning the enchanted wood for any sign of the mysterious little man calling himself Séamus. I stayed away from the fairy-tale bridge.

My brain buzzed through each dilemma. My life had become a series of supernatural events. But the dreams haunted me before I arrived, faces and places I could never recall the morning after. Those garbled voices were now succinct, the visions flowing freely in technicolor. I had conversed with imaginary people. *Call me crazy, but hello?*

I quieted my mind, drawing inspiration from the peaceful landscape. Blue hydrangeas climbed the walls of the caretaker's building, almost hiding the stone structure from view. Low stone walls marked the boundary, and from there, a vast meadow spread in a westerly direction, the long grass swaying in a cooling breeze—a blend of soothing, rustling sounds interspersed with bird-song. Beyond the meadow, a rugged forest-covered mountain touched a clear blue sky.

"Niall, do you know a man called Séamus?" I smoothed a wrinkle from my dress.

"Séamus O'Malley runs the bike shop in town." He closed the van's side door and looked up at me.

"The bike shop? Hmm. Did Dermot have a helper, a farm helper?" I pinned my lips together, glancing at each car filling the parking lot.

"Dermot? I'm not sure. Why do you ask?" He collected his violin and double-tapped the key fob. The beeper dinged, and the lights flashed.

"Hmm, no reason." I nibbled my lip, deciding against sharing my crazy with him. Perhaps it was another hallucination. The whole thing. All of it. Huh.

I followed the cobblestones beyond the grave

markers and raised tombs toward a family plot, ready for burial.

"Niall?" I glanced sideways, reconsidering my earlier decision. Niall was local and had lived in these parts his entire life. I considered him a neutral party. The question burned my lips. "Tell me about Ciarán O'Donnell."

"Ciarán? I haven't heard talk of the boy in a long time." Curiosity lifted his brows.

"I heard he disappeared?" I shifted my gaze beyond the blue hydrangeas and past the cemetery walls to where the meadow faded into a green forest.

"Look at ye, not here a week and getting caught up in the rabble." He grinned. "He had the sight, that one. Some say the Faeries took Ciarán."

"So it's true then? He just vanished." I studied Niall. He believed.

"Aye. It was a sad time. We're good here, Calla." He unsnapped his violin case and stood beneath the broad branches of an ancient Yew.

The tree symbolized immortality, living, and breathing, protecting and purifying the dead buried beneath its boughs. The darkness called to me, and the ground swayed. I lifted my hand—the need to touch the ancient one overwhelmed me.

"Calla? Are you all right?" Niall's words broke the spell.

I tore my mind away from the ancient one. A procession approached.

Six brothers, cloaked in black, walked in unison, their heads held high, their backs straight. They carried their late father's casket on their shoulders, sharing the weight equally. Sweat trickled down their foreheads, yet united in their grief, they persevered.

The mourners congregated beneath the protective shadow of a Celtic cross. The brothers laid their burden onto the bier and then stepped back in reverence.

Enough time wasted.

Niall tucked the violin under his chin and drew the bow across the strings, releasing a cascade of clear, soothing notes that stretched through the air and captured the mourners' attention.

We began with a traditional hymn—"Amazing Grace."

Some dabbed their eyes while others wept. My heart skipped a beat. Among the attendees, the blond-haired man—Ciarán—stood behind Saoirse, casting her in a protective shadow. Ciarán and Saoirse. Saoirse and Ciarán. My inner voice hitched a treble beat. How did I not see that?

Niall drew out the crowd with the soulful notes of "Danny Boy," always a crowd favorite. I rose to the occasion, belting out the familiar lyrics.

Our final tribute to the dearly beloved, a haunting melody—I sang to the angels, the Faerie people, and Ciarán himself. There was not a dry eye in the place except his. He turned his back on his father's grave, Saoirse and his brothers, and walked away. I chewed the inside of my mouth, losing sight of him in the distant tree line.

I twined my fingers and squeezed my eyes shut, knee-deep in Colm's and Saoirse's sadness and my mysterious beginnings on that green island.

"May the road rise to meet you,
and the wind always be at your back.
May the sun shine warm on your face
and the rains fall softly on your fields.
And until we meet again,
may God hold you gently in the palm of his hand."

The robed priest recited the Irish blessing.

"And may you be in Heaven, Da, a full half-hour before the devil knows you're dead!" A dark-haired lad shouted a requiem, transforming the mood.

The mourners smiled and laughed, and even the priest clapped his hands. The crowd mingled, sharing hugs and chatting. Our job—fait accompli.

"Hi, Calla. Do you remember me? I'm Breda. We met at the wake." Her voice rose in sing-song notes, turning my head away from the O'Donnell clan.

"Of course. I'm sorry for your loss." A girl with stunning black eyes fringed with snow-white eyelashes thwarted my escape. White hair tumbled over her shoulders, reminding me of winter's snow. The black crepe jumpsuit exuded elegance, belted with a glimmering strand of black beads. Flowing chiffon sleeves engulfed her slender arms.

"Thank you for the beautiful songs. Uncle Hugh would have loved it." Her ruby lips rocked a smiley piercing, the bejeweled barbell sparkling in the light.

"You're welcome. I'm glad we could be here." I scanned the crowd, looked for Saoirse, and spotted her standing next to a large gray dog and one of Colm's brothers, a man named Tadgh, looking in the direction Ciarán had gone.

"We're off to the pub. I hope you'll join us. My nephew, Connor, the young fella, plays the ukulele. He wants to marry you." She twirled her finger through her loose tendrils.

"It's true what they say, then." Colm towered over Breda, the circles under those shiny blues hinting at deep sadness. With his hair swept back and the black suit enhancing his muscular build, he looked more than dashing. I stared at his polished leather shoes.

Not my fault. I did nothing to cause his father's death. Foretelling was a psychic ability—a gift, not a curse. My conscience haunted me, nevertheless. All the shrinks in the world could never convince me otherwise.

"What are they saying now, Colm?" I said with more attitude than necessary. What I would give to be somewhere else. Wrapped in his arms, maybe?

"Your voice. I've never heard anything quite like it." He took my hand, drawing his thumb over my knuckles.

I saw rainbows and unicorns.

"I was after inviting Calla to the pub." Breda looked quizzically at Colm, her lip ring glinting in the sunshine.

I pursed my lips, exhaling slowly. Do you. Be

me. I sang myself to sleep each night with those words running through my mind.

"And I hate to say no, but Niall's my only ride home." I ran through the possible options: duck and run or face the reality of an impossible situation, and why was Colm O'Donnell still holding my hand? I stabbed him with my best death stare and yanked my hand away. He suffered from the same psychotic issues as I did.

"Oh, too bad... Connor will be so disappointed," Breda seemed unaware of our interaction. She smiled at a little boy with shiny copper hair, standing beside a bit of a girl who hid behind her mother's skirt. "We could give Calla a ride, that is, if you'd like to come." Breda nudged Colm with her elbow.

"Of course, no trouble at all." He appeared deep in thought.

That was a collision course with a fucking disaster. Duck and run had always been my motto, but that was before.

"I hope we see you again, Calla. Thanks again for the songs. They were grand." She turned and walked away.

An army of blackbirds dropped from the branches, descending onto the open earth of his father's grave. The mountains, purple shapes cloaked with mist, walked toward me.

I waited until Breda was safely out of earshot before I leaned in real close, my mind scattering buckshot in all directions. "Sorry for your trouble, sweet cheeks."

"Daughter of the wind. It's so like you. I've never seen anything... anyone so beautiful." His outstretched fingers grazed the starry flowers of my crown.

"Excuse me?" That was my bad. I should have escaped when I had the chance. I stepped back from the dangerous man, the ground squelching beneath my white sneakers.

"The flowers. It makes sense you would choose them." He whispered, his voice barely audible over the chirping birds.

"It does?" I wondered where the conversation was going.

"You're one of Them, one of the Good People. Of that, I have no doubt. But you're something more." He blinked as if seeing something for the first time.

"What are you talking about?" I lifted the hem of my dress and turned away from his intense stare. 'One of Them.' Where did he get those ideas? My confidence slipped with every step.

"You don't know, do you?" He trailed behind me.

"I can assure you I'm not a Faerie, and I'm not good." I removed the holly crown and placed the starry circlet on the upturned earth.

"You're a *Bean-Sidhe*." His penetrating stare burned a hole through my shoulder blades. His accusation should have scared me, but I was used to the name-calling: sticks and stones and whatnot.

I gathered a handful of earth and then opened my fingers, dropping each granule. One year ago, I stood in his place. I had lost everything I loved. *Things cannot replace people.* For a time, I believed they could. A giggle tickled my throat. "A banshee? Are you for real?"

"But you're flesh and bone. You're a woman." His words carried a note of wonderment. His eyes appreciated my every curve, enhanced by the clinging velvet.

I tossed my head and pouted my lips. Two could play that game.

"Well, I'll take the compliment." Is that what I was? What did I know about the banshee? Who was the legendary woman from popular Irish myth?

I visualized the times I'd blurted prophecies to

unwelcoming ears. In those moments, did my essence travel to where it was needed? No, no way, not the same. That would require powerful magic.

I rose to my feet, scanning the distant parking lot, searching for the cosmic blue family van.

"The *Bean-Sidhe* came when my father died. If you don't believe me, you can ask her." He nodded toward his mother, a slight woman shrouded in black, surrounded by mourners. "The house shook. The *Bean-Sidhe* keened. Wailing cries, like fingernails on a blackboard. She went outside thinking a storm was coming. When she returned, Da was gone. You were that storm, Calla."

I recalled our first touch. He clutched my forearm, propelling me to safety and saving me from falling. I could not account for those lost moments. I closed my eyes, calling upon the sensation to return and hit the wall.

"You remember, don't you?" His rumbling voice demanded an answer.

"No. I don't remember anything." I glared at him. Where did I go? Those moments were lost to me.

"Your eyes flashed silver. You told me I was too late. You left me, Calla. Only a *Bean-Sidhe*—a faerie woman possessing extraordinary powers— could do that." He lifted my wrist, drawing his thumb along the center of my palm. His gaze narrowed. "Your cut has healed."

"What are you saying? I'm a shapeshifter? That I traveled in ethereal form to your family's home. That I, Calla Sweet, sing the song of death? How is that even possible?" I clenched my fingers into a fist, refusing to acknowledge the abrasion that bled profusely and healed seamlessly overnight.

I laughed, but my laughter sounded hollow. It was all I could do not to cry. If what he said was true, I wasn't crazy. I was something else entirely. I gathered my skirt and walked away.

"Calla, wait. Please, listen. I want to apologize." He dropped his hands to his sides, his expression sheepish.

"Excuse me?" I lifted my chin, gazing into an azure ocean. A warm breeze caressed my face. The mountain crept closer, the mist calling me. "No. No. No." I huffed a loud breath, pushing the salacious fantasy six feet under.

"What you said about Ciarán blew me away." He seemed not to notice the heat flooding my face.

"Okay." I bit my lower lip, stilling the hum.

"Which does not justify my behavior. I dropped by your place uninvited. It was inappropriate. I hope you won't hold it against me." He spoke in slow, melodic syllables, soothing my mind.

"Look, I have to go." I combed the parking lot for Niall.

"I would like to start over," he said in a voice that would charm most women.

"Start what over?" I raised my eyebrows, reminding myself of one obvious fact. I was not like most women, and even though I was falling in lust with him, I would not be his fool.

"Give me a chance, Calla. I'm not a bad guy." His rugged features framed in copper were bewitching.

"Why do you think there's a 'you and me?' Did I ever give you that impression?" I snapped. The sooner I rid myself of Colm O'Donnell, the better.

"Something happened, Calla. We have a connection. I don't understand, but I want to." He extended his palm, his eyes beckoning me to go with him.

"Do you have any admirers I should know about?" I took one step backward, unwilling to admit he was right.

"I dream of you, Calla. It's the strangest thing. I feel I've known you forever." He loosened his tie, his face turning a pretty shade of pink.

"So, let's get this straight. I'm the scary banshee, yet you want to be what? Friends?" Heat tore through me—dizzying heat.

"The *Bean-Sidhe* is a source of pride for many families. Some say only the ancient clans have them." A lick of longing tore through his gaze.

"Really?" My stomach coiled. The edges blurred, and I feared I might pass out.

"She warns of coming demise. She doesn't cause death. The way I see it, she's the most industrious of the Tuatha Dé. She has a job to do, and she does it well. It could be worse. You could be a *Leannán Sídhe*, the Faerie lover who takes men's souls." He shrugged, bristles shadowing the underside of his jaw.

Silence rippled between us.

I noticed the intricate Triquetra inked behind his right ear, hidden beneath those copper locks. I had seen the same tattoo on Ciarán.

"What does she do with them? The Faerie lover?" I ran my index finger over my eyebrow, considering the thought.

"They say she takes them back to the Other-world, where they cannot find peace even in death. Look, could I buy you a beer? Can we go somewhere?" His voice was a soft seduction of luring notes.

I found him hard to resist. Eye candy aside,

there seemed more to the affable tree farmer than met the eye.

"I hate beer." I struggled with his theory. Could I be a Faerie? Faeries had magical powers—magical powers I did not possess.

I gazed into his starry eyes.

"There's a place nearby. They have a nice selection of wines and good food. Can we go there? There's so much we need to discuss." He offered his hand, enticing me to follow. Skilled in the art of persuasion. Hmm.

The moment had lasted too long. Walking away from Colm was the only choice left to me. I rejected his accusations, closing the door on that fairy tale.

His brother, Ciarán, however, left a mystery to unravel on another day.

"Listen up, Colm. I'm all about the Faerie tale, but you and me? That is not going to happen. Make a good life choice, okay? I can almost promise you will never see me again." I needed time—to think—to process. Call it self-preservation. So why did I feel so sad?

"Calla? Calla, Darling! What are you doing here?" A voice called out, an Irish voice I'd known for as long as forever.

Storey O'Donnell, *the Charming Prince* my mother called him.

"Storey?" I faced him, engulfed by waves of relief. His presence felt like a warm hug on a cold day. Who'd have thought a familiar face could bring such happiness?

"What great craic." He swung me into his arms, planting a kiss on my forehead.

I landed on my feet, Storey, my financial advisor...a busy man since my adoptive parent's untimely demise. And an O'Donnell. I shook my head—another one I could touch yet not see. Maybe Colm was right. For better or worse, my visions centered around death, just death, and only death. The realization freed me in a sick kind of way.

"What are you doing here?" I murmured, turning my gaze toward each man. I noticed the resemblance at once—the high cheekbones, the clear blue eyes.

"How are you, mate? Sad times. Sad times." He shook Colm's hand, his voice undulating like the backbone of the surrounding mountains.

He reminded me of what I'd lost.

"It's good to see you, Storey. Polly said you'd be here." Colm's brows creased. "How are you acquainted?” He directed his question at me, his tone flat.

“Storey, you’re coming to the pub?” Breda waved—behind her stood the three black-haired O’Donnell men.

Her approach saved me from answering Colm’s question.

“Of course. Of course. Calla? You’ll come? Say yes, darling. You wouldn’t miss a pub night with the O’-Donnell clan, would you? Loads of craic!” He hooked his elbow around mine and almost skipped down the cobbled path. “Feast your eyes on this beauty. Isn’t she stunning?” He extended his long fingers toward a luxury Silver Phantom, glinting in the breaking sun.

Storey’s voice ebbed and flowed, and I was grateful for the distraction. The distance between Colm and me increased with every step, yet our connection endured. I didn’t know what to make of it.

Colm

I held Mam’s elbow until the last mourner said their goodbyes.

“We’ll be seeing you, laddie.” Eamon tipped

his flat cap and climbed into the luxurious backseat of Storey's vehicle.

Calla and Storey? I wasn't expecting that. Polly's conversation floated through my mind—one plus one equals two, and simple logic couldn't be denied. "It's about time the boy settled down." Polly's voice brimmed with excitement in the kitchen of Mam's house—something about Storey and a big announcement. I punched the accelerator, passing the Silver Phantom on the next straightaway. One glimpse through the rearview mirror showed Calla's pretty face in animated conversation.

"Do you have to drive so fast, Colm?" Mam clenched her hands together.

"Put the peddle to the metal, Uncle Colm." Connor jumped up and down in the backseat, grinning like a mad hatter.

"Yes, Mam." I took my foot off the gas and coasted down the big hill, making a sharp turn at the diamond and gliding to a stop in my brother's driveway.

"Connor, help *Maimeó* from the car." I gave the rambunctious hallion a job, which he performed admirably.

"Let me help." The boy hooked his elbow

around hers, leading his *Maimeó* down the sidewalk.

Brake lights flashed, and Storey stepped out of his vehicle. He circled the luxury car, opening the passenger door. She slipped her delicate hand into his, rising into his waiting arms. An aura glittered around her, like black diamonds falling from the night sky. She threw her arms around his neck, pecking his cheek with a playful kiss.

Wrapped in silence mere moments ago, the street came alive. Like bees at the hive, the gathering crowd swarmed their queen. Passing cars honked their horns, and the butcher's dog howled.

Her face turned pink.

Wee Connor stood on the sidewalk, strumming his ukelele for the admiring crowd.

Her aura glimmered stronger today than yesterday, yet she seemed oblivious to the glamor surrounding her—what it was or what to do with it.

I spent last night trying to solve the puzzle, but it was not until I held her hand in mine that the pieces fell into place. She was innocent—the terror in her eyes confirmed that.

Calla Sweet could only be a halfling fathered by one of the *Aos Sí*, the mystical beings of Irish folklore. The Irish believed that magical folk interacted with mortals—it wasn't hard to imagine the rest.

Her return to Ireland was a mistake. The consequences were dire. How long before the wrong people took note? If her heritage were discovered, she would be taken—studied like a lab rat in a cage—all in the name of science. Even more terrifying, she would be exploited by those seeking to misuse her magical abilities. A pang of guilt flowed over me. Was I no better than them? I had sought her out for my benefit, for Ciarán's.

My heart stilled. Whoever sent her away as a babe knew the truth. But someone or something had engineered her return. My eyelids fell for a brief second. Accusing her of being a *Bean Sídhe* was the wrong approach. I had not intended to scare her.

My cousin—a complication I had not anticipated.

"Uncle Storey, can I ride in your car?" Connor ran ahead, tugging Storey's hand, beaming up at him.

"You bet, mate. We'll take her for a spin a little later. Just you and me." He mussed Connor's hair, then held the door to Pete's Pub open for Calla. They entered together.

Voices rang, welcoming Storey home. I listened intently, waiting for the impending announcement. Suppose he was her man, well, good on her. I couldn't compete with his likes. Expensive clothes and flashy cars were not me. I preferred the low-brow approach, which easily fit in with the local punters. I settled onto the bar stool, intending to lash down a few pints. Refusing to admit, that woman gutted me.

"You're about the right age for my grandson, no? He's off to college in the United States on a full scholarship." Old Eamon walked ahead, leaning on his shillelagh.

"Sit with us, Eamon." Storey offered him the bench seat against the wall at a cozy table for three. "What can I get you? Whisky? A pint?"

It struck me odd that he didn't ask her what she would like. I looked away. What had she said earlier? Get a life. Live your best life.

"I bet he has a lot of girlfriends." Calla gave Eamon her full attention.

"Here we are. Whisky for you, Eamon." Storey sat in the chair opposite Calla.

The server followed him, balancing a platter in one hand, whisky neat, and two glasses of rosé wine.

"Aye, he's a right handsome lad." Eamon

smoothed his charcoal blazer with his free hand, black bifocals resting on the end of his nose.

"I think I'm too old, Eamon." Her smile dazzled the room.

"Aye? No. I don't believe it. You're what, sixteen, seventeen?" He nudged the plastic frames with his forefinger.

"I turned twenty-nine last week." She cranked up the charm, laughing silver bells.

"You look like you can sing. Aye, well, now. What am I saying? You sang at the burial." He tipped his glass toward her.

"It was an honor." She lowered her eyelashes, her stare finding me.

Heat crept up my neck. I pretended to have a conversation with the bartender.

"You probably are not aware that we don't use all the alphabet letters in the Irish language?" Eamon raised his glass once more.

"No." She worried her lip and then returned her attention to Eamon.

"Aye, you'll never find j, k, q, v, w, x, y, or z. Our language comes from the old Ogham alphabet. You'll sometimes see runes inscribed in the odd fence post thereabouts." He stared deeply into her eyes.

"It must be hard to learn." She sipped her wine. Her attention belonged to Eamon alone.

"Aye, that it is. Do you hear that one over there?" He lifted his bushy eyebrows, jutting his chin toward the barber's wife sitting at the bar. "You hear her before you see her. We call her noisy. Talk your ear off, that one."

"What do you do for fun, Eamon?" She laughed, the cadence of her voice reaching over the din, touching me, folding over me.

I lapped up every intonation, her every expression. My thoughts scattered, and I knew I had lost. I ordered a whisky from the busy server.

"Woot. Woot. Eamon, sing us a song." Someone shouted, noticing Eamon in the crowd.

"They say I suck all the fun out of the room. Aye, I do." Eamon murmured to Calla and rose to the floor.

The place quieted, and all eyes turned toward Eamon. He sang of heart and country, blood-stained valleys and mud-soaked hills, his low voice consuming every breathing soul. He bowed his head for a moment of silence, and when he lifted his eyes, it was with a smile. "And now, how about a nice round of happy birthday for Ardara's newest resident? The lovely Calla, with the voice of the angels."

Her birthday? She hadn't mentioned that, but why would she? We were not exactly friends. I pondered how many more birthdays she might celebrate, how immortality would affect a halfling like her. These were intricacies I knew nothing about.

Storey whispered in low tones something about long-term investments and hedge funds.

"Here you go, luv." The server set a glass before me.

Eamon started the celebratory song. Faces turned, and voices rose. Wee Connor strummed his ukelele out of rhythm and off-key. Voices joined in, happy for something to celebrate. Everyone clapped.

"Thank you." She offered an exaggerated curtsey to the crowd.

I imagined what kissing her would feel like. The top of her tousled head would tickle my chin. I would run my fingers down her slender arms, relishing in the honeyed softness of her skin. She would gaze into my eyes, wanting me as I wanted her. I studied her clunky white running shoes. Why would an otherworldly being be interested in a chancer like me? I threw back the shot and ordered another.

She whispered to Connor and then faced the

crowd. "This young man would like to play a song." She placed her hands on Connor's hips, lifting the young fella onto the bar top. He strummed the first stanzas of "It's a Beautiful World," and a hush fell.

She sang out, her voice kissing every corner, enchanting every soul. I straightened in my seat, my gaze glued to the boy. He plucked each string as if touched by an angel himself. Her magic flowed through her fingertips into wee Connor, gifting him with newfound grace. Connor's mother spoke to Breda, and Breda breathed to Polly.

Calla returned to her table, unaware of what she had done. Connor remained, kicking his legs, strumming the sweetest strains imaginable.

I looked into the shadows and found what I searched for—Da's spirit threading through the crowd. I lifted my glass.

"Join us for a pint, bro?" Tadgh placed his brawny hand on my shoulder, tearing me from my fantasy.

"What?" I murmured, gazing into his wide blue eyes.

"Colm, will ye come by? Play a game, won't ye?" Oisin yelled, calling me into the billiard room.

I slid from the bar stool, intent on stealing a

look at the Faerie girl. Did Storey know what she was? Someone would have to tell him.

Oisin's brow furrowed when I met his stare.

"What's the bet, then?" I removed my suit jacket and tie, unbuttoned the top three buttons of my starched shirt, and rolled up the sleeves.

"Rounds. What else?" Cillian laughed.

"Aye. You break then." I selected a cue, unable to shut out Calla's silvery voice. It followed me around the pool table, echoing in my mind with every shot.

The server balanced six pints of the Black Stuff on a silver platter. Cillian dumped a handful of change into the tip jar. I added twenty euros to the mix.

"Brilliant shot, mate." Tadgh held up the back wall, commenting on the bank shot.

The boys cranked it up, tossing back their pints and ordering another round.

"Right corner." I shot the cue ball off the left bank, sinking the eight ball and winning the game.

"Deadly. Who'll play the champ?" Oisin lifted my arm high into the air.

"I'll play you, Colm O'Donnell." The queen of the night glided across the room. Her fragrance hit me first, a warm, citrusy scent crafted to lure her victim.

I met her gaze and drowned in limpid silver pools.

"You know her?" Oisin's eyes popped out of his head.

"This is my brother, Oisin." I stumbled over my words—so much for playing it cool.

"Was it you who ran my sheep from the road?" Oisin's eyes glazed over, captivated by her charms.

"Yes, it was. I'm so sorry." Her voice unlocked the spell, and Oisin returned to himself.

"Ach, no worries. The damn beasts get me into all sorts of trouble. Just glad you're all right, lass." He nodded his head, handing Calla his cue.

"There's Cillian, Hugh Jr., and Tadgh." I pointed at the three brothers leaning against the back wall.

"Hello." Her gaze flickered from one to the other, acknowledging them.

"I didn't know it was your birthday." I gazed at the Faerie girl because that's what she was. Was I enchanted? Captivated? I was all of those things.

"Are you ready to lose, Mr. O'Donnell?" She chalked the tip, then blew dust fragments through the stale air, enchanting the room.

"Aye, she's good craic." Oisin chuckled, a wave of heat filling his face.

Her eyes bored into mine, setting my heart on

fire and my nerves tingling. 'Tingle,' a word not part of my vocabulary.

"G'wan, ya hoor, there's a fiver in it for ye." Tadgh nudged my elbow, offering a bet.

"He's got it bad, aye?" Pádraig sallied forth, offering a tray of chocolate-covered scones. "Hello, Sweetheart. I'm Pádraig, the most talented O'Donnell brother. Did we meet the other day?"

"From across the road. I've heard all about your sticky buns." She winked, sending Pádraig into a fit of chuckles. She took a bite of the flaky delight, closing her eyelids and murmuring her enjoyment. "This is amazing."

"Are you married? Not for me, mind. There are several eligible bachelors in the room." Pádraig turned his eyes toward me.

"Nope, not married." She twirled one cascading lock behind her ear. "Would you like to break?"

"You go ahead." I nodded toward the table, unable to keep my thoughts straight.

She tapped her fingers and then, without hesitation, bent at the waist and lined up her shot. She thwacked the cue ball, sending stripes and solids flying in all directions, sinking two solid balls in the corner pockets.

"Deadly." Oisin's face showed a blend of wonder and fear.

Cillian nudged Tadgh.

Pádraig placed his platter of sweets on a nearby table.

She circled, the hem of her dress swishing with every turn of her hips. She languished, resting the cue on the curve of an uplifted thumb while sinking one solid ball after another.

I scratched my forehead, studying all the striped balls decorating the green felt.

"Game shot." Pádraig shuffled across the floor, gaining a better view.

The eight ball sat in a precarious position, blocked by two striped balls.

"Impressive." I circled the table, eyeing up the difficult shot.

"Easy peasy, hurling boy." She chalked the cue one more time.

Pádraig snickered, his face beaming like the second coming of Christ.

Oisin whistled.

Cillian slapped his thigh.

I watched the way her lower lip shifted to the left. The way she had blinked before every shot.

"Left corner pocket, lads." She pointed her cue. Tilting her chin, she gave me a teasing smile, then drew back, driving the white ball into the cushion, making the most spectacular-looking bank shot I had ever witnessed.

Hollers and shouts broke the silence the moment the black ball disappeared into the left corner pocket.

"Thanks for the game, boys." She moistened her bottom lip with the tip of her tongue, then slid away.

I took my hands out of my pockets, picked up my pride, and followed her.

"Where'd you learn to play?" The frog in my throat croaked sincere congratulations.

"I'm good at a lot of things." Sparkles danced in her eyes, but she didn't elaborate.

"I'm sure you are." I extended my arm, leaning on the doorway, stalling for time.

"What's wrong, buttercup? You don't look like you're having much craic." Her words whispered over me.

She was a temptress, that Faerie girl.

"Why didn't you tell me?" I knew what defeat looked like. I took one last look at that enchantress.

"Pardon?" She challenged me to express the obvious to everyone.

"Your Storey's wan." I nodded toward my

cousin, who seemed oblivious to Calla's presence. It made sense: the playful kiss, the hug, and the big announcement Polly was so excited to share.

"I'm what?" Her smile teased me.

"I'm not naïve, Calla." The trusting fool seemed oblivious to Calla's whereabouts. If she were mine...the thought played with my mind before I could shut it out.

"Storey and me?" She handed me the pool cue, a smile teasing her lips. "You need to work on your game, buttercup. Rounds on Colm O'Donnell." She lifted her chin, making an announcement for all to hear. Her voice rang out as she floated away, her graceful swish daring me to follow.

My pride, the only thing I had left, stopped me.

I observed my cousin from afar, studying his movements and enthusiastic conversation with the barkeep. I should rise above my disappointment and congratulate him. Fair play to him. I should, but I failed to do so. I weaved toward the empty bar stool.

"Such a nice send-off for him, aye?" Breda handed me a foaming pint of the Black Stuff.

"Aye. Thanks." A cloud hung heavy over my head, and I wallowed in it.

"Don't thank me. This is your treat." Breda

tugged my sleeve. "It was nice to see Eamon get up and sing. Did you notice his hands shake?"

"Aye." I took a long sip of the tall blonde in a black dress, one of many I would drown tonight. Tomorrow, I would share my concerns with Storey.

"Colm? What's wrong?" She prodded.

"Things aren't what they seem, Breda." I took another long pull.

"What things, Colm?" She gazed into my eyes. "Are you having visions again? You don't look good."

"No." I tossed Breda my car keys, settling in for the next round or two or three. She owed me one.

"Let's talk about it." She planted her palm on my forehead.

Dear Breda, she deserved better.

"No." I caught the server's eye for another refill.

"Touchy. Touchy. Well, I'll leave you to it, aye?" Breda left me to drown in my sorrows.

I couldn't say I blamed her.

SAOIRSE

I ran the brush through my hair for the umpteenth time while the bathroom mirror stared back. Water dripped from the leaky tap, echoing throughout the tiled chamber. Spending that much time with the O'Donnells hurt. I had longed for that sense of belonging my entire life—the laughter, the noise. Only to have it pulled out from under me when Ciarán vanished. It was Da and me from when I was seven years old. He had done his best raising a wee lass, but it was hard.

"Saoirse? What are you doing?" Breda rushed into the first available stall. "You've been out of sorts all day. What's going on?"

"Is it that obvious?" I popped open my lipstick tube and touched up my crimson lips. "I shouldn't have come. Everyone is so nice. It hurts."

"You're part of us, Saoirse. It will always be so." She washed her hands and then ripped the paper towel from the dispenser. "I'm proud of you. Running that pub. All of it. Bringing *Ceilidh* back...gets people out at night instead of glued to the telly. Serving food was bloody brilliant. 'Bout time Brandy's had some competition."

"I guess there's that." I turned sideways, tugging my shirt sleeve. I smoothed my short skirt and plucked lint from my black stockings. "Can I tell you something?"

"Always. What is it, luv?" She grabbed my lipstick and smeared the vibrant shade over her lips. "Hmm, what do you think?"

"Nice. You've got too much there." I handed her a tissue.

"C'mon, Saoirse. Spill the tea." She plunged her hand inside her black V-neck, adjusting her bra strap.

My mouth dried. She would think I'd lost my mind if I said the words aloud. "I think Ciarán is alive."

"Did the crystals tell you?" She didn't even blink. She knew me too well.

"No." I hung my head. Since when did a witch of my caliber believe in hearsay? Colm's visit replayed in my mind. Charged. Anguished. Another level of pain.

"Then what?" She grabbed my hairbrush, proceeding to straighten her snow-white curls.

"It's not wishful thinking. It's something Colm said." I turned from the mirror and leaned on the counter.

"When were you talking to Colm? Want a candy?" She searched through her handbag.

"He came by the pub. He talked about Ciarán. Accusing me of the same old shite. But then. I can't explain it. He wanted to know about Calla. He says she's a Faerie."

"And you believed him?" Her black eyes flashed as she handed me a clove candy.

"There's more. He said Calla spoke to Ciarán at the wake." I swallowed hard.

"Are you serious? You are, aren't you?" Her words garbled together. She dropped her arms to her sides and looked at me.

"Yes." Pandora's box had been opened. I could never close it again.

"A Faerie? Aye, makes sense." Her tongue played with the candy. "Jaysus, fecking Christ."

"What?" I stepped back. When Breda was on a roll, you gave her the floor.

"Did you hear Connor playing the ukulele?" She planted her hand on her hip.

"Yes," I recalled the lively tune the boy played.

"He's five, Saoirse. The wee chisler can't play like that. Touched by the Faeries, isn't that what they say?" She lifted her eyebrows.

"And you think Calla did that?" I almost whispered. Tales of old spoke of Themselves gifting the angel music to mortals—my father told of the fiddler who fell asleep on this side of a Faerie rath, a tumulus of earth covered with hawthorn branches, thought to be an entrance into the Faerie realm. They were common in these parts, feared, and left untouched. Bad luck or even death would come to the poor bloke who tampered with the Good Folk. The fiddler of my father's tale was one of the lucky ones, waking in the mortal world gifted with song.

"What did I do?" Calla glided into the bathroom, a glass of wine in hand. She looked back and forth, smiling between us.

"Calla, we need to talk." Sparkles danced in Breda's inky eyes. "But first, would you have a candy?" The pink cellophane bag crackled.

"Candy? Sure. Is this about Colm?" She giggled.

"Yes, it is about Colm. He came to see me at the pub. He said things, Calla. I need to know if what he said was true." I wrung my hands together. Where did my bravado go? She was Calla. She was my friend.

"Look. I know what he thinks. But Storey and I are not a thing. We're just friends. Business associates." Calla crunched the hard candy and then grimaced. "What is this?"

"Storey? What about Storey?" Breda's eyes bugged out.

"Colm thinks we're a couple." Her laugh sounded like church bells on a quiet morning, ringing over the land, calling everyone to listen.

"Is there something going on between you two?" Breda eyed Calla, her mouth hanging open.

"Maybe. Yes. I suppose we're due for a crash

test." Calla set her glass down. "I have two main hopes, and Storey isn't it."

"I don't understand." Breda rested her palm on her face.

"Storey swings the other way, ladies," Calla revealed Storey's preference in a matter-of-fact voice.

"Oh dear, what will Polly say? She's over the moon, talking grandkids and the lot." Breda sighed.

"You didn't know?" Calla gazed from me to Breda.

"As long as he's happy, Breda? Aye?" I added, knowing full well Breda had her suspicions. Why else had the lad left home and hearth? Not much happened in the little town that didn't get dissected around the back fence. I should know.

"Storey's significant other is Jonathan. A great guy. He's a big player in pharmaceuticals. And he's coming to visit next week." She applied pink lipstick to her perfectly formed lips. "Saoirse? Why are you looking at me like that?"

"It's not about Storey." My voice trembled. I inhaled deeply, gathering my wits.

"It's about Colm's brother. Saoirse's fiancé. Ciarán." Breda said the words that broke my heart.

"Ciarán?" Calla's gaze held mine. "What did Colm say?"

"He has this crazy story. That you spoke to Ciarán—at the wake, he thinks you're one of the Other Crowd." My breath lodged in my throat.

"Yes, I know." She clucked her tongue inside her cheek, and then she sighed.

The cold water tap dripped. I counted five pings before anyone spoke.

"I'm not sure about 'Them,' but yes—he's right. I saw him in your pub, Saoirse. He stood at the end of the bar. I didn't know who he was. Just a guy staring at you. He watched you all night." She leaned on the counter, her face paling.

"Jaysus Fecking Christ," Breda muttered.

"I saw him again at the wake, standing beside the coffin, mumbling to himself. I spoke to him, and he answered." She spoke softly, believing everything she said. "And at the burial, standing behind you."

"Dear goddess." I clutched the sink, stars dancing behind my eyelids.

"Do you always see the dead?" Breda's words stung. The dead. The bloodless dead.

"Is he with the angels? Is he happy?" I dug my fingernails into the broken edge of the counter. I refused to believe Ciarán was dead. I wanted to believe he was alive and well and living in the land of the young, *Tír na Nóg*.

"I tried running from my past. But it catches up with me wherever I go. But this, this is an add-on to my talent list." She chuffed a halting breath.

"What talents?" Breda pounced on Calla, her voice quickening.

"Is Ciarán dead?" My throat ached.

"No. No, Ciarán isn't dead, Saoirse. He was there." Her eyes were bright.

"How did he look?" I clenched my elbows, my heart bursting.

"Well, he wore dirty sneakers, blue jeans, and the craziest-looking cape, purple with silver stars. Was he happy? No. I don't think so. He said everything was his fault." She paused, then exhaled a long, silvery breath. "I'm having a real hard time with this Good People thing. I left Canada because of my gift because I scared people. Colm thinks I'm one of Them because I saw his father's death and because, at the same moment, a *Bean Sidhe* visited his mother."

"The wizard costume?" My knees wobbled. There's no way she could have made that up.

"The Banshee? Yes, it was the weirdest thing. A howling cry came across the meadow, rising in pitch. I thought the damn dog got caught in a gopher trap." Breda's eyes widened.

"Yeah? Colm is convinced I'm a *Bean Sidhe*, and

those keening cries were me. But I don't remember any of it. And let's double down, yeah? I met a guy at the wake who everyone thinks is dead. Well, let me tell you. He's not dead." She shook her head, convincing everyone.

"What do you mean, you see death?" Breda prodded deeper.

I sucked one breath after another into my lungs.

"It started when I was young. If I touched someone, I would see death, not theirs...someone close to them. But that was scary enough. My mother did her best to keep me away from kids my age and from people in general." Her eyes shadowed, and she shrugged. "I was homeschooled until I went to university. I was a loner. Kept to myself. Friends were not part of the deal. But the truth comes out, eventually. My gift raised its ugly head one too many times."

"You're clairvoyant, which is likely why you can see Ciarán. There's power in this land, and your abilities have grown since arriving here." Breda nodded her head. Her wide smile told Calla she believed in all things.

"You're not afraid of me?" Calla's voice cracked. She gaped at us.

I gazed into her shimmering eyes. Faerie or mortal made no difference to me.

"Afraid of you? No way, girl. We call it *dá silleadh*. It means two looks. You see spirits, ghosts. You see the past, the present, and the future. We won't banish you from our island for having the sight." She laughed, then sighed happily.

"I don't know what to say." Calla's gaze cut toward me, unsure.

"Being 'different' is almost expected. Look, we're all different. Saoirse's a witch. I'm an empath. You'll fit in just grand." Breda offered her another candy.

"We're friends, Calla, and Breda is a friend." I piped up, adding my two cents worth.

"You mean that, don't you?" Calla's eyes glowed.

"Yes. Oh my God. Yes." I wrapped my arms around her, and Breda hugged the two of us. Calla flinched, her every muscle turning to stone.

"Breathe, Calla. You're one of us," Breda murmured.

What she said made sense, except for one thing. Sympathetic souls exuded the energy of the world, but Calla's aura was something else entirely. The crystals hinted at the truth, and the flames confirmed it.

"We have to find him, Calla. Somehow. There must be a way." I placed my hand on the green velvet covering her upper arm.

"I don't know, Saoirse." She flinched and then circled her lips, blowing a cool, calming breath. "I can see him, I guess, when he wants to be seen."

"We'll figure it out. I know we will." Hope tore through me.

"And you're a witch?" The corners of her mouth lifted into a small smile.

Her furrowed brow told me she remained unconvinced. What would happen when she learned the Otherworld does exist? I dallied there once and almost got burned.

"She's not just a witch. She's a high priestess. Tell her the news, Saoirse." Breda nodded.

"It's not important right now." I hugged my arms around my chest, my heart full.

"Oh, for God's sake, Saoirse. When will you learn to blow your own horn? She's now licensed to reside over wedding ceremonies." Breda clapped her hands.

"Wedding ceremonies? That's amazing." Calla smiled.

"C'mere to me, Calla Sweet. We have a lot to celebrate." Breda grabbed Calla's hand, gesturing toward an open-air courtyard.

The narrow passage behind the pub held six painted picnic tables and exited to the alley behind. Pub memorabilia fastened to the century-old bricks added hometown charm.

"It's plain to see we need refreshments, aye? Espresso martinis all around. My treat. Grab a seat, aye?" Breda circled away, humming a lively tune.

"I've spent my entire life hiding from this. This ability, as you call it." She folded her long legs under a red picnic table.

"But none of it matters if you're one of Them. You just 'are.'" I took a step back, literally speaking. Approaching the Other Crowd should not be taken lightly. And yet, when my arms wrapped around that regal one, I felt no evil. Calla exuded darkness, yet a healthy degree of light shone within her.

"I just 'am?' You'd think I would know. You'd think I'd feel something. Something more than this. You believe, don't you? In this Other Crowd. This Otherworld?" Her gaze narrowed, only half convinced.

"I do. I'm a pagan and a witch. The old gods are part of that. I believe in the spirits of the land and the spirits of nature. It's all around us. Connecting with the magic and the earth's power has given me my life back," I admitted freely.

"Here we are, ladies." Breda placed a tray on the picnic table with three espresso martinis foaming over the rim. "*Sláinte!*" Breda clinked her glass to ours.

"The gods? You mean the *Sidhe*?" Calla rubbed her thumb over her chin, then swallowed.

"Yes." I smiled at the simple human response.

"Eamon leaves an offering every night 'to stay on good terms.' Potatoes and milk. I thought he was pulling my leg. He seemed almost afraid to talk about Them." She opened her mouth but then furrowed her brow.

"Eamon knows the old ways. His people knew them, feared them, and loved them. People nowadays think fairies are cute little winged creatures from Hollywood movies." I ran my finger over the rim of the pretty glass.

"Granda knew how to keep us in line: "Don't go out at night. Don't follow the twinkling lights," I was utterly terrified." Breda shivered and chuckled, recalling a rule that all schoolchildren lived by.

"This is going down way too fast. How in the hell are we going to get home?" I giggled, then threw it back.

"Storey. My very only best friend, until now." She shrugged her shoulders. "How about a ride in a Silver Phantom, girls?"

"Cheers to Storey," Breda lifted her glass.

Calla tapped her phone, sending a text message.

"Not so fast, Calla. It's my round." I left the two of them sitting at the picnic table. Breda smiled, and Calla played with her fingers.

"Three espresso martinis." I leaned on the bar top, and while the bartender prepared the order, I watched the O'Donnell men minus one: Hugh Jr. and Pádraig playing darts, Oisin talking up the pink-haired lady with purple glasses, Cillian and Tadgh shooting billiards. Tadgh lifted his gaze from the game, catching my eye. His smile warmed my heart.

I searched the room and found Colm alone, staring into his stout in the darkest corner of the pub. I studied him from a distance. I knew what love looked like and what losing someone felt like. Real or imagined, love hurts. I walked toward him and whispered into his ear. I owed him that one truth.

6

Ciarán

The grand hall, draped in billowing black silks, exuded a gothic grandeur. Marble columns crowned with inverted pineapples welcomed revelers to the ball. From the pages of dark fantasy—demons—gargoyle-like creatures leaped from pillar to post on disjointed limbs, their misshapen mouths dripping stardust onto the crowd below. Androgenous beings, neither male nor female, stroked pockmarked organs, hissing for release, which would come when their ruler gave the nod—the machinations of a depraved mind.

The beautiful people below seemed unaware of the baseless creatures above. They lounged on modular marshmallows, some in deep conversation, others in various states of undress. Strobe lights whirled pink and purple beams across the marbled dance floor, distorting reality—continuous motion broken into flashing still frames—the effect was mind-bending.

The ultimate trick for the trickster himself—Finvarra, the King of the Faeries.

Servers served enchanted wine while waiters dressed in black tuxedos cleared empty glasses from the glowing cubes.

The pounding beat enticed Finvarra's guests onto the floor. Scantily dressed women doused in fragrance. Lust-crazed men flitted between partners. Each revolution of the circular floor took five minutes, the gentle motion leaving minds blurred. Pleasure became pain, and pain became pleasure.

The guitar player saturated the hall with screaming chords, and bodies thrashed to the head-banging riffs. Neon lights pulsated in sync.

I stared too long at a blue-haired nymph lost in the throes of a climax. The human, stationed between her thighs, planted his hand on the arch of her black velvet open-toed pump. He lifted her leg over his head, exposing her black lace garter and taut thigh. Suckling her pink flesh with hollowed cheeks, he gave her glistening core a thorough lashing. Her orgasmic screams heightened with the pulsing rhythm of the flashing strobe.

Enticed by magic, drunk on the wine, the mortals within didn't stand a chance. They had been here too long, feasting and dancing. Playthings for the immortals. They no longer knew their names.

"Oooh, pretty, so pretty." The White Woman hearkened to those drunken fools. Beneath her gossamer gown, her bones were liquid, her skin translucent, giving her an otherworldly appearance. Neither dead nor alive, her kind existed on the threshold of both realms. A direct ancestor to the Tuatha, the *Bean Fhionn* served the boundary between life and death, and in recompense, one human soul was owed every seven years.

I froze on the spot, too late.

She extended her arms, her spindly hands reaching for the stardust. Her eyes were white glass, and her skin appeared spidery beneath the blinding lights. She teetered on the edge of sanity, of life. The one remnant remaining was the cascade of black hair reaching her lower back.

"Aren't you a handsome one?" Her lips parted, her breath sweet with wine. Her blood-red nails curved into sharp talons, digging into my chest. The dancing fools did not notice her intrusion.

"My lady, how can I help you?" My blood

chilled as her essence prowled beneath my skin. I held her unseeing gaze, willing my mind to resist.

"Hmm." She clung to me, searching for what I did not know. She lifted her lips in disdain, retracting her claws and releasing me.

She did not differ from others in the room. Snuffing out life meant nothing to them. But that was too harsh. Finvarra's playthings were well-nourished and happily cared for. And to give him credit, none were stolen from the mortal realm. Willing humans who were no longer of sane mind. Perhaps that was what they sought.

I studied the White Woman and almost felt sorry for her. I had lived among these beings for seven years. Having the sight gave me an advantage over the other mortals within. I knew their kind. I had built a rapport with many, some of whom I considered friends. Yes, they held me against my will, yet I had only myself to blame. That was their world. Beneath the pomp, they were a mystical people, at heart, a warring people. I questioned myself. What would I give to hold on to life's breath? Would I become that?

She lost herself in her ecstasy and forgot my presence.

In seven days, the supermoon would be upon us, and to celebrate the goddess, the great hall would transform into an ice castle of silver stars wrapped in gossamer silks. A masquerade ball with jesters, bards, and mythical beings of all shapes and sizes would go well into the night, but the players would remain the same: queens and kings, an entourage of immortals from every kingdom would attend.

I turned away, cutting across the dance floor toward the solid wall of ivory, the only constant in Finvarra's palace.

I slipped unnoticed through the castle's kitchen and the servant's entrance. I sensed a 'quare wind sweeping through the glen— streamers touched with darkness. Beyond the Faerie rath, the moon cast a silvered glow, and stars sparkled in the night sky.

Human hands hadn't touched the Tuatha's side of Ireland. Mountains were thick with forests, meadows abundant with elk, salmon-filled rivers, and a million other unearthly horrors.

I remained in the shadows, preferring to avoid detection. My nightly sojourns were tolerated, but tonight came with risk. Others were about, and an alarm would sound should a visitor to Finvarra's kingdom discover my presence. I gazed at the crenelated walls and soldiers stationed in every turret and gave no thought to the guarded drawbridge.

Another portal, one few knew about, existed on the other side of the vast estate. A path I knew well. Cian, Finvarra's bastard son, had shown me years ago. *"Can't have you fading away, O'Donnell. We need you, mate."* Although he referred to an up-coming hurling match between the Faerie king-doms of Ulster and Connaught, he understood what maintaining my humanity meant, if only to me. With his blue eyes, a rarity among his kind, he might have been more connected to the mortal realm than he cared to admit.

Beneath the boughs of a feathery pine, the druid's altar revealed itself. The capstone, grooved to allow sacrificial blood to escape, the two portal stones were tall enough to enable a man to enter. The passage narrowed at a shimmering rift. I slid sideways, a restless breeze following me, its sigh haunting.

Passing through the portal proved a disqui-eting experience. As I had many times before, I held fast to the belief that I would survive the jour-ney. I willed my mind, preparing for the sensation of knives cutting through me and the inferno of wind.

My lungs burst, and I coughed up hell's fire. I

stood in the shadows beneath the same moon and waited for normalcy to return. With each journey, the effect of crossing over took more of a toll. I could smell the poison in my blood and taste it on my tongue.

The shadows danced among themselves, and the wind sang. I skirted the dark path unseen by human eyes. The glamor imposed on me prevented interaction with those I loved.

For that, I despised them.

The whippoorwill flew past, its lonesome song filling the gloom. From somewhere above, an owl hooted.

I shivered, not yet back to myself, my gaze following the mottled bird's flight through the dark hedges. The curious bird would have to wait another day to capture my departing soul and take me to the underworld—a place I had no intention of visiting.

Eamon's barn loomed before me, a dark silhouette against the inky blackness of the night sky. I slipped silently through the barn door, the only sound being the soft nicker of the cow, a gentle melody that greeted my ears.

Eamon's offering to the Other Crowd, a substantial helping of mashed potatoes, and a mug of unpasteurized milk sustained my existence. Without it, my fate would have been sealed, and I would join the ever-growing band of lost souls. I banished the faces haunting me and glanced at my watch. Time was running out.

I sensed her presence before she appeared. I scanned the quiet, searching for the otherworldly being. From the highest rafter, as a black crow, Nemain, the halfling daughter of Finvarra himself, watched me through beady black eyes. The bird pounced, the air buckled, and she transformed into her true form—a golden-haired princess any man would kill for.

"Whatcha doing, Ciarán?" She drawled my name through crimson lips, her sultry voice enticing.

"Faffin' about, Nemain. Just faffin' about." I gave nothing away lest she use it against me.

"Like my dress?" She trailed manicured nails over the body-hugging slip of miniature black diamonds.

"Aye, it's deadly. What do you want?" I couldn't hide my smile. Of Finvarra's two daughters, she amused me most. Before she entered her own, she would follow Cian throughout the castle, begging for his attention. Her instincts were ingrained from birth to charm and cajole and to suck the life from unwary mortals, male or female; she showed no preference. Her appetite was insatiable. Finvarra considered her his equal, in trickery at least.

"I long for the same things as you, Ciarán." Her voice chimed low and sweet, meant to seduce even the most robust soul. She sought the love of mortals, knowing full well that if they refused, she would become theirs. None refused.

"And what is that, luv? What do you think I want?" I watched the wee vixen. She gave that look that had been the end of many mortals—the *Leannán Sídhe*, the faerie lover. Fair play to her.

"You're such a bore, Ciarán. Why can't you have a little fun now and then?" Her eyes lit with darkness.

"Why are you following me?" I lounged in the rickety chair Eamon had left in the corner. I pictured him there on a summer's day, a straw stick in his mouth, nodding off in the cool shade.

"Because it's fun. And because I can. Why are you eating such ghastly slop?" She seethed, eyeing me with disgust.

"How many souls are enough? Those are people with families who need them. They are not puppets meant for the Tuatha's pleasure." I blasted her, continuing the conversation we had the night before.

"Tell me about it, boyfriend." She smiled lazily, twirling a golden curl around her finger. She would take me to hell if I let her.

"I'm not your boyfriend. How many souls have you taken, Nemain?" I turned my back on her alluring gaze—eighteen at last count. I sighed and shook my head. At least they died happy.

"I know. I'm not your type. You could have anyone in the realm, yet you pine after a mortal witch. You know she's getting wrinkles? And grey hairs on her privates. She is. She is." She jutted out her chin.

"Have you been spying on Saoirse? What have you been up to?" I narrowed my gaze. Reading thoughts was her forte, not mine.

"Nothing." She pouted.

"And now you're following me? What would your father say?" I knew the answer to that. Finvarra knew not of my existence; I was a pawn in the grand scheme of things.

"I don't care. I am an independent woman." She batted her eyelashes, but doubt flickered in her eyes.

"Of course you are," I smirked. Raised by an

adoring father and ignored by a spiteful step-mother, Nemain and her sister Macha were alike, yet different—both dangerous in their own right —two sides of the same coin.

"And you know that slop is an offering to my people. As if the Tuatha Dé would touch lips to that. Such a silly belief." She huffed.

"This is my only hope of returning home. You know that." I stretched my legs. Time drew near.

"You could have anything or anyone: sex, love, whatever, and here you are. Why? Life is good for you in the Kingdom." She jutted her pretty chin.

"I never asked for this. I agreed to help—one tournament game. I kept my promise. They didn't." I sighed through my nose.

"Buck up, Ciarán. Take one for the team. Be-sides, you have more freedom than the rest. Hmph. Don't think your sneaking away doesn't go unnoticed." She held her head high.

"This is my world. This place. These people. This is where I belong." I drained the remaining warm milk from the ceramic mug.

"I don't get you, Ciarán. Satisfied with a life of drudgery. This cesspool of sadness. Why don't you hook up with someone? Odette follows you around like a wee lost puppy. Aye, and she's not the only one. And yet, here you are. Feasting on sour milk and cold mash. Like a common barn animal." She tossed her golden mane.

"Nemain, you will never understand." Raised in the royal household, how would she know the difference?

"But I do, Ciarán. I want what you want. Freedom." She whirled her hands in the air, giving me room for pause. Halfling or not, she wielded mighty powers.

"Nemain," I said her name. She was not my enemy. She was the king's daughter. "You have no cause to leave your father's realm. You are free to come and go as you like." I left the empty bowl where it was. Best not to frighten Eamon.

"And if I did, I would face banishment. Father would never forgive me." She lingered outside the box stall. The brown pony raised its head and nickered.

I realized the horse knew her.

"Oh, I doubt it. You and Macha are the chosen ones." I considered her words.

The king's bastards would never succeed him. Queen Nuala did not recognize their existence, never gracing that court, preferring the grandeur of Knockma.

I recalled my visits there with trepidation. The hurling jamboree brought the four kingdoms together and lasted over seven days. The grueling tournament was exhausting—a culling of sorts. Finvarra sat upon his dais, surrounded by the kings and queens of the realm. Win or lose, he selected the strongest hurlers from the Ulster team, banishing the rest. Had they banished me, would they have set me free or sent me to another realm?

"Macha? With her nose stuck in a book all day. You're kidding, right? She would never leave. I can't believe we are related. I want to experience life. I want a man who bleeds. Not those pansy-ass creatures calling themselves men." She loosed a breath and slipped into the pony's stall, landing on its broad back in one easy leap, her nimble fingers twisting the pony's mane into tiny braids.

"You just told me Middle Earth is beneath you. What did you call it? A cesspool of sadness?" I smiled for the first time today.

"Yeah, well. I'm bored. I want new friends. You understand, don't you?" She didn't look up from her task. Her fingers twirled, tying more and more intricate knots.

"I met someone. She saw me." I leaned on the half-door, admiring her work. Had I become blind to the cruelty? Hardened to their ways? Accepting of Them?

"So?" she graced me with a regal stare.

"She has your eyes," I recalled my encounters with the dark-haired beauty. Her dove-grey eyes and Elven voice enchanted the crowd.

"Aye?" She looked at me with a passing interest.

"She saw through the glamor. She spoke to me." An awareness flowed through me, one I should have seen. The girl carried herself as Nemain did, and her mannerisms were strikingly similar. "She sang at my father's burial."

"What's her name?" Her gaze narrowed, and I wondered if she read my mind.

"Calla. Calla Sweet."

COLM

The local radio program, "Good Morning Ardara," was broadcast through the television's surround sound system. Poppy, the show's host, engaged in a lively conversation with the most recent caller, discussing the importance of carbon sequestration and the rewetting of raised boglands.

"Mam, I had to go." I sat back in the high-backed chair. Taking her hand in mine did not calm her ire.

I had left Ireland for one reason only—to escape the pain.

Poppy reiterated that increasing the water table could transform a compromised site from a carbon source into a carbon sink.

"Did you, Colm? You spent a lifetime away from us." Mam spoke the hard truth.

Back then, I saw no way out. My head was a dark, foreboding space. My life revolved around one thing—finding Ciarán.

"There was nothing left for me, Mam." The words sounded selfish, even to my ears. I had left Ciarán and everyone I loved behind. My brother looked up to me, and I let him down.

Swept away by the Faeries—the old folks say. The tales lived on in that little town. The young girl from Glenties on the eve of her wedding. Jim McGovern during the hurling championships of 2012.

Ciarán on Samhain—when the passage to the underworld opened, and the undead searched for breathing souls.

"You had your differences. What father and son ever think alike? I know how he was when an idea struck him." She hugged me, pressing her greying head against my chest.

"It was for the best, Mam." I left with what

money I had and started a new life. I tossed about for months and drank myself into a dark place. Women. Whisky. None of it mattered, but then the clouds cleared. It began with a phone call. The voice on the other end of the line was Eamon. "I have a job for you, laddie. If you're able." He threw me a lifeline, and I took it. I buried myself in other people's pain and, in doing so, escaped from mine. I settled into my new life, neutralizing risk and executing covert operations—as a ghost.

Eamon—I pictured the unassuming man, the mastermind behind black operations for the Irish government. Some would call him a doddering old man.

"Would you be playing with the internet again?" She peered over my shoulder at the computer screen. "'Tis the lass who sang at your da's burial." Calla's face smiled back. The headline blasting... Calla Sweet, Rich Girl Lost. The scathing article purported Calla—a spoiled debutante with a checkered past, alleging mental illness and excessive substance abuse.

"It is Mam..." My Faerie girl, an heiress to one of the most enormous fortunes in North America. Yet there she was, living in a crofter's cottage in the small town of Ardara.

I saw her: bright-eyed, sharp as a tack. My

mind denied those accusations. I was, in a word my father would use—gobsmacked. I considered every conversation, her actions, and her reactions.

An inheritance from an older man who, by all accounts, had led a simple life. The connection eluded me, yet the possibilities seemed endless, daring me to dig deeper and to stay.

"Such a lovely girl, Colm." She placed her hand on my shoulder, squeezing gently.

"Why would you say that, Mam?" Her aura haunted me, pressing down on me, consuming me.

"Ach, a Mam knows such things. Did you see today's paper, luv?" She flattened the newspaper on the table, smoothing the corners with care.

"Calla Sweet and Niall York, headlining tonight at the Black Horse Pub. Join us for great food and drinks. Liquor sales from tonight's event will be donated to the local Donkey Sanctuary— because their survival is in our hands."

"Didn't your da love those donkeys? Remember, wee Bingo?" She mussed my hair, then laughed.

Calla's photo stared back in grainy black-and-white.

"Oh dear, that wee boy is still missing from near Malin Head." She traced her finger over the child's black-and-white image in the right-hand corner of the opposite page. "Well, I'm after the messages. They've got pork backs on sale this week. 'Twas Da's favorite, remember?"

"Aye, aye, I remember. Have a good time." I leaned back in the chair, brushing my fingers against hers as she walked away.

"Will you be home for dinner, luv?" She turned, her eyes shining bright.

"I wouldn't miss it, Mam." A muscle twitched in my jaw—an involuntary reflex I couldn't contain.

MY DREAMS HAD ESCALATED into something more.

The wind sang, her whispers calling me. Brazen, salacious thoughts flooded my mind, yet I could not express them. Held down by a mysterious force, I could not respond to her teasing touch.

Her need slammed into me, and time lost its grip.

Her hair, braided into delicate spirals, fell into my face as her pink lips brushed mine. She slipped her graceful fingers between the buttons of her blouse, spilling her breasts and rocking her heated flesh over my bursting erection. I woke semi-conscious, locked between her thighs, my cock straining at the seam of my boxers, her breath ragged, her ecstasy near.

She left my balls burning and my mind crazed.

I woke each morning—worn out and used up—my desire for her flaming out of control. I convinced myself those dreams resulted from an overactive imagination and simple infatuation.

ARDARA'S main street had stayed the same over the past seven years. The chippy truck was still parked illegally. The Blue Bonnet Grill closed by three o'clock. Pete's Pub was always an excellent place for a pint. From Pádraig's bakery, a light shone beneath the kitchen door, telling me my brother worked late into the night.

I clenched the concrete railing, gazing into the flowing waters of the Owentocker, singing toward the sea. Breda might have had the right idea. The fishing boat Ciarán and I dreamed of represented an end to the madness.

My father's death weighed heavy on my conscience.

Had I lifted that burden from his shoulders—would he still be alive?

"The blame game doesn't suit you, brother." Ciarán's voice whispered. How many times had I talked to Ciarán? Imaginary conversations. Unanswered questions.

"Where are you, brother?" The question played on repeat, over and over.

I willed my mind to stay in the present, but instead, I relived the past.

Samhain's frigid breath had poured over the land. While Mam twisted wood and bits of straw into protective crosses, Da stirred the bones of the past year's slaughtered cattle into the fire. The flames consumed everything. Blue smoke curled into the air. The time to usher in the dark half of the year had arrived.

We ran for our lives, Ciarán and me, chased by ghouls from the Otherworld. The Sluagh sought to steal our souls. The Faerie Host aimed to take us away. Our brothers chased us, their faces hidden behind flour sack masks embellished with horsehair and sheep's wool. Concealed in shadows, we flattened our bodies against the cold earth. I intended to surrender to the Púca's wrath, but a shout was raised, our brothers whipping by. Fear curdled our screams as we crept on our bellies through the tall grass, searching for more friendly ghosts.

Rain lashed down, a sharp wind howling in from the sea, the ocean's roar adding another dimension to the Púca's fury. A ghostly apparition floated through the haar, a faceless woman cloaked in gossamer silk. If ever the dark was frightening, it was then.

Ciarán's face whitened, and I looked in the direction of his fear.

A beast from the Otherworld, a giant wolf-like creature, approached with quiet stealth. His almond-shaped eyes shone like fiery flames, the night glowed in his black fur, and the moon shimmered in his wild ruff. The creature guided us to higher ground, where we huddled through the storm.

The following day, a farmer tending his sheep found us two missing O'Donnell lads. I still remember the ride home in the back of the farmer's truck, wrapped in a heavy wool blanket, and the steaming bowl of porridge Mam shoveled into my mouth.

No one knew who the black dog belonged to. My father said the Faeries came that night. We placed an empty chair at our supper table to thank them, and a full meal was prepared for Themselves.

I headed toward the witch's lair, The Black Horse Pub—my second visit in two days. I smiled, half expecting the witch would give me the boot, no questions asked.

The latch stuck but then gave way, the creaking hinges granting access. Faces shifted, accepting me into the din. Laughter spilled from the inner depths of the pub. Glasses clanked together. The front end was jammed tight with sweating bodies, a mixture of musty body odors and cheap perfume. A girl's voice reached out, the guitar player strumming in accompaniment.

"Colm O'Donnell. I heard off Rollie that you were back." Joseph, a school chum, slapped my shoulder.

"How're ye getting on, mate? Haven't seen you in a donkey's age."

The conversation turned to sheep prices and people who had died in the next parish. I excused myself from the rambling conversation and approached the back of the bar.

"What will ye have?" The bartender turned his thick neck toward me.

"The Black Stuff, please." I settled onto the stool, resting one laced boot on the foot rail.

The bartender slid a tall glass toward me.

I rested my forearm on the bar and watched the crowd, waiting for the head to settle.

"What are you doing here?" She stood at the end of the bar, the dark scent of orchids and moonshine emanating from the pores of her satin skin.

I gazed at the skimpy dress knitted to her every curve. The icy blue shade reminded me of a twilight sky. She had my full attention.

"Nice dress." I was lost in those shimmering eyes. There was no turning back from that. I would go to war for that woman.

"Thanks. I found it at the Treasure Chest." She moved the air with her fingers, making my thoughts whirl.

"Hmm." An heiress shopping second hand. Nothing she did should surprise me.

Uber-aware of her presence, the bartender dispensed a pint into a tall glass and ambled our way with a handful of napkins and a bowl of mixed nuts.

What other powers did that Faerie girl possess?

"Thanks, Gerry," her sultry voice hung in the air. They treated her as one of their own, not someone from away.

"Anything for you, luv." The man nodded and turned away.

"Why are you here?" Her soft laugh weaved

havoc. She gazed into my eyes, a small smile playing on her lips.

"For the craic." My ears popped, and the sensation subsided—I loosened my fingers, extending each one. It took everything I had to break the spell.

"You look good, O'Donnell. Have you broken any hearts lately?" She raised her glass, taking one long, breathtaking pull. The gold spheres circling her earlobes caught the light. My thoughts slowed, making words difficult.

"I thought you didn't like beer." My gaze skated over her shining locks—the two braids wound around her head and the third hanging down her back. I studied the silver comb, which joined all three together.

"I lied." She popped one candied beer nut into her mouth.

"You lie about a lot of things." Her bell-like voice made my heart ping.

"I do not." She chewed thoughtfully.

"You made me think you and Storey were an item." The edges blurred, and a realization crept over me. I had never considered myself a jealous man.

"Um, no. That's on you, O'Donnell." Her smile

lit up the room—her presence more potent than the day before.

"Hmm." I rubbed my chin, considering what may come.

"Maybe you can't see the forest for the trees, huh?" She arched one delicate eyebrow, considering me right back.

"How do I repel your powers? Should I wear my clothes inside out? Walk backward around the pub? Two? Maybe three times?" Protecting oneself —Faeries 101.

"Look, you're mesmerized by my charm and wit..." She ran her tongue back and forth across her lower lip—unknowingly, I think. There was something provocative about that.

"Do ye think?" Playing hard to get was not my forte, and hiding my smile was nearly impossible.

The crowd grew. I scanned the perimeter, gazing over the bobbing heads—people talking over one another, laughing and shouting. A bottleneck of so many worried me. This was a night out for so many. That was home.

"Okay, I'll play your game, O'Donnell. Why are you here?" She rolled her eyes and smiled at me alone.

"Like I said, I'm supporting the fundraiser." My

thoughts ran riot, my obsession growing by the minute.

"Why doesn't Saoirse like you?" She planted her hand on her hip and studied me.

"We have history." The conversation with the witch seemed a long time ago.

Concern grew in Calla's gaze.

"Sounds like you accused her of sorcery. Take my advice, buttercup. Kiss and makeup. You want a mad witch talking shit about you?" She lifted an eyebrow, sizing me up for a fight I couldn't win.

"What are you doing after the show?" I smiled, throwing my masculine charms her way.

Another wave entered the pub, adding to the deafening roar. Some escaped the melee, finding refuge in the long hall. Others stood their ground, claiming the real estate close to the bar. Shoulder to shoulder, they closed in on one another. It was claustrophobic, the atmosphere suffocating.

"Are you asking me out?" She lifted her chin.

"You owe me a raincheck," I held her gaze.

"A raincheck? And what did you have in mind?" Her eyelashes fluttered.

"A moonlit stroll on the strand?" I drew the pad of my thumb along the curve of her jaw.

One enthusiastic punter jostled another. The burly lad with a tweed newsboy cap would collide with the Faerie girl in seconds. I reacted, thrusting my palm forward, striking the clown between the shoulder blades and, at the same time, pulling Calla out of harm's way.

"Oy, sorry, mate." The culchie tipped his hat, making amends.

"You saved me, O'Donnell. Twice." She pressed against me, her hands on my shoulders. Beneath the clingy knit, her nipples rose into delectable nubs.

"Aye, and I'll do it again. You're a fine lass, Calla Sweet. You need to take care." Blood rushed through my veins, making my balls burn and my cock react.

"I do?" She smiled sweetly, making no move to retreat.

Her scent made my head spin, my mouth water.

"Aye, there's a wee rabble out tonight. Shnakey shitehawks. Bleedin' melters." I chuckled.

"Shnakey shitehawks?" She stumbled on the Irish slang.

"They'll be after taking advantage of a lass like you." I pressed the heel of my hand into the small of her back, seating her position between my thighs.

"And what would you be wanting, Colm O'-

Donnell, from a fine lass like me?" Her fiery gaze stared through my soul.

"I want what's beneath this slip you'd be calling a dress." I leaned close, the bristles on my chin scraping the soft skin of her cheek.

A cacophony of voices babbled around us. Another day, I would slip through the kitchen, escaping through the back door. Crowded places were not my thing. But that was not the time to abandon a lady in distress.

"Hmm. I wasn't sure if I was your cup of tae." She pinned her soft lips and smiled.

The voices faded, and in that moment, that fracture of time, the crowd dissipated, leaving us alone. She was the wind whistling through the trees.

"Why do you visit my dreams?" The Faerie girl and I were in a precarious position, yet she made no move to escape. Drifting lower, I brushed the edge of her skimpy dress with my free hand. Unseen and unnoticed, I explored freely, finding a wee bit of lace and her bottom bare. She rewarded me with a low laugh.

"You don't want to know." She writhed silently against my hardened erection, her breath mingling with mine. This was not a hookup in a bar. This was a pleasure, long overdue. The dreams we shared had only escalated my need. The point of no return loomed near.

"I want everything about you." I swept my fingers through the soft folds of her wee vagina, parting her labia and finding her wanting. My mind left the room when she gave me a hot flush of wet heat.

"No, you don't." She held fast to her denial, but I sensed her resolve wavering.

"You're wet for me, Faerie girl. Don't forget." I dragged my thumb over her clitoris, coaxing the hooded bead to swell.

"You don't play a friendly game, do you?" She dug her stiletto fingernails into my bunching trapezius, a shudder wracking her inner thighs.

"Fair game to you, luv." I buried my face into her silken locks and nibbled on the golden sphere circling her earlobe.

"What? Oh, God." She closed her eyelids and hummed.

"Come for me, sweet Faerie." I eased my first knuckle into her weeping channel. Her pussy contracted, the inner walls clenching.

"This is better than dreaming. Oh, God. What are you doing to me?" She flexed her hips, her movements barely indiscernible.

"Let me ease the ache." I slid my thumb over

her clit, circling the swollen bud with gentle pressure. What I would give to languish in her sweet release, to fill her pussy with my hard cock.

"Colm." She murmured my name, her breath rasping. Still, she held back, denying herself the pleasure of release.

"Make my dreams come true, Faerie girl." Shattering her became the prize. I rolled her hips with one hand while stroking the roof of her pussy with the pad of my forefinger.

Her eyes shimmered, and her lips half-parted. I closed my mouth over hers, inhaling her hungry sighs, her ecstasy slid down my throat, and her tongue brushed against mine.

She tasted like heaven's breath.

I gasped when her pointy eye teeth, all four of them, clamped down, sending a line of fire straight to my soul. Or was she draining my soul? I wasn't entirely sure.

A curious bystander would see a passionate kiss between lovers.

A shudder flowed through her, and her pussy twitched, flooding my fingers with wet heat. Far too soon for my liking, she pulled away.

"I'll tell you what, Colm O'Donnell. Find a new dream, okay?" Her bottom lip quivered, and for one long moment, her stare drifted––across the sea of heads, to the stage, to the girl with curly brown hair, and then back to me. She released me and walked away from our embrace, her expression—calm, cool, and collected.

"Lunch tomorrow, Faerie girl. Brandy's at noon." My balls burned. I offered a public, safe place to meet—a dark place where lovers lingered. I gazed at those lush lips, swollen from our kiss.

"Hmm, don't get your hopes up. I'm super busy right now." Cool air rose from the floor, drifting between us. She skimmed her palms over her hips, adjusting the hem of her skirt.

"This fella bothering you, Miss Calla?" Two lean and clean, muscular young men wearing white T-shirts emblazoned with a black donkey kicking ass flanked one another. A cloud of dark floral fragrance preceded them.

"I'm not looking for a hassle, boys. Take it somewhere else." Rising, I curled my fingers around her rounded hip, willing her to stay. For a mere moment in time, I believed.

"Put your big boy pants on, Mr. O'Donnell, and go home." She pressed her index finger against my lips and then turned away. Darkness followed her, an aura so great that the dead woke, and the daemons rose, the specters taking their place among the living.

I watched the crowd. Some cringed and jerked sideways, sensing the disruptors.

"Raise your glass, friends. To a man lost to the angels. May his life be a blessing; may his soul rest in peace." She picked up the microphone and whispered a sultry welcome.

The cadence of her voice haunted the room, swelling with sadness. Her song stirred a memory, one long forgotten, one buried with my brother's memory—a ballad of love and loss—Ciarán's favorite song.

Calla

The air stirred, and the mist weaved around me—undulating black motes surging forward, ravaging my body, claiming me. I welcomed them, riding the cresting waves of desire. My clit throbbed, and my sex ached. His face came into focus, sculpted and hard. With each penetration, my core shattered. His need was mine, and mine was his. I sank deeper into dreamland, my whole being tingling for him, wanting what I could not have.

Did I initiate the dream, or did he? What did it matter? Our imaginary trysts were becoming increasingly frequent, and I couldn't stop them. I didn't want to. The thing with Colm and me proved an entity of its own. Unstoppable. Inevitable.

The days turned into nights, with the minutes and hours blurring together. Hiding from the outside world was easy when there was no cell signal and endless time to fill each day. I rarely ate and slept a lot. I found myself craving the dream world, hiding from my own. The past consumed me, not my own, but someone else's.

Branches tapped the windowpanes, and voices called my name. The walls spoke to me.

Orlaith's vision revealed the woman in the photo as Ériu. Her possessions were scattered everywhere in Dermot Sweet's cottage, each holding a memory. The blanket box at the foot of the bed sat, filled with trinkets, keepsakes, and one baby blue wedding dress.

I refused to touch them. The dreams were enough.

"Did you think I wouldn't find you, my sweet Ériu? That I would let you go?" His voice ran the gamut of human emotions: frustration, joy, and relief. His image taunted me—gleaming black hair swept back from a strong face and the golden diadem adorning his head, glowing like the rising sun.

On the morning of the fourth day, the sun crept through the bedroom window. I peered through my lashes at the puzzle crossing the floor, a tapestry of sunbeams and diamond shapes. The lilac fragrance teased me, and the bees hummed.

All of that I could ignore.

Krrrex-krrrex. Krrrex-krrrex. The corncrake's incessant call dragged me from the arms of the dead.

I lurched upright, my skull throbbing, my heart pounding. The inside of my mouth tasted like desert sand.

Caw. Caw. Caw. Caw. Ravens took to the sky. They screamed and screamed and screamed.

The curtains moved with the fragrance of spring—soft air filled with sweet honey scents.

I stumbled across the wood plank floor. No one was coming to save me. I was alone, truly alone.

There was a quiet about the place. The cozy room looked the same: tweed pillows tossed over the sofa and the fringed throw folded into an olive-green square.

The chessboard, the black-and-white marble slab, claimed my attention. My thoughts flew across the board. Which army would win? Which royal family would fall? The pawns gave their lives freely. The knights rode gallantly into battle. The bishop protected his king. My inner voice whispered, "Kill or be killed. Defend and protect." I crossed the bloody field, striking down the enemy king. The walls tumbled and fell. The voice inside my head cheered.

I clawed through layers of doubt, unable to shake the feeling that someone was watching.

I left the slaughter behind and dragged my feet into the shower room, and while I waited for the water to warm, I stared at my reflection in the oval mirror––my ratted hair, my too-bright eyes. My thoughts were mired in a distant place. I shrugged out of the baby-doll nightie and walked into the water spray, lifting my face and relishing the full brunt of the heated water. Rivulets poured over my shoulders, running along the curves of my breasts, down my stomach, and over my hips, pooling on the shower floor, sloughing the dead from my skin.

I summoned the secret I had hidden from my entire life. I reached for it. I strained my brain until my veins pulsed. But I couldn't remember. I couldn't find it. I let the water run cold, and only then did my mind awaken.

I returned to the bedroom, wrapped in a towel. Sitting on an ivory-painted stool before Ériu's vanity, I pulled a hairbrush through my hair until my scalp stung. My braid hung haphazard, but I didn't care. I dug through the closet for a pair of sweatpants and a crop-top hoodie emblazoned with the words *boys lie,* another prize from the Treasure Chest.

Somehow, a bee had found its way inside. I watched it perch on the windowsill, sunning itself. I even spoke to it, describing where I planned to go and why. The man with the golden diadem had shown me a mountain that touched the clouds. I left the cottage on a quest to discover the truth.

The screen door thwacked shut behind me, and all around the croft, calla lilies danced in the gentle breeze. Every time I saw them, chills licked my spine.

A rabbit darted away, leaping from flowerbeds and landing beneath the sprawling lilac tree. Sitting on its haunches within a purple carpet of periwinkle and glossy green leaves, it studied me with its beautiful amber eyes before bouncing away.

Beyond the barnyard, past the sheep pens, along the mud track, a stone hedge snaked the hillside. I would find the stone shieling from Orlaith's vision on the mountain's summit.

I ducked, hugging my bared midriff against the gusting winds. I climbed upward, following the zigzag trail carved by the black-faced sheep.

I stumbled over the crown and found what I knew had always been there—the skeleton of the same stone shieling. There were boulders, field grass, pink and purple heaths, and heathers. Where once glass panes glittered in the sunlight, black holes stared back. Holly fought Ivy for possession of the tumbled walls. The wooden door had long fallen from its hinges, and the thatch had blown from the rafters.

I stood at the entrance, the gnarled vines holding me at bay—the air shimmered, an unseen force protecting the shadows within. I projected my will, breaking free from the tangle and hurling myself onto the stone floor. The glass shattered, and the shadows moved. My vision came to life.

A man and a woman lay together in a little bed built into the stone wall. But it was not Ériu lying in the little bed. It was me. Am I Ériu? Are we the same?

She cried out, her ecstasy peaking. She weaved her fingers through his black mane, tenderly caressing him.

I hovered in the haze, a creeper watching, unable to move forward or escape.

The man making love to her was not of the mortal world. I knew him.

Finnbheara—Finvarra, the High King of the Faeries.

My breath came in short, ragged bursts.

Smoke and mirrors.

Shadows and sunshine.

Bees hummed in every bloom—too many bees.

Laughter played through my mind.

His laughter.

Who was he to take such liberties with that woman?

"Ériu? Are you awake?" The door burst open, and Orlaith stuck her head into the adjoining room. "Dear gods, it's stuffy in here." She lifted the latch, pushing the sash upward. Lightning bolts cracked the sky.

At the same time, a hooded crow landed on the sill, majestic in its grey-black plumage. A screech, a rasping gurgle, rose in pitch, ending with a snap of its hooked beak. Bold, beady eyes pierced mine.

The lump in my throat turned to stone. Running was never an option. Whatever that was, I was part of it. Forevermore.

"Jesus feckin' Christ. Go away. Go away." Orlaith shooed the crow away with the flat of her hand. "What is with these bloody birds? They're everywhere today. It's an ill omen, let me tell you. Ériu, luv? It's time."

Ériu rested her hands on the lace hem of a black silk nightie, which touched her knees. Her golden hair cascaded over the scooped neckline.

"My sweet, Ériu." He bent his knee before her, his fur-lined cloak pooling on the cold floor. A diadem of gold sat atop his regal head, taming a black mane.

Orlaith seemed oblivious to his presence. They appeared unaware of hers.

"Release me from my vow." Ériu's eyes blazed, and her words were laced with fury. She stood before him, the lacy hem swishing against her slender thighs.

"How do you ask that of me? Dear Ériu. You are mine, and I am yours. I love you, and you love me." He lifted her fingertips, resting his lips on her knuckles. His silver eyes shone.

"My heart bleeds—for him. He needs me. You, Finvarra, do not. Release me from our bond and let me go." She extended her arm, touching the gilded broach pinned to his shoulder—tears welling in her blue eyes.

"A vow cannot be broken, my sweet Ériu. Come. Let me take you home." He cupped her heart-shaped face in his hands, wiping her tears with the pads of his thumbs.

"Any woman would be proud to walk beside you. Choose another." She planted her palms on his gold-threaded tunic, holding him at arm's length.

"Another? There could never be another like you." He clasped her hands within his, his full lips lifting into a smile.

"I do not want this." She enunciated each word, her nipples peaking against the delicate silk.

"You would deny your rightful place among our people? You would deny your king?" He released her *and paced back and forth, his deer-skin riding boots silent on the stone floor—regal in every way.*

"They are not my people. And you are not my king. You are Tuatha Dé, banished beneath the mounds by my people. My people. Remember who I am. I am Ériu, Princess of the Dead."

"You are a rare joy, my sweet—a refreshing pleasure—but this folly has continued too long." He wagged his ringed finger toward her. "I offered you everlasting life, and you accepted. You came willingly, and you were never forced. How soon you forget, dear Ériu." He closed the distance between them and wrapped one arm around her narrow waist, pressing her against his noble frame.

"I loved you then." She whispered soft, honeyed words.

"You love me now." He lifted her hands, twirling her around the little room. "You are my consort. You are my love. Come. Let us dance. Let us make love." He sighed a sonorous breath, swinging her backward and into his chest. He explored freely, smoothing his palm over her flat belly and heavy swells.

"No longer." A sigh left her lips, and she moaned, bowing into his touch. Taking ownership of his hand, she guided his fingers lower.

"You are mine, Ériu. It is as it should be." He

dragged his other hand through her hair, turning her face toward him.

"You are Tuatha. One day, death will find you. Perhaps your soul will live within the House of Donn. Or not. You may pass through the gates of hell as others have. Some willingly. Some not." She hissed a ragged breath.

"But that is not today, my sweet." He dropped a kiss on the corner of her lips. "Look at me, Ériu. Only I can give you what you seek." He dragged his lips across her tear-soaked face. "Children. Yours and mine. Our line will be strengthened—our immortality ensured."

"I am promised to another." Her voice sounded hollow.

"You are promised to me, my love." He met her lips, swallowing her sighs.

I squeezed my eyelids shut.

"Thank goodness. You're up! Here, let me help you. You're going to miss your wedding. Dear gods, you're flushed. Are you feeling all right?" Orlaith placed the back of her knuckles over Ériu's forehead.

"I'm fine, Orlaith. I need to shower." Ériu dropped her head, hiding behind a curtain of blonde hair. She twisted her fingers into rumpled silk.

The air sparkled as two planes of reality became one.

"Hurry. Hurry. The day is slipping by. Dear gods, listen to those birds." Orlaith clucked her tongue.

Beyond the window, a vast flock of hooded crows crowded the sky and blocked the light.

The Sluagh––the unforgiven dead, here to feast on my soul? How did they find me?

"I will come for you, Ériu, before day's end." Finvarra's voice rang out. He urged the black stallion onto his hind legs, the horse's nostrils fiery red. Tossing his flowing mane, the crazed horse kicked his forelegs into the air, taking Finvarra into the ether.

"Orlaith, lock the window." Ériu rose to her feet, then fell backward.

"Look at that, will ye?" Orlaith gazed through the window.

"What should I do, Orla? I don't know what to do." Her wild eyes searched the room.

Her heart beat with mine.

The winds moaned—the windowpanes rattled. Flapping wings darkened the sky. The Sluagh? Finvarra?

"We must fly, Ériu. It's your wedding day. Look at ye. Flushed so." She plunked her hands on her hips. "Wedding jitters. It's plain to see. I'll be along with your dress." Orlaith left the bedroom, returning one moment later with a simple blue gown.

The pieces fell into place. It was a love triangle of mythic proportions. Ériu and a Faerie king. Ériu and a sheep farmer, a man named Dermot Sweet.

Lightning struck the clear blue sky.

I huddled into a ball against the tumbled walls and buried my face in my hands, unable to stop the tears from falling.

"Calla? Calla?" The echo of his voice pierced the fog, waking me from my fever. He knelt before me, his gaze searching. He was flesh and blood. He was whole and sound.

"Colm? What are you doing here?" I wiped my face with my sleeve, unable to process what had happened.

Sunlight rained through the open rafters. Living, breathing vines slithered through the arched door, hiding the entrance to another world. Buzzing bees left their hives swarming overhead.

He seemed not to notice. He looked just as he had the day we met, dressed in khaki-colored cargo pants and a neatly buttoned shirt. The only difference was a blue ball cap turned backward, embellished with a blue and white maple leaf, a tuft of copper hair poking through.

"Looking for you. We had a date, remember?" He scooped me into his arms and sat in the tall grass, his long legs stretched out. He pressed his lips to my head, his arms encircling me. Safe. Warm. Protected.

"A date?" I floundered through those seconds, nestled in his arms.

His nearness brought me back to the evening in the pub when he had taken full advantage of the melee, the jostling crowds, and the roaring clamor. It was dangerous and exciting. He made me forget the world existed, taking me to the point of no return in a shattering, life-altering moment. The way he stroked my thighs—in plain view, for all to see. My core clenched, sending heat coursing over me. Lusting over the man had given me something to focus on instead of the past and the visions that came with it.

"You stood me up." He held me close, his breath tickling my hair.

"I did? I'm sorry." I ran my palm down his bristled cheek, taking comfort in his strength. That last time we spoke, I snubbed him.

"Brandy's? Three days ago? I waited, but you failed to arrive." His chest rumbled, and his voice soothed. "I called, but you didn't answer."

"You waited? You called?" I swallowed my confusion. Was that what I hungered for? A man who showed no fear of me?

"Saoirse hasn't heard from you in days. She came by, but you didn't answer the door. When you missed the *ceilidh* last night, I thought I should check on you." He caressed my hair as a lover might.

"She came by?" The warmth in his voice touched my heart. Sure, he made me feel things others could not. But could I trust him with my heart? Not yet. Not yet.

The ravens took flight, leaving the tall grass and scattering through the blue skies. Screaming. Screaming. Screaming.

"Like I said, you owe me a raincheck." He stroked my cheekbone with his thumb like one would caress a panicked bird.

The sigh that left my lips broke the heavens. The bees stopped buzzing, and the wind gurgled and sighed. I wanted more than anything to feel his touch. I squirmed in his arms until I could better face him.

"Calla." He kissed the corner of my mouth, coaxing my lips to part. His tongue roamed freely —deep licks that awakened my wanton desires.

My breasts grew heavy, straining the lace fabric of my bra. Heat bloomed in all the right places.

"*Mo grhá.*" His voice growled and purred, intense and dreamy at the same time. His eyes blazed, dark and dangerous. His length was hard beneath his cotton pants, demanding against my backside.

"I want you, Colm." I whimpered, my breath a hollow moan in the wind. Only he could ease the ache.

He planted one kiss after another along my nape, dragging his lips across my throat and igniting a fire that could not be quenched. His hand slid beneath my hoodie, roaming across my bare skin until he found my breast.

"You are beautiful." He brushed his lips across my temple, squeezing the heavy globe, pinning the arrowed nub between his extended fingers.

I exhaled a shuddering breath, leaning into him and rocking against that hard staff.

"And this." He slid his free hand beneath my waistband, gliding over my hip and clasping my bottom with five calloused fingers. He squeezed and squeezed again, imprinting his palm into my flesh. Swift heat settled in my core.

I braced myself, curling my fingers into his packed muscles.

He snarled low in his throat, sliding past the corded thong and teasing my heated entrance with his fingertips, parting the swollen cleft and eliciting a flood of wet heat.

I stifled a cry—every nerve ending on fire. I couldn't get enough.

He kneaded the heavy swell, making my soul ache. But what he did with his fingers had left me breathless. He entered my sex knuckle deep, stroking the roof of my vagina with exacting pleasure. And then filled me, plunging two thick fingers deep within.

"Do you like that, *mo ghrá*?" He growled, licking the seam of my mouth.

I could only whimper.

"Show me what you like." He closed his mouth over mine, flicking my tongue with his own.

My vagina clenched the girth of his fingers. I bucked against him, driving his fingers to the end of me again and again until the heat spiraled, and I could only ride the cresting waves.

"Come for me, *mo ghrá*." His thumb scraped my nipple while his erection strained between us.

Heat pulsed through my sex, and I lost myself completely, my mouth open in a silent scream. Voices whispered, and darkness fell. I could barely breathe.

And then he took away what I craved, leaving me empty inside.

"This is what I want." He displayed his glistening fingers, wet with my release, and then ran his tongue in lazy circles around his long digits, savoring every last drop.

Some part of me went wild with animalistic lust. I grabbed his hand and fought his tongue for the remaining sweet heat. I tasted myself. I tasted him. My pussy tightened, wracked with thunderous waves. I shoved his fingers into my mouth and sucked those long lengths, plunging deeper and deeper until the waves crashed onto the shore.

The clouds shifted, and the sun beat down. I left the past where it belonged, my heart alive with unfamiliar sensations—the why and what for seemed unimportant.

"Take me home, Colm. Please." That breathy moan belonged to me?

He rose, lifting my limp and liquid body with him. He set me on my feet, cupped my face in his big hands, and nibbled my lips. "Are you all right?"

"You made me come." The shattering waves of pleasure left me replete. I eased my grip on his arm, my gaze dropping to his still-hard erection.

"You were exquisite, *mo ghrá*." He offered his hand.

"But?" I motioned with my eyes toward his rigid member.

"I have become accustomed to this state of distress." He twined his fingers with mine and grinned.

His meaning was not lost on me. My imaginary soirees into the land of lust involved him as well. His comment confirmed it.

We left the tumbled walls behind, following the mud track down the mountain slope.

A black billy goat lifted his bearded head, holding me in his fiery gaze. I looked away from those chocolate eyes. The landscape blurred into a canvas of emerald shades and blue skies.

"What were you doing up there?" At each rocky outcrop, he sent me an anxious glance.

"I was looking for Ériu." We continued down the narrow path.

"Who?" He lifted an eyebrow and locked his fingers around mine.

"My mother. The Princess of the Dead. Her portrait is above the fireplace." I chewed the inside of my mouth, realizing how insane my words sounded.

"What?" He tipped his head, his eyes widening.

"I see her everywhere, Colm. She's trying to tell me something." Her image showed itself—a golden-haired girl on the cusp of womanhood with rosebud lips and lily-white skin. She belonged to another world, a faraway place of verdant forests and sapphire skies.

"What is she trying to tell you?" His lilting voice chased away the shadows. He made me question everything.

"I don't know." My voice rose. "I don't even know how long I've been here."

"Shh...it's okay. It's okay." He clasped my elbow, halting our descent, and rested his hands on my shoulders. "Tell me everything."

"She wanted to marry Dermot Sweet, but he wouldn't let her," I remembered her conversation with the ghostly visage.

"Who? Who wouldn't let her?" A muscle ticked in his jaw, and his eyes darkened.

"Finvarra, the King of the Faeries." I glanced into the sky. Black-feathered ravens rode the wind, cresting sideways, jagged feathers floating upon every current. I knew them.

"Finvarra. He's one of the Tuatha Dé." He waited for my response. He seemed curious and fascinated. "The Tuatha Dé Danaan, the People of Danu."

"Danu?" I paused to catch my breath.

"The mother of all gods." He grinned. "Pagan gods."

"Finvarra was with Ériu the day she was to marry Dermot Sweet. They were together. I saw everything. Oh God, he's my father—the King of the Faeries is my father, and Ériu is my mother." My knees buckled, and I swooned. Only his grip saved me from falling.

The air shimmered, glinting in the sunlight. White clouds skiffed across the sky.

"Then who was Dermot Sweet?" His brows creased.

"Ériu wanted to marry him." I cringed, reliving the memory. "How did you find me?"

"You left a trail of breadcrumbs, Calla." He chuckled. "No, I'm kidding. Your dog led the way. What's his name? He's very friendly."

"I don't have a dog." The heat left my face, and a wave of dizziness threatened.

"The red collie sitting in the driveway when I arrived? He led me up the hill." He scanned the courtyard, searching for the mysterious dog.

"It was Seamus." I swallowed hard, accepting the little man had many faces. "He's one of them. I'm sure of it." Any doubt I might have had vanished, along with the King of the Faeries himself. I wavered in Colm's arms and swallowed hard. The world between worlds existed, but what of the underworld? Ériu stated plainly, her tone demanding respect. *"Remember who I am."*

"Who is Seamus?" Colm's eyes filled with shadows.

I could see that even he who believed in pagan gods was unprepared for a shapeshifting immortal.

"He looks after the place. He looks after me. Am I going crazy?" My gaze ventured beyond Colm, but I saw no sign of my little friend.

"You're not crazy." He planted a simple kiss on my forehead, enough to ignite the flames. Heat raged between us—so much heat.

"What? Why are you looking at me like that?" I moistened my lower lip with the tip of my tongue.

"I'm just wondering about this man called Seamus. How did he reveal himself to you?" He considered his words, shadows drifting in his eyes.

"He was here the day I arrived. He's not tall and wears the strangest clothes, like from another century." I swept my hair behind my ears and looked at him, really looked at him. Maybe, just maybe, I wasn't crazy.

"He could be a spirit, but more than likely, he was sent by someone else." He led me through meadow grass burnished with gold tips.

"He said my father wanted to meet me. Oh,

God. It's true, then. Finvarra is my father. I have to know what happened to Ériu. I have to talk to Orlaith." I gazed at the smoke curling from the chimney, the purple pansies trailing from each window box, the calla lilies blooming vibrant pink and virgin white.

Colm's blue rental car sat parked in the courtyard. He had stolen my heart so quickly and confidently. What did I even know about him?

"I'll go with you. I don't trust this, Faerie King." Suspicion coated his words. His chiseled features hardened, and his lips curled into a tight line. He seemed a man used to drawing first blood.

"What does that make me, Colm?" My thoughts danced between realms. The Tuatha. The Dead. And Colm. *Where does he belong?*

"You're one of Them, Calla. You're part of their world." His gruff voice soothed my spiking emotions. Light returned to his baby blues.

I wondered if I had imagined the whole thing, but the weight stayed put, pressing down and making breathing difficult. Colm wanted something. I closed my eyes and fought the shadows. For him, my "gift" was a means to an end. The heat raging between us could not be denied, but neither could the truth.

"That's what Saoirse said. She said, 'You just

are.' How can I be part of an invisible world? What does it mean? What world do I belong to?" I turned into him, drawn to him. I placed my hands on his biceps, fingering the smooth cotton sleeves.

"We'll figure this out together." He pulled me close, tucking my head beneath his chin.

"Colm...would you? Would you like to come in? I have tea." My mind calmed, and I saw a future with him. He had shattered my mind with a single touch.

Sunlight broke through the clouds, lighting every leaf in dappled shades.

"I burn for you, *mo ghrá*." He drew his thumb over my lips, tearing my soul to pieces—pieces that belonged to him.

"I've never." Liquid heat flowed through my veins, and desire caught flame.

I should tell him this would be my first time. I swallowed hard, unable to voice the words. My gut burned with indecision, confusion, and shame. I ran through today's events: my father was an immortal god of the *Sidhe*, and my mother was the princess of the dead, *and by the way, I'm a virgin*— all that in one day.

"Never what, luv." He dipped his head, closing his lips over mine, filling me with his taste.

I threw my hands into his thick curls, knocking

his hat to the ground, and kissed him back, fully and completely. My tongue found and battled his. A whimper rose low in my throat, hunger burning in my soul.

He came for me. He wanted me. That was all that mattered. I didn't care about the rest.

"Shh." He nosed my nape and then traced his lips along my throbbing pulse. "You taste like no other."

"I want you. I want to be with you." I inhaled his scent, musk mixed with shadows. I melted into him, wanting what he could give. I yearned for what others took for granted: intimate contact, the shattering pleasure of release.

"And I you." He glanced in one direction, then the other. He held my hand, leading me away.

"Where are we going?" I would go anywhere with him, and he knew it. I rubbed my forehead, blocking the sun's rays.

The waterfall trickled down the mountain gash, tumbling onto the stones below. The sun beat down, too strong for late April. I spied the bee hives Dermot Sweet cared for, ten square boxes hidden in overgrown brambles.

We walked across the courtyard and behind the barn, where the grass grew long.

"This will do." He threw his arms on either side of my shoulders, caging me against the wall.

Only the circling ravens could see. They cawed and screamed, throwing shadows onto the meadow.

"Here?" I twisted my neck and looked longingly toward the cottage.

"You're not afraid of me? Are you, Faerie girl?" He dragged his tongue across the seam of my lips, his voice rough-hewn and hard.

"I'm not afraid." Arrows of heat shot straight to my core. He made my mind lust.

"Good." He slid his hands beneath my hoodie, lifted my arms over my head, and tossed the fleece away. It landed front-side up.

I read the words—boys lie.

My skin prickled and burned.

"Should I be? Afraid?" My bottom lip trembled. The weight of his hand grazing my flesh made my sex quiver.

"You've been riding me for days now. Bespelling my mind. Haunting my dreams. Leaving me in a wee bit of distress." He slid his index finger beneath the pink band of my bra, flicking the snap free and spilling my breasts.

"Well, that's your fault. You didn't give me a chance to remedy your discomfort." I tried not to flinch. Instead, I arched my back, jutting my breasts toward him, tantalizing him.

"Look at me." His eyes filled with luminous light as he caressed each swell with his knuckles.

"You're not the boss of me, O'Donnell." My mouth watered, my nipples hardening into taut nubs. I was ready, so ready. I wanted to have my way with him, yet it appeared to be the other way around. As much as he pointed out his distress, he seemed to want me—at his mercy.

"Let's pretend I am." He dragged his lips down my face, suckling my lower lip into his mouth.

I lost what remained of my mind. I wanted him to touch me again, to squeeze my breasts, to suck my nipples into his hot mouth.

"Take those off." He released me and stepped back, motioning toward the sweatpants hugging my hips.

"Now? Right here?" My mouth watered, fueled by insatiable need.

"Aye." He peered through half-slits, his smile devil-made.

"Okay," I whispered under my breath. "You're enjoying this, aren't you?" I pushed the sweats down, leaving them pooled at my feet. I slipped my thumbs into my lace panties, intending to bare it all. Like, why not? I had everything to lose.

The V-Card had been in my possession far too long.

"No, *mo grhá*." In one fluid motion, he bound my wrists in his left hand, raising my arms, pinning me against the barnboard wall.

My breath hitched. Dreaming of Colm was never like this.

"What do you mean, no? Don't you want me?" My bare bottom pressed into the jagged boards, the triangular slip of lace the only thing concealing my sex. The sun shone between us, red-orange with fiery heat.

"Aye, but not today." He held my hands, his beautiful face angled and hard.

I lowered my gaze to the apex of his cargo pants. His erection strained the fabric, the length threatening, the width imposing. I did that to him. My presence. My will. That I could do that made my heart sing.

"Close your eyes. Tell me what you're feeling." He drew his index finger between my breasts, over my taut belly, and snapped the elastic waistband of my panties.

"I'm throbbing." I pressed the back of my head against the wooden boards, my sex clenching in anticipation.

"What's throbbing?" His breath mingled with mine. He was hot. So hot.

"My sex. My pussy." My mouth watered for a taste.

"What else." He leaned close, searing my nape with a hot lick.

"My breasts are on fire. My skin tingles." I bowed my hips, seeking his bulging erection.

"You will burn for me, *mo grhá*, and no one else." He traced a hot path over my collarbone, circling my breast, scraping his teeth over one pebbled nub.

"Yes." I arched into him, floating in a sea of desire.

"I'm going to make you come." His rumbling voice demanded obedience. He dragged my nipple into his mouth and suckled the arrowed peak. He dropped one hand, containing me with the other, working his thick fingers into my aching flesh, stroking the outer cleft, rousing my need.

I threw my head back against the wall, my breath rasping, my sex quaking.

He didn't stop. He angled his mouth over mine and suckled my tongue, taking my breath away.

The walls of my pussy fluttered. That. That was what I wanted. When I thought he would release me, he tightened his grip in full control of my pleasure. I arched and bowed, the heat ratcheting higher. In his eyes, I saw a man obsessed. Predatory. Hungry.

His breath raged with mine.

"Come for me, *mo ghrá*." He entered my sex with one long finger, sliding between the slip of lace and the corded thong, cupping my pussy in his curved palm as he had before. He rocked and squeezed and made my body thrum.

I was unaware of when he released my arms. They were dead weights clenched around his neck. I bucked into him and ground into that single digit. He made me work for it.

When he suckled my bottom lip, I shattered against him, and a fury of heated embers burst through the sky.

"How did you do that?" My voice was unrecognizable.

This man enjoyed wreaking havoc.

"The next time, I will taste your sweet nectar." He traced my cheekbone with his lips.

"You made me come just like that." I swept my tongue over my dry lips, thirsting for more of him.

"The next time, you will part your legs for me. Your sweetness will be mine." He kneaded my wet pussy. "Your nectar will flow over my lips, over and over again."

"What's wrong with now?" My breath hitched, surprising even me.

His hands circled my breasts, his fingers pinning the arrowed nubs, and then he kissed me again, exploring deeply, flicking the roof of my mouth, his hunger insatiable.

"You will take pleasure from no other." He murmured into my ear, leaning into me, planting me against the rough wall.

"What?" I let my arms hang loose at my sides and took comfort in the solid wall holding my weight. Warmth brushed my skin, fire racing from one pleasure point to another.

"I will not take you that way nor lose you to another." He splayed his big hands on my rib cage, his thumbs sweeping over my breasts. He grazed each nub with his warm tongue.

"Hmm." I ached for him.

"Call me old-fashioned, Calla Sweet, but I intend to have you forever." He scraped each nub repeatedly, suckling the arrowed peaks until my knees buckled.

"Forever?" Forever flowed through my mind. What he wanted thrilled yet terrified me: a promise, a commitment. Yesterday, I would have jumped at the chance to touch a man to experience such pleasure. But my entire world had changed. How could I promise forever when I didn't know what I was? When I didn't know him?

"You will know your heart when the spirits rise. Under the full moon, with the sea lapping the shore, you will give yourself to me, and I to you, this coming Bealtaine Eve." He rolled the peaked tips of my breasts between his fingers, drowning me in desire. "Now, *mo ghrá*, let's put you back together."

He left me undone.

8

olm

"Lord Jaysus, laddie. I wouldn't ask if it wasn't important." Eamon sat at a wide oak desk, resting one withered hand on his shillelagh while the other lay on a thick manilla folder.

Blue light illuminated the perimeter of a circular room almost twenty feet in diameter. Within the domed walls of that medieval dovecote, a row of monitors hummed, with one constantly in motion, tracking lines of information over the screen. The fiber optic cable entering the building transmits data at the speed of light. Beneath the false floor, a six-foot-high storage space housed classified files.

The domed structure stood alone in the land-scape, far enough away from avian, animal, and human predators. The castellated roof, topped with a cupola, where rock doves entered at leisure, nesting in various ridges and alcoves. The interior resembled an ocean cave. The soft croon and constant feather ruffling added another dimension to the meaning of clandestine operations.

Who would have thought the nation's security would befall a man issuing orders from a pigeon coop? The smell of bird droppings was something I would never get used to.

A red border collie lifted its head, slapping its tail on the stone floor and watching the older man's every move as he rose from the desk and shuffled from one nesting box to another, whispering soft words, the pigeons cooing in response. He returned with a basket brimming with speckled eggs. "For your mam, laddie."

"She'll love this, Eamon. Thanks." I looked into his eyes, unreadable behind heavy plastic frames. I often wondered if he wore them to throw people off.

He nodded silently.

"I wasn't expecting your call." I tilted my chin, observing the older man.

His mouth was set in a hard line, and his knuckles were white on the horn of his shillelagh.

"I require your services, Colm." He peered over the rim of his glasses.

"Eamon, it's not a good time." I shifted my weight, the chair's legs scraping against the stone floor—six years as an independent contractor. I went wherever the old man sent me. No questions asked. Rescues. Extractions. A short stint in security. Time had taken its toll, and I found myself yearning for normalcy. Whatever that might be.

He slammed his closed fist on the desk, shaking the table lamp from its moorings. I watched a spider skitter along the thick folder. The doves cooed.

"You're the best I've got." His voice reverberated within the round chamber, the tenacity of a much younger man lingering on each note.

"You have others more qualified than me." Turning him down was my only option. I would admit to no one the effect Calla Sweet had on my mind.

"Are you familiar with reconstructionism?" His eyebrows twitched.

"A bunch of loons reliving pagan times." I huffed but smiled inside. My father followed the

Celtic calendar closely, holding those same rituals close to his heart. I sat back in my chair.

He remained silent, but his thoughtful expression prompted me to continue.

"Modern pagans believe everything on earth is connected, and the natural world is imbued with spiritual presence. Academics would call it animism." I was raised in a household steeped in old beliefs and superstitions. But did I believe trees had souls? "Where is this going?"

"An English bloke named Sean Hamstead is bent on proving that those 'spirits' have shape and form and can indeed affect the world we live in." He picked up a pencil, holding it between his thumb and index finger.

"That's far-fetched, isn't it?" I saw the humor, but warning bells rang just the same.

"He's a dangerous man with unlimited funding." His grip tightened, snapping the pencil's spine into two jagged pieces.

"Funding?" My brain throbbed as I watched the broken pencil rolling across the desk.

"If Hamstead could control those spirits, consider the consequences." He swept the pencil pieces into a trash can and then looked up.

"What's his background?" I was almost afraid to ask the question.

"He was a researcher with the Global Health Organization. Sources tell me they let him go, citing questionable practices." His gaze never left mine.

The dog Eamon called Finnigan left his station and rested his head on Eamon's lap.

"What kind of questionable practices?" I placed both hands on the edge of the broad desk, steadying myself.

"Genetics. He hijacked specific samples found in archeological sites. More importantly, he's suspected in the disappearance of a young lad from Malin Head—the boy was accused of being a changeling by his parents." He opened the manilla file, revealing a shiny eight-by-ten photograph of a balding man.

"A changeling?" I scoffed at the idea. An ancient pagan belief—a child stolen away by the Other Crowd and replaced by a sickly faerie child enchanted with a convincing glamor. The parents left none the wiser. It was better to believe your healthy child lived in a crystal palace than waste away before your eyes.

"The child has been missing three days, taken from his bed in the wee hours. The investigation is ongoing." He tapped his index finger on the photo, and the resounding thud echoed.

Is that why Eamon sought me out? To search for the missing child? Dread consumed me. The longer an investigation, the less likely a successful outcome.

He continued his analysis of the subject.

"What supernatural beings do we, the Irish, immortalize to this day?" He took off his glasses and set them down on the desk.

"The Tuatha Dé," I admitted to their mysterious presence. They existed. They exist. My brother spoke to them. Is that where he was now?

I turned Eamon's synopsis over.

Faerie belief was alive and well in Donegal County and was looked upon fondly as part of our heritage. How many ideological and fantastical books have been written? But what would happen if those beliefs were proven to the world?

Calla's image came into focus—my Faerie girl was already mired deep in their mystical world, a world she knew nothing about. I caught the last part of his sentence.

"Think of the power one man would have if he proved the existence of the immortals. Of the Tuatha Dé Danaan?" He patted the collie's head.

"Wait, are you saying Hamstead stole the changeling? That he has control of a Faerie being?

Then where is the child?" My stomach clenched with horror.

"That is a concern." He tilted his head, giving me a hard look.

"Alright, what would you like me to do?" My arms hung loosely at my sides.

He gave me a history lesson from Christian priests in the fifth century.

"St. Patrick, the patron saint of Ireland, banished the slithering reptiles into the sea. He is credited for enlightening the pagan people and bringing Christianity to Ireland. Priests succeeded Druids. Christian celebrations supplanted Pagan ones. It was the end of paganism." He lifted his shillelagh and scratched his head with the horned staff. "But now the Church is losing its grip on the masses. People are looking for other spiritual avenues. The time is ripe for zealots like Hamstead."

My throat closed, grasping the magnitude of the situation.

"Do you know what adoration and power do to a man verging on madness? Suppose he is successful in his pursuits. The trail of destruction would be catastrophic."

My thoughts turned in another direction. If inanimate objects had souls, the Tuatha Dé were gods and goddesses of the earth.

"Are your sources reliable?" I looked up from my musings.

"Of course they are, man. Do you take me for a fool?" His eyes were bright.

"My apologies." I held up my palms, acknowledging my faulty judgment.

"The Tuatha Dé is a secret the Republic must protect." His tone turned venomous.

"We are admitting the Other Crowd exists?" The Tuatha Dé, a race of mystical beings banished beneath the mounds by our ancestors, was rarely spoken of. I found his willingness to broach the sensitive topic astounding.

"If you met him, you'd pass him by and consider him a bumbling fool." He turned the photo in my direction.

I looked upon an unassuming man who would blend into the crowd. I etched his face into my memory. "If one man could harness the power of the gods, the world as we know it would end."

"His following is growing, with people departing from the Christian fold in search of other spiritual paths." He sighed through his nose.

"So he's their savior?" I chuckled, making light of the situation.

"Don't laugh. What will his next step be? A promise of immortality? There's more at stake than you realize." He steepled his hands against his chest.

"Immortality?" I hadn't given any thought to immortality. "It would make him a global force. You want me to bring Hamstead in?" I sighed inwardly. The older man knew me too well.

"No. We've penetrated the upper echelon of his organization. We have a source on the inside." He reached into a drawer and pulled out another file.

"Who?" I scanned his eyes, searching for answers.

"I can't tell you that." His tone didn't waver.

"Then why am I here?" I scratched my head.

"You're acquainted with the girl, Calla Sweet?" He pushed the folder in my direction. I gazed at the tidy label imprinted with her name.

"Excuse me? What is the connection with Calla?" My stomach coiled. He had my full attention.

"I'm an old man, Colm. I've seen more than my share, but your Calla-girl is one of Them, but I think you know that. Some fool likely meddled in their business and stole her away as a babe, aye? It's a dangerous thing messing with the Good Folk. Ach, that it is."

The dog lifted his head and whined.

"I don't understand, Eamon. How does that

relate?" I rubbed my chin, pondering his words. How did he know what she was? Was it that obvious?

"Intelligence suggests he's coming after her." He leaned forward.

"What?" I realized my worst fears.

"Your girl sent away for her DNA. Her genetics confused a lot of people. The results were flagged, but before we could investigate, the file disappeared. Likely taken by someone on his payroll. This whole DNA business, ripe for the picking by fanatics like him." His breath rasped, heavy in his chest.

"And you think he knows about Calla?" Fear tore through me, which I suppressed.

Finnigan seemed to listen to every word.

"Her identity is about to become a matter of national security. I'll do what I can to keep this hushed, but I'm counting on you to keep the girl from harm's way. I expect you're up for the job?" He rapped his shillelagh, and the dog rose.

I flipped through the manilla folder containing a Canadian birth registration in the name of Calla Sweet, her school records, and a partial job history. There was nothing there I didn't already know.

His diatribe struck a more personal chord. My

thoughts drifted to Calla and how she cast her spell of enchantment over those lust-filled males at the Wild Horse Pub. And what of her claims? Finvarra, the King of the Faeries, her father? I accepted her revelation without question, without any fear of the consequences. I left her unattended and unprotected. How would I forgive myself if anything happened to her on my watch? The revelation thawed my frozen heart.

In our last encounter, I had woven an illusion of my own over the Faerie girl, tantalizing her the way she had me. I resisted giving in to her desires out of spite. The promise I made—that her pleasure would be mine, that she would be mine—gave me the upper hand, at least in my mind. It appeared I may have outsmarted myself. How reckless. How naïve.

I met Eamon's gaze.

"Keep her close, laddie. Let me worry about Hamstead." The words crackled on his tongue.

CALLA

On the south bank of the River Liffey lies the Temple Bar District of Dublin, a pedestrian walkway lined with galleries, colorful shops, and brightly painted pubs. Cafes filled to bursting spilled onto the cobblestones.

Colm hooked his elbow through mine, navigating the narrow laneways with expert precision.

"For the lady?" A woman cloaked in a black shawl stood beneath a streetlamp, a trail of smoke rising from the cigarette dangling in her mouth. She extended slender, ringed fingers and offered one long-stemmed red rose, the velvety petals vibrant against her black shawl. She spoke in the gravelly voice of one who smoked too many cigarettes.

"Aye." He nodded, his gentle voice bringing a smile to her hard lips. He handed her five euros, and they made the trade.

"This wasn't necessary." I held the fresh bloom to my nose, savoring the honeyed scent.

"*Is tú mo rogha, mo grhá.*" He pressed his lips to my first knuckle.

"What?" I ran my tongue over my bottom lip.

"You are my choice, my luv, you and no other," he murmured, his eyes shining.

I pulled him close and kissed the corner of his mouth. We walked hand in hand, people passing by, blurred in color. I could almost forget the reason for our visit.

Orlaith's sister lived in a three-story brick

building on the banks of the river, bordered by an imposing wrought-iron fence. I studied the intricate welds and thought of Saoirse.

Envy consumed me. Anonymity, living in the thick of it all, unseen, and yet in plain sight. Was that not what I wanted? But that was before Colm. My breath caught in my throat when I thought of him. My path forward seemed written, or did I simply want to believe? I held Colm's gaze and wished I could read his mind.

He lifted the latch, and the heavy gate closed behind us. We walked up the path past budding greenery and flower pots overflowing with pink pansies. Ivy crawled up the brick face.

"After you." He opened the tall entrance door and stepped back.

We crossed the marble foyer together and waited only a minute for the elevator doors to open. The lift rocketed upward, leaving my stomach on the floor. Entombed in that lacquered box, the air stilled.

Colm stood inches away, his hands tucked into his pockets. Poker-faced, he gave nothing away.

I glanced at my maybe-lover, puzzled by his demeanor, wondering what he was thinking. He seemed unfazed, as if questioning a woman about a Faerie king was an everyday occurrence. I threaded my fingers through my hair, tidying the ends into a sleek braid.

The elevator doors opened with a sudden whoosh. My ears popped, and I swallowed hard. Blue carpet led in both directions down the spacious hallway.

Colm's blue-eyed gaze filled with ready kindness.

When was the last time kindness looked my way? Genuine kindness aimed toward me alone? Even now, my past haunted me, and I spent every day waiting for the sky to fall. But going backward was not an option. I had to press on. The truth lay in the moments ahead. Orlaith, Ériu's friend, held the keys to the future and the past.

"Are you all right?" He planted his hand on my lower back, each fingertip radiating heat.

"I'm good. Great, actually." I clamped my lips together, convincing myself.

"Does she know why you're here?" He looked one way and then the other and headed down the hall to the right, his sense of direction spot on.

"No. Not really. Saoirse arranged the visit. Said it would be easier that way." My stomach fluttered. Needles pricked the surface of my skin. Two questions danced on my tongue. *Who am I? What am I?*

"Hmm. Why is Orlaith in Dublin?" He looked at me, questioning.

"Looking after her sister's cat." Uncertainty occupied my thoughts. The idea of asking those questions terrified me. Sharing my visions with Colm was one thing, but that would make them real.

The door on the left opened before we knocked. Orlaith wore a mint green frock adorned with delicate white daisies that swished when she moved.

I gazed at the braided carpet flowing down the hallway and the sleek black cat weaving between her legs.

"Come in. Come in. I've been expecting you." She brushed her palms over her flowered dress while voices blared from a television inside the apartment. She guided us into a sun-filled reception room, where she picked up a remote and muted the television noise. "Have a seat, both of you. The tae is wet." She gestured toward a yellow-striped sofa and a china tea service on a glass tabletop.

Etched into the sides of the ivory pot was a whimsical scene featuring flying dragons in soft, muted blue, pink, and orange hues. The tea set appeared very old.

Colm cleared his throat, jolting me out of my trance.

"Orlaith, thank you for meeting with me." I took a deep breath, released the tension from my shoulders, and lowered myself onto the plush sofa.

Colm remained standing until Orlaith settled, then sat beside me. The cat purred at his feet and jumped onto his lap.

"He's a wee hallion, always acting the maggot. Ye don't mind, do ye?" She looked between us, pouring tea into white china cups adorned with a landscape scene of high mountain peaks. Steam curled from each teacup.

"Not at all. I love cats. What's his name?" He placed his big hand on the cat's shoulders.

"Collins. He's been with my sister for years." She clucked her tongue.

The cat twitched its ears at the sound of his name.

"He's fine. No worries." Colm caressed the cat.

"I knew this day would come." Orlaith broke the silence, her gaze darting from Collins to me.

"I have questions, Orlaith, about Ériu." I balanced the saucer on my lap. "You were Ériu's friend."

"Aye. We were. How did you learn Ériu's name,

luv? Was it Dermot? Was it in his papers?" Her blue eyes deepened in color.

"No. Um, there's a photo of Ériu over the fireplace, and her wedding dress...is in the cottage." I pinned my lower lip beneath my teeth and held it there, forgetting to breathe.

"I don't understand." Her face paled.

"I see things, Orlaith, things others can't see." I didn't know where to start. Her vision? Seamus? How about the mist coming to take me away?

"Aye?" she encouraged me to continue.

"The day you fainted. I saw you with Ériu, preparing for her wedding. I'm sorry." I admitted my intrusion into her mind. I considered sharing what I'd learned since but decided against it.

"I see." Her hand trembled, clinking the teacup against the saucer.

"I'm sorry, Orlaith. I didn't want to intrude. I just...I have to know who she is." I placed my teacup on the table.

"Ériu is your mother. She's gone, luv. She's with the angels." She crossed her chest in mourning and then rose. She walked across the shining floor, her flat shoes soundless.

"She's gone?" I absorbed the weight of her words, the finality in her voice. My heart sank. I had clung to a thread of hope that my mother was alive.

"Would you like a scone, luv? Fresh made this morning." She returned with an oval platter overflowing with golden puffs dotted with plump raisins.

"Thank you." I placed the scone on a napkin, leaving it untouched.

"Colm, luv, you must be famished." She offered him a scone before setting the platter on the glass table. "I have had a sense of things since that day." She placed her palm over mine for a brief second.

What I would have given to be somewhere else, anywhere else.

"What day, Orlaith?" The silence deafened me, and then she spoke.

"The day you were born, child." She tilted her chin, recognition shimmering in her eyes.

"The day I was born?" I repeated her words.

"Aye, would you like a spot more tae, luv?" She lifted the pot and raised her eyebrows.

"Yes, thank you." I gazed into my empty cup, not remembering drinking the fragrant tea.

"You're so like her, you are. In every way." Orlaith filled mine and then Colm's. "You are so."

"What became of her?" I sipped the hot liquid and scalded my tongue.

"You shouldn't be here, child. For the life of me, I don't know why Dermot did what he did—leaving the croft to you and bringing you back to this place. She didn't want this." Orlaith frowned.

"What does that mean?" I dared to ask. I needed the truth, all of it, every last bit.

"You were safe and away, but now here you are. Himself knows, don't think he doesn't." She twined her hands together. "This land belongs to Themselves. What happens, they know."

"Are you talking about Finvarra?" I asked, confused by her nervous ticks.

"Don't speak his name, child." She lifted the teapot, filling her cup.

Darkness spread along the floor, a dark mist creeping closer and closer. A hollow moaning filled my ears.

Orlaith placed the teapot on the table but failed to set it down properly. It teetered precariously on the table's edge.

The dragons' scales glistened rose gold. Three of them pondered my existence through slitted yellow eyes and then, in unison, lifted their spidery wings—iridescent pink and boned with blue. I willed my heart to keep beating when they turned their horned heads and spewed fiery orange flames in my direction.

Colm reached forward, spilling the cat from his lap.

"Don't touch it." I knocked his hand away and caught one dragon by its tail, subduing the rest and saving the teapot from crashing onto the floor. Searing heat blistered my fingers. I lifted them to my mouth, easing the burning sensations.

"Calla? Calla? Are you all right?" He squeezed my forearm, calling my attention to him. His concerned gaze calmed my erratic thoughts.

I licked my lips and stared at the teapot, wondering what the vision meant. Flying dragons. Orange flames.

"Ach. Be gone with ye, crazy woman." Orlaith placed her hands on her cheeks. "Forgive me, luv. 'Tis the medication throwing me off."

"Orlaith, what can you tell us about Ériu?" Colm interjected, his voice low and soothing. None the wiser after my escapade with the flying dragons.

"Himself took her the day of her wedding." She dropped one spoonful of sugar after another into her cup.

"Took her?" I stared at the teapot and saw nothing but a fairytale scene.

"Taken, child. Swept away, by Himself." She pushed her glasses onto the bridge of her nose. "It broke Dermot's heart. Took to tipping the bottle, but who could blame him?"

"Then what happened?" I closed my fingers into fists.

"It was long ago. People forget." She pushed herself to her feet.

I watched her walk across the room and straighten a painting hanging on the wall—white sails billowed from the mast of a tall ship, the prow cutting through crashing waves.

"What about Ériu's friends? Her people? Did they not look for her?" Colm's brows creased.

The cat butted his head against my chin.

"Ériu was from away. Not one of us." She looked away, tears filling her eyes. "People forget what they don't want to see."

"I see." I did not see anything at all.

"Nine months later, a man came knocking at my door. Said his wife needed help with delivery. I thought nothing of it at first until I saw what he was driving—a black carriage drawn by four black horses. I didn't know at the time who the gentleman was—dressed fine and all the like. Such a way about him. He said his wife asked specifically for me. We traveled for hours, and I found myself dosing off. When I woke, we were in a dark forest. A footman dressed in the finest of garb led the carriage away. I still remember the clip-clop of the horses' hooves. He took me to a palace, the like I'd never seen, sparkling with silver and gold. I was terrified until I saw it was her, my Ériu. So full of pregnancy and in such pain, the wee thing was."

"Finvarra came for you?" Colm's face turned bedsheet white.

"It was Him, the King of the Faeries himself." She nodded at Colm, twisting her fingers together.

"Ériu was pregnant?" My vision from the stone shieling rolled over me, Finvarra's laughter filling my mind. I squeezed my eyes shut, but the truth shocked me.

"Aye. It was a difficult birth. The wee thing was frail. Too frail. I knew right off Ériu wouldn't make it. She knew it, too." Her gaze held mine. "She gave birth to three beautiful girls."

"Three? Three girls?" My heart beat faster.

"Aye. She called them 'the three' as if each would serve a purpose. She held you to her breast, luv. I remember the moment like it was yesterday. Your eyes were silver then. Shiny, like stars in the night sky. You grasped her finger so tight. I could hardly break your wee grip. Ériu named you Rioghain. She called you the dark one." Orlaith poured more tea.

"The dark one?" I rubbed my forehead.

"Aye, named after the Morrigan herself." Her gaze softened, and she placed her hand on my knee.

"I have sisters." I sat back on the sofa, my thoughts racing, and for a moment, I couldn't catch up.

"Why did he come for you, Orlaith?" Colm prodded.

"Ach. Well, you see, I was a midwife back then. Birthed most of the babes in this parish." Her eyes beamed with pride.

"How did Calla get away from the Faerie palace?" He glanced at me and then at her. He seemed to realize that I had lost my words.

"Ériu was powerful in her own right. She had a way about her. She did. I think that's what attracted Himself to her in the first place. She looked into your wee silver eyes and then called you Rioghain, the others Nemain, and Macha. Heartbroken, she was, and so weak. She kissed your wee cheek, and then she made me promise. I was to keep you safe, Rioghain. May I call you Rioghain? Ériu would like that."

"Safe? Safe from what, Orlaith?" I shut my eyes and saw what I didn't want to see—a flash of light and Finvarra's face.

"Why would Ériu worry about Calla?" Colm interjected.

"She said they would use your dark heart against you. She made me swear I would take ye with me. And to send ye away. Away from this place." Orlaith looked far away as if the memory caused her pain.

"And you took Calla to Dermot Sweet?" Colm's eyes gleamed, awed by her part in the puzzle.

"Aye, that I did. It broke Dermot's heart to give ye up. You were part of his Ériu. She was all that mattered to him." She relived the memory, her voice haunted.

"You knew who I was all this time." My ears rang. It was a constant buzz that wouldn't let go of my mind.

"I knew when ye said Dermot's name." She removed her glasses and set them on the table.

I gazed into her soft eyes, taken aback by the emotions welling there.

"How did you get Calla away from the Otherworld without Finvarra discovering?" Colm rested his hands on his knees.

"Ériu had her powers. She did." Orlaith swept her hands over her silvery hair, her thoughts passing into another time. "She pressed her pale lips to your face and placed a glamor over you that the Others could not see. The other two babes were taken to a nursemaid. Beautiful ones, they were. All three of you. One dark. One light. One touched. Rioghain, Nemain, and Macha. Aye—the Morrigu." She whispered the name with reverence.

"Touched?" I exhaled a long breath. Colm's words rang true. I had to accept it. I was one of Them.

"A ginger. A redhead." Orlaith nodded.

"And Finvarra knew nothing of Calla's existence?"

The cat pounced, extending his claws into Colm's forearm. Colm didn't budge.

"Not a thing. The coachman delivered me home in the fancy carriage, unaware of your existence. The glamour, you see, kept you safe from Themselves." She tsked. "I was able to make Ériu happy in her last moments."

"What happened to Ériu?" I asked. I needed so desperately to learn every detail.

"Himself knew she wouldn't last the night. He loved her, he did, in his way. Sat by her bed, holding her hand. Horrible anguish it was. For all that he stole from her, she loved him too. He wept at her feet like a wee babe. He wasn't a bad man that way." She shook her head and tsked.

"And Dermot Sweet sent me to Canada?" My mouth dried as I comprehended the unbelievable.

"Aye. Dermot had family in Canada. He took you himself to your new family—a cousin of a cousin. Nice people, Dermot said. They were told a young girl in the village got herself in the wrong way. He insisted we send you across the pond to a place not touched by Themselves."

"What happened to Dermot?" Colm exchanged glances with me.

"He led a solitary life after Himself swept Ériu away. Dermot considered himself married to her memory. He would have raised you as his own had he been able. He called you Calla, after Ériu's favorite flower."

"The calla lilies." My eyes grew hot, and I blinked back the tears. "I'm sorry. This is a lot."

"Ach now, dearie, 'tis fine, 'tis fine. You wait here now." She left the reception room and walked down the hall toward the bedrooms. When she returned, she held a small wooden box. She lifted the lid, revealing a silver bracelet ensconced in a black velvet tomb. "This is for you."

"The bracelet you gave Ériu on her wedding day." I stared at the glimmering horseshoe and swallowed hard. It looked brand new.

"How did you know that? Never mind, it

doesn't matter." Her mouth dropped open. "The wee thing tucked this in my hand before I was to leave. She wanted you to have it. To know her."

I rubbed the horseshoe, and the sapphires, as dark as the ocean, warmed my fingers. "Thank you, Orlaith. Thank you for this and for telling me about Ériu."

"Aye. It is as it should be." She clucked her tongue and then poured another cup of tea.

S*AOIRSE*

"Could stand a lick of paint." Cillian O'Donnell shielded his blue eyes from the midday sun, looking at the peeling boards of the empty storefront with a keen gaze. He spoke to no one, yet everyone listened. He commanded an unerring eye and a quick mind.

His tattoos and half-shaved head declared a rebellious image, but his clothing contradicted that. He looked fine, dressed quietly in a close-fitting black turtleneck, straight-legged black trousers, and supple leather loafers.

Cillian was the silent one, charming when he wanted to be—hunger burned in his eyes and raged in his soul. A rage pent up for so long, one could only imagine what it did to the mind. The fact Cillian intended to stay in Ardara town bewildered me. I didn't know what to make of it.

Tadgh, shorter than his brothers and mack-truck-wide, shadowboxed with the Faeries and then threw a solid punch, nailing Cillian in the upper biceps.

"Are we doing this again?" Cillian didn't even flinch.

"Big match Saturday." Muscles rippling beneath an olive-green tank, he fancied back and forth in white high tops and ripped jeans—always smiling, always happy. He fancied me a little too much.

"Have you signed the lease, bro?" Pádraig rubbed the red bristles sprouting from his chin with his index finger and the fat pad of his thumb.

"Aye, moving in today." Cillian glanced at the gold watch on his wrist, the designer wristband glinting in the sunshine.

"What do ye mean? Does Mammy know?" Pádraig lifted his eyebrows, surprise in his eyes. He was his mother's son.

"What are your plans for it, Cillian?" Old Eamon sat on the bench outside the Black Horse, one hand resting on his shillelagh.

"Tattoo studio, Eamon." Cillian jingled a key ring in the air.

"A tattoo parlor? Aye. A nice addition to the town. What's the name of the place?" Eamon rose to his feet, taking slow steps forward. He tapped his stick on the dirty window and peered inside.

"How about the Black Rose?" I looked sideways, inspecting my work—today's special scrawled across the sandwich board in white chalk.

Colcannon Mash and Champ: the traditional dish of floury potatoes blended with butter and milk and a generous dose of kale, served with Irish sausages. Our very own Ulster Fry served in a cast-iron pan.

A hearty all-day breakfast consisting of Irish sausage, rashers of bacon, soda bread, and white pudding, all surrounding a yellow-faced egg garnished with vine-ripened tomatoes, would fill a hole in many an empty stomach.

"I was thinking something more like Body Art Tattoo & Design." Cillian's gaze bored into mine.

"Pure shite, mate. The Black Sheep Returneth Home. That's more like it, aye?" Tadgh grabbed the keychain from Cillian, tossing it high overhead.

"Whatever, man. It's great having you back."

Pádraig threw his broad shoulder toward Tadgh, knocking him off balance.

"Why don't ye put that energy behind a paintbrush?" Cillian caught the jangling ring with one hand.

"Painting? Jaysus, man. I'm no painter." Tadgh dropped onto the sidewalk, giving his brothers ten quick pushups, then popped onto his feet.

"Does Mammy know you're leaving home?" Pádraig said in a worried voice.

"Poker nights every Wednesday, aye? I'll bring the whisky." Tadgh gave him the thumbs up.

"Are you on the card this weekend, Tadgh?" I jostled the sandwich board again, positioning it perfectly on the sidewalk.

"Aye. I'll be there. How about a kiss for luck?" Tadgh shifted his stance and planted a quick peck on my cheek.

Since Ciarán disappeared, Tadgh O'Donnell had taken on the role of guardian angel, stepping in whenever I needed a shoulder to cry on.

I left the O'Donnell shenanigans behind and entered the pub. I smiled, breathing in the faint aroma of last night's dinner, and looked over the premises: the polished tables, the gleaming copper accents. I grabbed the broom from the closet, giving the stone floors one last sweep before the day began.

The door creaked, shaking me from my quiet reverie. I faced down two men, not from these parts.

"Are you Saoirse Dunne? The owner of this establishment?" A man dressed in a slim-fitting grey suit and a white-collared shirt peered over the rim of dark sunglasses.

The other man gave me a warm smile. He wore a red plaid sweater vest sandwiched between a white button-down shirt and a navy blue cardigan, cuffed chinos, and white tennis shoes. He forgot to wear socks.

"Yes, I am, and you are?" I relaxed my shoulders, composing myself. I focused my attention on his horn-rimmed glasses while taking note of the selection of colored pens in his cardigan's breast pocket.

"Sean. Sean Hamstead." Sweater-vest returned my smile, crinkles fanning from watery blue eyes. He handed me his card, which read Dr. Sean Hamstead, University of Oxford, Biologist. "I'm with Oxford. The University."

"And what are you? The bodyguard?" I glanced toward the grey suit, sensing trouble with a capital

T. He loomed over the Doc, black leather folio in hand.

"We understand a person named Calla Sweet stayed on these premises." He pinched the corner of a glossy photo of Calla's smiling face.

"Yes, she was here. She stayed two nights. Last week. Is there a problem?" I stared at a professional headshot of a different Calla—one who appeared to have stepped out of a Hollywood movie.

The suit gave nothing away. The Doc, on the other hand, shifted from foot to foot.

"Did she leave a forwarding address?" He took out a folded tissue, carefully unfolded it, and dabbed the corners of his eyes.

"No, I don't think so." The hairs on my nape rose. The mad scientist seemed too affable, and the suit breathed evil. There was no way I would dish out on my new friend—no way in hell.

"We would appreciate your cooperation." The suit placed the photo on the bar top and stabbed Calla's smiling face with his forefinger. "Where is she now?"

"Like I said. Calla Sweet checked out." I eyeballed the guy. Who did he think he was?

"What do you know about her? What was she doing here?" The Doc folded the tissue into a neat square and returned it to his breast pocket.

"She came, and she left. There's nothing to tell." I planted my hands on my hips, standing my ground.

The suit held my gaze.

"Did she happen to mention her plans? Where was she going next? Why she's visiting Ireland?" The Doc smoothed his flabby palm over Calla's photo.

"Hmm. What did you say you do?" I engaged him with a friendly smile.

"I am a specialist in DNA recovery. Evolutionary genetics. The reconstruction of extinct species." His watery eyes gleamed. His exuberance made my stomach heave.

"DNA?" My mouth dried.

"Ms. Sweet submitted a sample that showed extreme irregularities. We must find her and speak with her." He gazed lovingly at the glossy image.

"Are you talking about one of those ancestry kits?" I swept my hair behind my ear.

"Doctor Hamstead." The suit placed his hand on the doc's shoulder.

"Yes, exactly." He nodded.

"What does that mean? Irregularities?" I covered my mouth with my hand, my thoughts flying like a black cat on a broomstick.

"Ancient genomes were present. I'm sure you

understand the importance of this discovery. Perhaps the sample was compromised. Perhaps there was a glitch. Whatever the reason, further investigation is necessary. Where was Ms. Sweet going next?" The Doc looked over my shoulder, searching the corners of the pub.

"I have no idea what her plans were." I shook my head back and forth, willing them to leave.

"Do you have her contact information? A cell phone number? Did she pay by credit card?" The suit pressed forward, his stance threatening.

I considered my next move in that game of cat and mouse.

I thought of my friend and what I knew, what she had revealed in confidence, what she had just recently discovered. It wasn't hard to figure out how that happened. Calla arrived in Ireland with no friends or family. She had no idea she was not entirely human.

A DNA test would prove an unbelievable theory—that Faeries existed. I looked to the future and saw our little town swarmed with nut jobs of every kind. The notoriety would put Ardara on the map, not just for the Cup of Tae Festival.

Jaysus fecking Christ. That would ruin Calla's life.

"Let me have a look around. I might have

something." I turned toward the twirly-dex filled with yellow cards, flipped through Orlaith's recipes, and stopped at the letter S. "No. I'm sorry, we've nothing. It looks like she paid cash. If she comes this way again, I'll call you." I slammed it shut and sent it spinning.

"All we have is an email. It seems Ms. Sweet hasn't accessed the Internet in several days." The Doc searched for another tissue.

"Yes, well, the service is up and down. It's not very reliable." I picked up the Doc's card and slipped it into my pocket.

The hinges creaked, and the door swung open. Tadgh filled the frame, his shadow stretching across the stone floor. Behind him stood Cillian, straight-faced and scary in his own right.

I smiled with delight.

The suit didn't flinch. The Doctor took a step back.

"Is everything all right, Saoirse?" Tadgh's glance moved over the two men, his gaze resting on the suit.

"Aye. Aye. These yokes were just after leaving." I glanced at the suit, and my heart stopped.

"We'll be in touch, Ms. Dunne." He snapped the folio shut, curling his lips into a sneer. He seemed to gain inches, towering over the pallid doctor.

I held my ground, refusing to show any fear.

"Looks like you're finished here." Cillian's eyes held that fiery O'Donnell temper in check.

Tension hung in the air. It was steely and filled with a burning tang.

I could see where this was going.

"Doctor Hamstead, I'll reach out if Ms. Sweet returns." I weaved through the group of four, holding the door open.

"Thank you, dear. We'll speak again." The Doc's darting gaze changed from confused to penetrating. "Come along, Ramone."

A deep sense of dread quickly replaced the relief washing over me.

9

C*alla*

The aroma of rich leather filled my nostrils. The chrome gleamed, and the dark paint sparkled. I backed the sexy little coupe from the garage and sat idling in the courtyard.

I checked the rearview mirror for any sign of the mysterious little man but saw none. Since discovering the truth about my past, Seamus had made himself scarce, and his absence had me on edge. Questions plagued my mind. He had suggested my father wanted to meet me. Finvarra—if Orlaith's revelations were correct. I swallowed the lump forming in my throat. Meeting a Faerie King would mean exiting the mortal realm and entering another. Would it not?

I shifted gears, allowing the classic car to glide over the cobblestones, roll slowly down the long laneway, and enter the enchanted forest. The woodland bordering Dermot's property was a magical place filled with wonderful and horrible things, disconcerting and terrifying, and today proved no different.

The wind moaned, and time lost its grip. Daylight shifted into purple twilight. Mist appeared out of nowhere, weaving through the trees—long fingers seeking the dead. Haze crept in through the driver-side window, touched my face, and held my hands. I tightened my grip on the steering wheel.

Fluttering wings broke the silence as a trio of birds took to the sky. I debated punching the accelerator but faced the horror instead. I told myself that what I saw could not be real—a trick of the imagination—someone or something playing games with my mind.

I had laid among the soft ferns only yesterday, gazing at puffy white clouds accompanied by whispering winds and the singing stream.

But that was then.

Their voices prowled beneath my skin. An army of men, long dead, littered the scorched earth—soldiers from another time. The acrid scent of burnt flesh stung my nose. Tendrils of smoke clawed the sky.

My heart bled for all they had lost. I scanned the river banks for survivors but found none.

Carrion crows darkened the velvet skies. They descended, picking what remained of singed flesh and wasted bones. I forced my foot to engage the accelerator, propelling through the shadows of time. I hesitated at the stone bridge, unable to proceed. My hands trembled, and I reminded myself that the battle scene was imagined. And yet, the six decapitated heads impaled upon the stone spikes centuries ago whispered in unison, "O'Donnell Abú." Their resounding call to arms rose with the howling wind. "O'Donnell Abú." Their rallying cry rang through the greenwood.

I squeezed my eyelids shut, refusing to acknowledge the ghostly apparitions. When the car thumped over the last tumbled stone, I dared a glance over my shoulder at the verdant forest staring back. The mist had wandered away, and the sun blinded me.

When I pulled onto the road, I saw only the farm tractor hauling a load of turf. When I arrived at the crossroads, I sank deeper into the bucket seat, seeking the anonymity I had sought when landing at the airport.

And yet there I was, traveling to Donegal town,

obliging Colm O'Donnell his raincheck. I had dallied in front of the mirror. Black leggings or cropped blue jeans? The leggings won out, topped with the camel-colored canvas work shirt I had found hanging on Dermot Sweet's back porch. Washed and tumble-dried, the long shirt added an extra dimension to my simple wardrobe. I mused over Colm's anxious voice, insisting he pick me up.

My mind wandered with every twist and turn of the winding road. Somewhere along the way, I engaged the roof and drove through Ardara with the top down, the salt breeze taking away the last horrors.

Thoughts of him slammed into me—two encounters with that man, and I had lost myself completely. He had teased me and taken me to the brink of pleasure. Butterflies danced in my stomach, and bees hummed overhead. That was my kind of office gossip.

I pulled into Donegal town with my head on a swivel and found a parking spot in a public lot near the GPS location I had plugged into my phone. I slung my bag over my shoulder, hurried my steps, and realized I had arrived too early.

I stood on the sidewalk, admiring the quaint town. The cobblestone diamond intersecting the roadways surpassed Ardara's in terms of scale. Despite the absence of market vendors, the plaza was alive with chatter. People occupied every bench, engaging in lively conversation. I listened to the warm Irish lilt and smiled.

I left my imaginings behind and followed the sidewalk toward the castle looming in the distance —Donegal Castle, the O'Donnell's Castle. I recalled Colm's conversation. His ancestors had once resided within that fortress. I passed by the tearoom and the many cafes spilling onto the sidewalk. I pressed my face against a glass window and gazed at all the lovely tweed. I waited for the streetlight and crossed the road with a melee of other looky-loos. I walked beyond the gatehouse and peered through the iron rails, searching for a view of the castle grounds.

They had restored the Tower House to yesterday's grandeur with steep gables and bartizan turrets. The ruined English Manor house sat roofless, the stones blackened with empty mullions staring into a manicured yard.

The gatehouse beckoned, offering entry for a fee. I passed through the turnstile, lingering behind a group of children on a school field trip. Their guide explained how the site once housed a Viking fortress—later developed by Sir Hugh Roe O'Donnell, The O'Donnell of his clan and King of

Tyrconnell. He had built the O'Donnell castle on a bend in the River Eske, where sentries could guard against invaders approaching from Donegal Bay.

I followed the chattering group, taking in all the castle once was. Stunning gothic-style doors led underfoot across fifteenth-century cobblestones into a shadowed stone-and-mortar storeroom, where only half of the barreled stone ceilings remained. I hugged my chest, a shiver passing through me. Relics of the past stared back: barrels and baskets, crockery, stuffed fowl hanging on the walls.

I ran my fingers along the ship's mast, leaning against the ancient stones—the O'Donnells were called the Kings of the Fish. I studied the O'Donnell coat of arms, on display beside the Brooke coat of arms—the captain in the British forces awarded the castle for his service to the English. Hmm.

Spiral stone steps led to a banqueting hall with beamed ceilings and white plastered walls. The ornately carved Jacobean fireplace told a story of opulence and celebration. I climbed the wooden staircase to the great hall, where magnificent beams arched the ceilings and displays showcased the history of those ancient times.

I was drawn to the spiral staircase climbing the

corner turret, a series of uneven steps the brochure referred to as a trip staircase. My knees buckled as I envisioned the mighty O'Donnell, sword in hand, vanquishing the enemy foe on these same uneven steps. The arrow slits deep in the stones told of archers defending these lands. I left the castle breathless, yearning for more.

The expansive green lawn was crowded with tourists—I paid close attention to the schoolchildren's guide. Following the Battle of Kinsale, Red Hugh O'Donnell II, the young prince, set fire to his home lest the stronghold fall to the English.

I stumbled, landing on one knee, my hand resting on the manicured grass. Beneath the soft layer, something sharp jabbed into my palm.

A uniformed attendant who witnessed my mishap made his way toward me. I reached into the soil, closing my fingers around the culprit. A triangular spike the length of my palm glimmered in the soft light. My stomach flip-flopped, and an icy wave enveloped me. The whirring sound faded into nothingness, and time slipped away.

Black smoke drifted from the windows while flames licked the tower walls. Soldiers of war surged into the castle keep.

My throat closed, and my eyes stung. I witnessed the revenge of a young man, copper-haired and battle-

scarred. Filled with blood lust, he shouted orders to those under his command while the tower house burned.

Draped over his broad shoulder, a thickly woven Irish Brat, a fringe of silk threads layering the bottom edge. The hard-wearing cloak would keep a man alive on a frosty night or a woman warm beneath him. Through the heavy folds, the hilt of a short sword poked from a leather sheath, revealing his warrior status. He turned his head and looked into my eyes. When the smoke dissipated, he had vanished.

"Miss? Miss? Are you okay?" The attendant looked at me with worried eyes.

"I'm fine. Just fine. Thanks." I walked backward, away from his concerned gaze.

I had no memory of departing the castle grounds. Car horns honked, and brakes screeched as I ran across the busy road. I zigzagged through traffic with Red Hugh O'Donnell's ghostly image burned into the back of my eyelids.

I stood in the arched doorway of O'Donnell's Lair, a pub boasting gastronomic delights. I breathed through my nose, savoring the ancient scent of stone, beer, and hearty Irish fare. The pub provided a refuge for my unhinged mind. I navigated the dimly lit maze of aisles, pressing myself against the uneven stones as servers rushed past with platters held high overhead, oblivious to my searching gaze.

"Are you looking for me?" He rose from a wood-lined booth, his head grazing the lantern hanging from the timbered ceiling—a gentleman of noble ilk.

"I was." The bees hummed, and the butterflies danced. My mouth dried as I considered my present circumstance—a date with Colm O'Donnell, an actual date.

He ushered me into the dimly lit booth yet looked beyond me, casting his gaze into the dark corners of the long passageway.

"You look nice." I admired his cable-knit crew neck and dark tapered jeans. His copper locks shone in the yellow light.

"So do you." He grinned.

"Thanks. This belonged to Dermot. I thought I'd make use of it." I played with the caramel canvas.

"What's that?" He pointed at the spike clenched in my hand.

I dropped the pointed dagger onto the table, particles of dirt flying in every direction.

"I think it's an arrowhead. I, uh, found it at the castle. Well, I tripped and fell on it." The smile froze on my face. All I could see was the ghost of the bloodied young man.

"You went to the castle? Alone?" His gaze darted sideways, following a server down the aisle.

"I did. Why?" I brushed my hands together and let out an exasperated huff, swallowing the bitter aftertaste of fire and soot.

His expression softened as he picked up the arrowhead, brushing embedded dirt from the tapered shaft. "You're right. This is a bodkin arrowhead. It would punch through mail armor or the hide of an elk with no problem. I haven't seen an iron one in years."

"Huh, you can have it. It's giving me a headache." I pressed my hands against my temples, stilling the pulsing throb.

A serene silence filled the space between us when he moved his hand across the table and touched my fingertips. "I called you three times."

"Hmm...only one bar." I lifted my phone, gazing at the lack of data. "You're not worried about me, are you?"

"I could have picked you up and saved you the drive." He drew his thumb over mine.

"That's true." I moistened my lower lip. "But then, you would have to drive me home, allowing me to have my way with you." I batted my eyelashes. Pretending to be a regular person on a date with someone who wasn't a ghost was fun.

"Valid." He lifted my fingers, bending my knuckles to his lips. "And something I'm okay with."

"Hmm…I thought you were bent on driving me crazy." I referred to how he tantalized me. My thighs heated on the spot.

"Would you like to see the selections?" He chuckled and then passed the menu board to me.

"Sure. What would you recommend?" I scanned the listed entrees while Colm's gaze consumed me.

"Lady? What would you like?" The server, a burly man with a heavily accented voice, interrupted our romantic interlude.

"Water, please." I smiled into his broad face.

"Tap or sparkling?" He scribbled on his pad.

"Tap is fine. With ice, lots of ice." I grinned.

"Anything else?" He nodded at the menu.

"How are the oysters served?" I leaned against the high back of the booth, taking in the ambiance of the same castle design…stone floors, stone walls, and cross-hatched timbers beaming the ceiling.

"Raw." His eyes wide, he spat his answer.

I wondered what journey brought this man to O'Donnell's Lair.

"Yes, but what are they served with? Horse-radish? Mignonette?" I expected a response but received none.

"Lemon and a dash of hot sauce are all you'll likely find in these parts." Colm's textured locks caught the light, glowing every shade of gold. All I could think about was his soft lips brushing against mine.

"Sure, sounds great. I'll have the Gweebarra Bay oysters. Please and thank you." I nodded toward the server. I couldn't ignore the full-body quiver running from my toes to the top of my head.

The lights dimmed and then shut off, plunging us into shadowed darkness. Voices rose, and glass shattered before a generator kicked in, lighting up the aisles. Colm hadn't moved a muscle, unaffected by the surrounding pandemonium.

"And you?" The server remained where he was. He jutted his chin toward Colm.

"Fish and chips and a pint." He ordered, sending me a quiet smile.

The server turned his back and strutted away.

"How is this going to work, Colm? You and

me?" I wiggled on the bench seat, unable to ignore the heat striking my core.

"Let's eat, and then we'll talk. I need you healthy." His mouth quirked into a mischievous smile.

"Healthy? For what? Chopping down trees?" I considered my options. He knew more about me than any human alive. That thought made my heart thrum. Our lives had become so intertwined so quickly. Or were they? I studied him, wanting to believe his intentions were genuine. Was there more to that equation than met the eye?

"What is it?" He pinched his brows together, sensing my hesitation.

"I'm worried about Saoirse. She truly believes I can find Ciarán. I'm worried about you, too." Should I share my most recent vision with him, the young chieftain of the O'Donnell clan? The resemblance was uncanny—the set of his jaw, the copper locks swept back from his face. I rested my hands on the table's edge, deciding against it. How much crazy could one man cope with? I was a lot, too much for most, in a league of my own. I sighed through my nose.

"You don't need to worry about me, *mo grhá*." His voice sent fiery arrows straight for my heart.

"Am I a means to an end, Colm? Is that what I

am to you?" I popped the question, nagging my every thought. Why did I care? He made me hot. Was that not enough? I planted my palms onto the wooden table, freeing my mind of haunting concerns.

His silence sent needles of doubt prickling down my spine.

"No." He clasped my hands, dragging my elbows across the table until we were face-to-face.

"I'm not naïve. You've been all over me about Ciarán. About this whole 'Other Crowd,'" I whispered, my voice hollow. My stomach fluttered, and not in a good way. Finvarra's image floated through my mind. And what of the crazy visions? Some would have locked me up a long time ago.

"You don't believe Orlaith? That you're Finvarra's daughter. That you have sisters." He opened my palm, tracing the long lifeline. "Look at this vein, Calla. I do not doubt you're the glitterati." He circled the birthmark, marring the heel of my hand, a port wine blemish prowling under my skin.

"Trust me, O'Donnell, I bleed red just like you." How could I deny what I knew to be true? To say it out loud scared the shit out of me. What should I do with that knowledge? "It's not every day you find out you're 'not of this world.' Why are you looking at me like that? Like you've seen a ghost?"

He twined his fingers with mine. "What do you see when you look into my eyes? Do you see a scoundrel? A rogue? Please do not doubt my intentions, *mo grhá*. I would give anything to have Ciarán back. He's my brother. My blood. But if finding him meant losing you...that's not an acceptable option. Not now. Not ever." His voice hitched with an emotion he had never shared before.

I studied the bristles casting shadows over his chin, the jugular vein pulsating beneath the collar of his button-down shirt, and his eyes gleaming too bright.

"And seducing me? Is that part of your plan?" I heard the lunacy of my words and wondered if I was indeed mad, if somewhere between here and there, I had tipped over the edge, and he was fool enough to join the crazy train. I clamped my lips together, squashing the heated sensations racing over me. Why was I so attracted to him?

"Is this our first fight?" He played with my fingers, one at a time. His game had an unmistakably erotic undertone.

"You didn't answer my question." I planted my

fingers against his, opening his palm. His hand was so much bigger than mine.

"You've raised the bar. Visiting my dreams, holding me under your spell. I wonder sometimes if you are a witch. But then, when I look into your silvery eyes, I see the truth. I am a mere mortal. Could I ever be enough for you?" He closed his fingers, swallowing my hand.

"What do you want, Colm? Tell me the truth." My skin tingled from head to toe.

"I've told you, *mo grhá*. I want you, and only you." He leaned close, his breath tickling my ear. "Your sweet delight will be mine." The laughter returned to his voice, and the shadows walked away.

"My sweet delight? No one's ever said that before. You're quite the charmer, O'Donnell." My heart soared. My mouth watered.

"You're a greedy wench. You visit my dreams and take what you desire." He dropped his head and kissed my knuckles.

"I can touch you and not see the future." I shifted on the bench, imagining what my first time would be like. I gazed at his long, thick fingers, imagining what he had in store for me.

"You're wearing your mother's bracelet." He

didn't grasp my meaning. Instead, he turned my wrist.

"Look. Maybe this isn't such a good idea. All of this." I pulled away. "I don't 'connect' with other people. Not like this."

"But you have, Calla. How long have you been here? A week? You're part of the community. You belong. Even more than I do, it seems." His smile sent liquid heat fluttering over me.

The server placed our beverages before us and left behind napkin-wrapped cutlery.

"I don't know what you want from me." Playing dumb was not one of my strong suits, but I raised my eyebrows and gave it a go.

"Are you enjoying my company?" He stretched his long legs under the table.

"Maybe." I broke the seal, opened the napkin, and set out the utensils, refusing to commit.

"I want to be with you, Calla Rioghain Sweet, for the rest of my days." He said my given name with a full-on Irish lilt.

"Hmm, sounds like you're asking for another play date." That touching thing proved addictive. "Can I ask you a question?"

"Anything. My life is an open book, dog-eared and stained but always open." His grin touched my soul.

"Do you think Ciarán is with the Other Crowd?" I watched him through my eyelashes.

"It's a possibility. Ciarán was always one for the craic." He wrapped his hand around the back of his neck.

"How does that make you feel?" I whispered low so that he had to crane his neck to hear. I wanted the truth. I wanted him to think.

"What do you mean?" He shifted in his seat and flinched for the first time.

"You mourned him. Your family mourned him. Saoirse still mourns for him. What if he left voluntarily?" I bit into my lower lip and waited for his response.

"He might be trapped and unable to leave. If you believe the tales, those freed from the Otherworld soon fade away. The Faerie King keeps their souls." He teased me with a smile, but his eyes held sadness.

"Would you forgive him? If he did?" I refused to dive into that rabbit hole. God only knew what awaited me on the other side. The afterlife, perhaps? How often had the three horsemen come my way?

"He's my brother." His voice remained steady, yet the muscle tick in his jaw told me otherwise.

"I have one more question." Should I leave that one alone or go in for the kill? I grinned.

"Just one?" His gaze robbed me of courage. Not.

"Are you really a tree farmer?" I pressed him, delving into his personal life.

"Hmm." He drew his thumb between the cuff of my sleeve and my wrist, the gold flecks in his eyes deepening.

"The truth. The whole truth, and nothing but the truth." I drummed my fingers on the table.

"If I tell you, I might have to kill you." He covered my hand, stilling my tap dance.

"Really?" I grinned.

The lantern overhead flickered and then went out.

"Perhaps." His voice surrounded me.

"Perhaps?" My curiosity piqued. His past seemed shady and secretive.

The lights flickered and then sparked, bathing the booth in a golden glow.

"I do freelance work for the government." His face colored a delectable soft pink.

"The government?" The bench groaned as I sat back. "Whose government?"

"The Irish Republic. Dark ops," he murmured as if the world was listening.

My imagination fired in all directions.

"Dark Ops? Oh my God, are you a hitman?" I exclaimed in a loud voice.

"No." His matter-of-fact voice expected me to believe him.

"You're not going to tell me, are you?" I lifted his chin with my forefinger, holding his heart captive.

"I can't. I can tell you one thing, though. I'll be staying in Ireland for a while." He set his knife and fork on either side of his place setting.

"A while?" I ran my thumb over my bottom lip. That was a bombshell revelation.

"Here we are, folks." The server brought our order to us: Colm's fish and chips, my oysters served on the half shell, and a farl of dark and dense Irish Wheaten bread.

"Wow, that looks amazing." I reached for one of Colm's crispy fries. "I should have ordered some."

"Help yourself. I'm watching my figure." He slid half the fries onto a side plate.

"Your figure looks great. Have some oysters." I gestured toward the generous platter.

"I don't eat those things." He supped on his brew, watching me over the rim of his glass. His gaze told me one thing.

"They're an aphrodisiac." I bit down on my lower lip. Swallowing my hunger for that man became more impossible by the minute.

"My sex drive is one hundred and ten percent, and all appendages are operating at full capacity." He defended his virility.

"I love this bread." I slathered yellow butter on top of one thick slice. "Do you always hold your pinky finger in the air when you drink?" I slurped one oyster and washed it down with a hearty hunk of the moist and nutty bread.

"I guess I do." He chuckled.

"Is it a family trait?" I smothered the chips with ketchup.

"Can't say I've noticed." He peeled the crispy batter away from his fillet, leaving remnants piled on the side of his plate.

"What are you doing?" I wolfed down two ketchup-covered chips at a time.

"My brother, Hugh Jr., is on a mission." He parceled morsels of cod onto his fork. "He's on about 'healthy eating.' Low sodium. Low fat." He scooped another mouthful of naked fish into his mouth.

"You could have ordered the salad." I smiled with a vengeance.

"Not a fan of green things." He watched me impale two more of his fries.

"Are you eating that?" I pointed my fork toward the green mush on his plate.

"Want some?" He motioned with his fork.

"What does it taste like?" I studied his pained expression.

"Green peas." He smiled a crooked grin.

"And you don't eat them either? Don't tell me because they're green?"

"Tell me, how does this telepathy thing work? How do you do it?" He shrugged, offering me a spoonful.

"Not bad, kind of like mashed potatoes." I opened my mouth and teased my tastebuds with the savory condiment. I turned his question over in my mind. How did I do it? "I don't know. I've only encountered dream travel with you."

"Hmm." He chewed each morsel. "You agree with my demands, then. No other man will give you pleasure. You will 'visit' me alone?"

"I told you already, O'Donnell, you're not the boss of me." I twirled strands of my hair around my index finger.

"I will provide your pleasure." He lifted one eyebrow, a smile tweaking his lips.

"You're confident. I'll give you that. You made

me come. What once? Twice? Besides, assassins live a solitary life, don't they? A cash box stowed away in a Swiss bank, a stockpile of passports. Long-distance relationships don't work. Everyone knows that." I dabbed the corner of my mouth with the napkin.

"I am not an assassin." His gaze flowed over me, soothing and teasing all at the same time. "But yes, I work independently. I've given a lot of thought to moving back home."

"Moving? Why?" My thoughts scattered.

"My priorities have changed." He trailed his fingers over mine. He looked up, his gaze searching the dark hallway.

"You're freaking me out, Colm." I'd gone from solitary flyer to let's join the band. When did I become that girl?

"Anything else for you? Dessert?" The server stuck his head into our enclave.

Colm looked at me for a reply.

"No, thanks." I shook my head.

"We're good, mate, just the bill, please." Colm nodded.

"Let me." I pulled my wallet from my bag.

"No, this is my treat." He motioned, waving with his hands.

The server returned almost immediately,

handing Colm the check.

"I ate your lunch. Well, most of it." I lifted my eyebrows as he reached into his jeans.

"I insist." He plunked paper bills onto the table. "Shall we?" He extended his hand, guiding me into the aisle.

"Well, thank you, Mr. O'Donnell." I walked ahead with Colm in hot pursuit.

"Calla, wait." He touched my elbow as we reached the exit together. He stepped before me and opened the door, allowing the moody skies to enter O'Donnell's Lair.

"Wow! Would you look at that? Where has the day gone?" I stood on the sidewalk, my gaze straying toward the castle turrets. I swallowed hard, the vision of the young Red Hugh O'Donnell razing his home to the ground burning in my mind. "Thank you for lunch. It was enlightening, to say the least."

Colm

Convincing her to spend the day with me was one thing. But what of every other day and the nights in between? A woman of many talents, she enchanted those around her. Underestimating her wiles could prove foolhardy.

My intentions remained unchanged. Eamon tasked me with her safety, but he didn't have to. I was already there.

I sifted through the Chief's account, compartmentalizing pieces of information. The object of his investigation—an extremist with self-serving motives—a man who had amassed a cult following. Eamon said he had a source inside, but how deep had he infiltrated the man's organization? I chastised myself for not demanding more from the older man.

I had never considered the resurgence of paganism outside of Ireland. I reflected on the family rituals and festivals—key pagan gatherings: Yule, Samhain, Bealtaine, and many others. Those celebrations were a way of life. I considered the witch Saoirse, a practicing Wiccan, and many others like her. The problem lay not with the pagans but with one madman.

I imagined what such a man could do. And what of the missing lad in Malin Head? I considered the fantastic—what if the Faeries had stolen the lad and Hamstead's people abducted the changeling? It wasn't beyond consideration.

Talking about the Other Crowd was one thing; believing was another altogether. I stopped in my tracks, considering another facet of myth and lore, and followed Calla's gaze toward O'Donnell's castle. I could not deny my ancestors.

I accepted one thing. I was in too deep, and my judgment was impaired. Had I disclosed the true nature of my relationship with Calla, would that have changed the Chief's directive? One thing I could accept—I relied on another to safeguard the most crucial package in the world—the woman I love.

"Do you have plans this afternoon?" I cupped her elbow in my palm. My motives were utterly self-serving, which I wouldn't deny—the time for second-guessing had long passed. I made the only sane choice, the only one I could live with.

Her brazen confidence stirred my arousal, and yet our last encounter revealed her genuine innocence. I lost my breath along with her and focused on one thought and one thought only. I would be the man who made that vixen sing.

"What did you have in mind?" The corners of her lips lifted into a winning smile.

"How about a walk on the strand?" I offered my hand, yet she wavered, considering my offer.

"Sex on the beach? Is that where this is going?" Her gaze left the castle and returned to me.

"Do you know how to ride a horse?" I asked, even though I knew the answer. Snippets of Calla's younger life resurfaced in my mind. The deeper I dug, the more I learned. Calla's adoptive parents were well off and indulged their one and only child in every way possible. Raised on a rolling property in Ontario's Caledon Hills, Calla's love for horses blossomed into more than a passing fancy.

"The four-legged kind?" Her face bloomed like a rose.

"Yes." I hooked my hand around her elbow, escorting her toward my rental car.

"I love horses." She chewed her bottom lip.

"How about horseback riding on the strand?" My heart stirred. Pounding hooves over hard-packed sand? Her image flowed into my mind, her dark hair flying with the wind, her laughter ringing over the land.

"A pony ride on the beach?" Her voice sounded far away.

"Aye." I stopped on the sidewalk in front of the castle gates.

"Um, I don't know, Colm. I should grab my car. I could meet you." She stared at the castle, her eyes shining.

"I promise to return you to your vehicle." I glanced at the castle and the tourists swarming the gates, unsure what the cause of her distress might be. I held the passenger door open.

"Are you going to have your way with me, Colm O'Donnell? I've heard a lot about those dunes and the strand." She lifted her chin, inhaling the lavender-scented air freshener dangling from the mirror.

"I can't promise you won't meet my mam," I smirked, turning the key in the ignition.

"You're taking me to meet your mam? It's kind of soon, isn't it?" She twisted a dark curl behind her ear.

"You met her at the pub, Calla. Don't pretend you didn't." I grinned, my gaze finding hers.

"I met many people at the pub. Your family has horses?" She regarded me with an appraising eye. I found her enchanting.

"Aye. Irish Draught Horses. We keep a good breeding stock and offer stud services." My father's horses gave the family a sense of pride.

"Stud services?" Her eyes widened, and her interest peaked.

"Aye, the Irish Draught, when bred with a thoroughbred, produces some of the finest sports horses in all the world," I recalled my father and the hours he spent analyzing breeding records. I continued down the one-way and nosed into rush hour traffic.

"You must have a lot of property, then?" She looked confused.

"Aye, meadowland, coursing the sea." Gunning the motor, I left the town behind, following the familiar roads toward the coast.

"Yes, that's right. You live near the sea. I don't remember seeing horses. I remember little of anything. Jet lag, I guess." She rubbed her forehead and winced.

I gazed into those sparkling silver pools, sure of only one thing—I was a drowning man. Holding my head above water had become my only priority. Her presence overpowered everything and everyone. I couldn't stay away. I thought of nothing else. She was an illicit drug. Logical thought left me the day we met.

"Do you intend to answer the question?" Her braided locks tumbled like a waterfall over her shoulders. She rested her hands on her lap.

"Which one?" I drove leisurely through a tunnel of blue hydrangeas, followed by swaths of ragged robins dancing in the afternoon breeze, fingered petals blooming vibrant pink.

She looked away, extending her hand out the

open window, her beautiful face expressing pure wonder.

Calla had no idea that a madman hunts for her. I hid that information from her, thinking I could protect her from the danger. Glancing sideways, I questioned my decision. She was not a woman to be controlled. I couldn't keep her under lock and key or shadow her every move. I could try, but I would likely fail. I sighed inwardly. Protecting her meant sharing the brutal honesty of the situation. Leaving her in the dark was perilous and downright stupid. I would tell her—later.

"Here we are. This is Clonmara." At the end of a long driveway, a two-story white clapboard house sat on a cliff overlooking the sea—a surrounding patchwork of green meadows dove down steep banks onto the rocky shore below. I saw the rugged beauty through her eyes.

"Wow. This is amazing." She slammed the car door shut and left me, striding one step after another toward the horses grazing in one of the farthest pastures. She showed no trepidation.

I threw my hand over my eyes, blinded by the sunshine.

"They can be skittish, Calla. Be careful." I picked through piles of dung, following her silhouette through the green meadow.

The lead horse lifted his head, tossing his long mane. He flared his nostrils, inhaling her scent. Leaving his herd, he trotted toward her.

I watched, in awe, as she extended her hand, her palm radiating sunshine.

The horse cantered around her in a wide arc, stopped, and pawed the ground.

I swallowed hard, fear closing my throat.

The wind howled, lifting the sea. I turned, stunned by that wild force. The waves scraped the sky, fell, then rose again. But they were not waves. They were dark and dangerous and not of this world.

White horses, magnificent in stature, emerged from the turbulent froth, leaving their sea home and galloping one hundred strong. Thundering hooves. Whinnying screams. Beautiful beasts from the underworld circled their queen.

I rubbed my eyes, but the vision remained. I had seen nothing like it, not in my wildest dreams.

"Hello, big boy. What's your name?" She skimmed the stallion's brow with a feathered touch.

"He likes you," I whispered as the shadowy figures faded into the dark waters.

"Horses like me." The stallion lowered his head and nuzzled Calla's chest.

"This is Jack." I sidled up to her, my hands in my pockets. The stallion proved hard to handle, a challenge most days, yet the horse had loved my father.

"Jack? Well, hello, Jack. Aren't you a handsome fellow?" She stroked the crest of his powerful neck.

"Shall we tack up and explore the caves?" I searched the sky, estimating the remaining hours of daylight.

"The caves?" She expressed interest, her smile quick.

"Yes. Not far from here." I clucked my tongue at a white mare named Jezebel, who returned my call with a soft nicker.

Jack trailed behind Calla.

"I'm not wearing riding boots, Jack. You're going to be nice to me, okay?" Calla murmured in Jack's ear.

"Calla, this is James." I introduced our stable hand, a young boy from a neighboring parish. I pinned my lips into a tight line, inspecting the boy's bruised forehead—a conversation for later.

"Good day, miss." James nodded, moving like smoke between the two horses, slipping halters over their heads.

Jack didn't seem to mind.

"This is a beautiful property. Did you grow up here?" She gazed beyond the house toward the sea and then back toward me.

"It's called Clonmara, meaning meadow by the sea. That building there is the tack room." I gestured toward an old Irish clachan, a settlement of cottages in sight of the sea. The ancient stone buildings now served a different purpose.

"This is amazing." She brushed her hand over the tumbled stones. "When were these built?"

"Hundreds of years ago. Let's get you a helmet." I took her hand, leading her into the smaller stone building. "You're not afraid of spiders, are you?" I positioned my hand against the small of her back, noting her lower ribs, too pronounced through the canvas shirt.

"No, I'm not afraid of spiders." The gunmetal flecks in her eyes deepened to a molten shade.

"Calla?" I left my hand stationed on the rise of her butt, unwilling to let her go.

"I need you to kiss me, Colm." She turned, removing any distance between us, curling her fingers into my shirt as she had once before. She lifted her face, presenting her moist lips—more than a man could resist.

"Right now?" I stared into her eyes—starstruck. Would I ever get used to that feeling of helplessness? I pushed aside the absurd thought and buried my other hand into those snaking tendrils, cupping the nape of her neck.

"Yes. Right now." She slipped the tip of her tongue into my mouth, flicking the roof, tracing my tongue with hers.

When she arched her wee pussy into my swelling erection, I lost my mind. I swept my tongue between the sweet cleft of her lips, savoring her tender softness. Her scent overpowered my senses, nightshade, and black orchids. And something else—honey. My mind numbed, and my cock hardened instantly.

"I want you, O'Donnell. You've teased me enough." She shoved her foot between mine and kicked my legs apart, demanding a wider stance. And then shoved me downward, settling my butt onto one of the many saddle racks jutting from the tack room wall.

"This is a first. Do you do this often?" I planted my feet on the slab floor, anticipating the ride of my life.

She shimmied aboard, straddling my lap. Her intentions—crystal clear.

"There's a first time for everything, lover boy." The most adorable sigh escaped her lips.

A voice whispered, telling me to take what's

mine. I argued that only a fool would ravage such a sweet delight.

"Where did you get this shirt?" I ripped the placket open, revealing a lacy pink bra. Another flick unsnapped the front closure. Two circular globes surrounding rosy pink nubs spilled into my waiting palms. I swept my thumbs over the pebbled areola—my mouth watering for a taste.

"Do you like it?" She placed her hands over mine and squeezed the peaked darts. In a dream, that moment came back to me. We did that.

"You'd look beautiful in anything." I dragged my mouth along her nape, tasting her.

She rolled my hands over her breasts, her eyes closed, her lips half-parted.

From the courtyard, the horses whinnied. Wee James spoke to them in low tones.

"What did I tell you about your next orgasm?" I pinched her chin and closed my mouth over hers —Calla's need—my only priority. I intended to fulfill every one of them.

"You did this to me." She rocked against me, rubbing her clit over my hardened width.

The price I would pay to claim her here and now.

"Two more days, Calla. Bealtaine." I slid my

fingers beneath her waistband—the words I needed to say stuck in my throat.

"You want to hash this out right now?" Her sweet breath made my ears roar.

"Soon enough, I promise you." I sat deeper, friction building heat.

"Looky here, O'Donnell. Yeah. Oh, yeah. I'm gonna come." She bucked into me, grazing my cock with maddening thrusts.

"Calla." I swallowed her rising whimpers, my tongue drawn to those pointy canines. They seemed harmless enough. I suckled the length of her fluttering tongue—my lifeline. A tender kiss turned into an insatiable desire.

She plowed her fingers through my hair, her heart pounding with every swell of her breasts. Her thighs clenched as heat flooded her panties. She sagged into me, her breasts stabbing my chest.

"There. There. It's okay." I lifted her dark mane, twisting the wild strands between my fingers and gazing at heaven on earth. Her skin flushed pink, and her eyes glazed with lust.

"That was amazing." She popped off the saddle, fastened her brassiere, and snapped the buttons closed on her shirt. "I'm serious. It was good."

"I'm glad." My cock throbbed. My balls burned

for the woman—two more days. I would keep my promise.

"Okey dokey. Let's get this show on the road, shall we?" She turned her back, walking toward a shelf of various-sized riding helmets. She twisted her hair into one long braid and tried on one and then another.

"Sure. I'm just grand. Thanks for asking." I slid from the saddle rack, shifting my cock into a better place.

"Colm, are you all right?" She threw on a bucket helmet and smiled at me, her eyes shining bright.

"Brilliant, my queen." I bowed at the waist, extending my hand in a broad flourish.

"You're teasing me, aren't you?" she exclaimed, jumping up and wrapping her legs around my waist.

"What are you doing to me, Calla?" I held her close. Leaving Ireland and returning to my old life was seriously out of the question.

"The same thing you do to me." She held my face in her hands, then kissed me, her lips soft on mine.

My heart throbbed, the blood in my veins burning hot. She lied, that woman, her words twisting the other way around. She did that to me.

I closed the entrance door and threw the bolt.

Tasting her sweet delight would be my reward, and it would be enough. How long could a man play the teasing game?

I scooped Calla into my arms and laid her on the soft straw.

"What are you doing to me, O'Donnell?" She stretched her arms out, languishing.

Heat crackled between us.

"I will make you come, and this time, I'm going to taste you." I hooked my fingers under her waistband and pulled her leggings over her bottom.

A sweet honey scent wafted from her lacy undergarments.

I tossed those aside and gazed upon perfection. Her pussy glimmered, gossamer silk protecting her outer lips from abrasion.

My hard-on was instant. I itched to sink my cock between those soft folds and make Calla mine. Dropping on my hands, caging her beneath me, I whispered, "I'm going to lick your wee pussy. I'm going to suckle your wee clit. I will play with you, Faerie girl, and you will not come until I tell you. Do we have an agreement?"

"I can't stop it. It just happens." She shrugged.

"You are perfect, *mo grhá*, in every way." I

walked my fingers over her sweet folds and drew circles around her hooded clit.

"Oh. Oh." Her skin flushed with wet heat.

Her whimpers weakened my resolve.

"You can, and you will." I hooked my hands behind her knees, lifted her legs over my shoulders, and opened the gates of heaven.

"Oh, God." She peered at me through slitted lids, her long lashes resting on her cheekbones.

I separated the pink folds with the tip of my tongue, licking from the inside out, finding the softest flesh beneath. Deep licks that made her squirm.

"Oh. Oh. Oh." She rolled her hips, her eyes blazing with need.

I glided my hands over her perfect bottom, nibbling, pulling, and tugging her tender folds. When I pulled her clitoris into my mouth, her wee pussy spasmed with hot liquid heat.

"Yes. Oh, God. Yes." She fisted her palms, flexing her hips in response to my trailing tongue.

A man could lose his mind over a woman like her.

When I introduced the tip of one finger and then two, her belly tightened, and her skin rippled. Her whimpers were enough to make me lose my resolve.

"Do you like that?" I stroked her heated channel, curling my fingers until her breathing raged and her hips bucked.

"Uh-huh, I want to come." She squealed, calling the daemons to rise.

"No. Not yet." I drew circles with my tongue, flicking her wee clit from side to side. I swept my tongue through her soft folds, delighting in her soft moans. I paused, dropping soft kisses to her exquisite belly button.

"More. Oh God, I need you. Colm. I want you." She tossed her head back and forth.

Her heated gaze took me away from my task. She was more than beautiful, her hair in disarray and her cheeks flushed. She wet her bottom lip, causing me to lose concentration. I inched away, easing the pressure in my groin.

"I need to come." Her voice rasped.

"Soon." Soon, I would take her on one long, sensual ride.

"Now. Now, you don't play fair, O'Donnell." She bucked in rhythm with my gliding fingers.

I teased her flesh, pinching her clitoris between my teeth. When I suckled her burgeoning hood, her vagina tightened, clutching my fingers.

"Come for me, *mo grhá*." I stroked her slick heat faster with just the right amount of pressure.

Anticipating her orgasm made my cock pulsate. The beast throbbed, threatening to burst the zippered confines of my jeans.

"You make me hot, O'Donnell. So hot." Her eyes drifted open and closed, and a shudder rippled over her, the walls of her pussy clenching. I stroked her until she was replete. When her frenzy slowed, I withdrew my fingers and lifted her core to my lips, lapping and suckling her raw flesh, drinking up the last of her sweet nectar.

My hunger sated; I embraced her tightly and kissed the beads of sweat from her brow.

THE TWO HORSES stood beneath the canopy of a leafy oak tree, tacked up and hitched to a cedar rail. There was no sign of wee James.

"Can I give you a leg up?" I twined my fingers together, offering her a jump onto the horse's broad back.

She humored me, placing her foot in my cupped hands and taking the offered help.

She sat deep in the saddle, gazing down upon me, a smile lifting her luscious lips.

I adjusted her stirrups while Jack stood gallantly at attention as if he knew what precious cargo he carried.

Her eyes flashed, and a smile played on her lips.

I rested my hand on her calf, unable to resist touching her.

I mounted the white mare and, without further ado, leaned forward, giving Jack a firm slap on the buttocks.

Jack bolted toward the sea, his long stride sending Calla diving for the flying reins.

She regained her seat, as I knew she would, at ease with the big horse's rhythm.

The horses slowed, and we rode side by side across the rolling meadow to where a narrow chasm, a green gully blooming with pink and purple flowers, led us toward the sea.

White sand, flecked with black diamonds, glimmered in the sun. Towering cliffs embraced the cove, with jagged rock slabs pitching into rolling waves. In the faraway distance, tendrils of peat smoke wafted on a west wind.

Calla urged her horse into a full-on gallop, pulling up before the rising rock formations.

"What's this?" She dismounted with ease.

"These are the caves." I looped both sets of

reins over a protruding stack. "Would you like to explore?"

"Of course." She removed her shoes, leaving them on top of a rocky outcrop, rolled her pant legs over her knees, and then walked through the first tide pool, unaffected by the frigid temperature.

My heart jumped when I saw how far she had ventured into the narrow sea cave.

"Wow, this is cool. How far does it go?" She pressed her palms into the pitted wall, venturing knee-deep into the tidal basin.

"Be careful, it's slippery." I took one hesitant step, finding a foothold on bare rock.

"How many caves are there?" Her face glowed radiant in the reflective light. She seemed nonplussed by the colony of algae buffering the smooth surface.

"Fifteen. Depends on the tides. We're a little late for most." I scraped my toes on sharp dragon claws.

"Look, there's a crab." She stooped, studying the fast-moving crustacean. She hopped from one sloping rock to another, deeper and deeper into the cavern. "This is so cool." Her voice echoed from a faraway chamber.

"The last man who disappeared into this cave

never came out, Calla. I think it's time we leave." I called out, slipping and tearing my foot on a barbed rock.

"Really? We just got here." She appeared behind me.

I wondered how.

"You're lucky to have grown up in such a wonderful place." She scrunched her nose. "Not those bogs, though. I'm not a fan."

The waves crashed into the sand, rising higher with the coming tide, bringing the moss-covered outcrops to life. I dove for her hand, pulling her toward the light.

Jack whinnied, stamping his hooves.

"It's time to go, Calla. We can come another time if you'd like to explore." I clutched her wrist, urging her across the strand toward the rock stacks where the horses waited.

"No worries, O'Donnell." She rose onto her tiptoes, kissing the side of my cheek. Gathering Jack's reins, she leapt into the saddle. "Where to now?"

"I can show you the dunes." I rode my horse toward the low grassy hills abutting the strand.

"It's time you made love to me, O'Donnell. Don't you think you've teased me long enough?" She grinned.

"This is not the place." I gazed into her wild eyes, taken aback by the set of her chin.

"Look around you. The sun is shining. The bees are buzzing, and the world smells brand new. What could be more perfect?" She loosened her reins, giving Jack his lead.

Jack picked through the sand, stopping amidst the thick marram grass. A moth floated from one waving tendril to another, catching his attention.

"Did you bring a condom?" Calla slid from her horse, landing on both feet. She turned toward me, her fingers working the buttons of her shirt.

"No, Calla. Wait." I searched the distant landscape, the public parking lot at the end of the slat walkway. We were alone.

"That's okay." She dug into her pocket, offering a wrapped package. "Will it fit?" She bit her lower lip, looking at me.

"Are you blushing, Calla Sweet?" I inspected the condom. The heat dusting her cheeks confirmed my mounting suspicions.

"No." She patted her cheeks, then blew a warming breath in my direction.

The skies darkened, and black clouds coated the sun. A wind gusted, picking up the sea and washing the dunes with a salty spray.

The rising tide swept away any thought of ravaging her sweet delight.

"We should save this for another day." I stuffed the condom into my back pocket.

"What? Don't you want to?" She pouted her pretty lips, her arms glued to her sides.

Did I imagine the shadow of relief passing through her eyes?

"I want to, more than anything." I threaded my hand through her wild locks, clasping the back of her head and gazing into her silver eyes. What I would give to make her mine—right here, right now. I pressed my lips to the side of her face.

I sensed the temperature change. Once warm and soothing, the air shivered. Ice crystals formed and then shattered, blanketing the sand in a thick white layer—of snow.

The skies filled with a luminescent mist, a thick fog rolling over and turning into itself. A thunderbolt struck the rolling surf, followed by a resounding clap.

"Colm, something's happening. Do you feel it?" Her voice flowed through me, and her eyes glowed white-gold. She turned away, facing the unknown alone.

"Calla. No." I struggled to maintain my hold on her wrist.

The wind pressed against me, and shards of ice numbed my bones. I lunged forward, straining my elbows and every knuckle, realizing my worst fears.

The sky flashed electric blue.

Her essence lingered and faded, leaving only the memory of her soft touch and sing-song voice. She had vanished.

Winter's breath tore through me. An otherness, a cold rage, blinded my mind and left my limbs paralyzed.

My foe raised the tides, whipping the waters into a maelstrom. The waves lifted on command, pounding over me, throwing me face-first to the bottom of the sea.

I fought to break the surf, gagging on salty brine, only to find the sea floor again.

Anguished screams rose from the depths, the keening cries of lost souls. Voices called to me, familiar voices. The waves chased the ocean deep, and reality left me, oblivion extending its dark, cold hand, clenching my throat and dragging me under. Again. And again.

The ocean roar crashed one wave against another. Rippling, curling, and then retreating, the tides sucked the sand away from the land. The waves churned, and froth washed over me. I clawed the sand with shredded fingers, my jaw cracking on a rocky outcrop.

Her voice rang in my ears, an echo from a distant land—neither here nor there, but elsewhere. The emptiness in my chest told me she was gone. The quiet called to me. I had no fight left. Care left me long ago.

Laughter filled the air. Voices cajoled, whispering of happy times—throwing a ball on the strand, body surfing these same killer waves. My heart lifted, and light rained down.

"Colm, dear gods, mate. What are you doing out here?" The man's voice rang with familiarity.

Strong arms dragged me through the wash and lowered me onto the grassy dune. A voice soothed me.

The horses nickered, tossing their heads back and forth.

Sunlight streamed from the sky, searing my eyelids shut. I opened my mouth to speak, my throat burning with strangled breaths.

A man I had known forever, a man I had mourned, crouched before me.

"Can you ride, man? We have to get you home. You're concussed." Ciarán's piercing blue eyes questioned me. He held my head steady with one cool hand.

"Am I dead? Is this heaven?" I rasped, my mouth full of sand.

"Jeez, bro. Is that all you've got to say to a long-lost brother?" He lifted me onto my feet.

I lurched forward and then fell onto my knees. My vision blurred, my mind spinning with confusion.

Her sneakers, one tied to the other, floated in the wild surf.

Calla taken from me.

Ciarán returned.

"Calla." I stumbled and ran into the sea, screaming at the gods, but no one answered.

GUIDE TO NAMES & FOLKLORE

Names:

Breda — *BREE-da*
Ciarán — *KEER-awn*
Cillian — *KILL-ee-an*
Colm — *Coll-um*
Donn — *Done*
Éamon — *AY-mon*
Ériu — *AIR-eeu*
Finvarra — *fin-VAR-ah*
Maimeó — *MAM-oh* — grandmother
Oisín — *uh-SHEEN*
Orlaith — *OR-la*

Pádraig — *PAW-rig*
Rioghain — *REE-in*
Saoirse — *SEER-sha*
Séamus — *SHAY-mus*
Tadhg — *Tige*

Terms & Folklore

- **Aos Sí** — *ees SHEE* — supernatural race; people of the fairy mounds

- **Bean Feasa** — *ban FASS-a* — woman of knowledge / walker between worlds

- **Bean Sídhe** — *ban SHEE* — woman of the sidhe; a spirit who announces death

- **Clonmara** — *clon-MAR-a* — meadow by the sea

- **Donegal** — *DUN-ee-gawl*

- **Faerie Rath—Rath** — *rah* — fairy fort / ringfort

- **Féth Fiada** — *fay fee-AH-da* — magical mist or enchantment

- **Fomorian** — *foe-MOR-ee-an*

- **Is tú mo rogha** — *iss too muh ROE-a* — you are my choice

- **Leannán Sídhe** — *LAN-awn SHEE* — fairy lover

- **Mo ghrá** — *muh GRAW* — my love

- **Na Daoine Maithe** — *na DEE-na MAH-ha* — the Good People

- **Seanchai / Shanachie** — *SHAN-a-kee* — storyteller

- **Shillelagh** — *shil-AY-lee* — wooden walking stick or club

- **Sídhe** — *SHEE* — fairy mounds

- **Sláinte** — *SLAWN-cha* — cheers / good health

- **Sluagh Sídhe** — *SLOO-ah SHEE* — the fairy host

- **Tuatha Dé Danann** — *TOO-ah day DAN-an* — the People of Danu

Hey there, lovely reader,

Step into the enchanting Faerie realm and follow the bees as Calla and Colm's extraordinary journey unfolds! Their adventure is just getting started, full of magic, mystery, and unexpected dangers.

I'm thrilled to announce that Resurrection, the second book in the Beyond the Faerie Rath series, is coming soon! Get ready for more spellbinding twists, surprises you won't see coming, and a deeper dive into the magic that binds their worlds together.

Stay tuned—the bees have so much more to reveal!

With all my best,

Hanna

P.S. Turn the page for an exclusive sneak peek!

HANNA PARK
RESURRECTION
A BEYOND THE FAERIE RATH NOVEL

SNEAK PEEK

alla

Fog clung to the earth, drifting in a circular formation, shielding me from whatever dangers lived within the dark wood. I lifted my hand and extended my fingers. The mist responded, flowing backward, then drifting closer, playing a game of cat and mouse. The haar lived and breathed and had a purpose. The life breath of a being unknown within the mortal realm, called upon to collect and bring me here, to this unknown land, this Otherworld, the one the Irish whispered of in hushed tones.

I scoured the darkness for any entity accountable and found none, neither ghostly nor human. I was alone, and yet I was not.

I stared upward into a lacy green veil, tried to piece together the last few moments, and came to one conclusion—this was a different Ireland, untouched by the hand of man, by civilization. Lush ferns captured the forest's spirit, and emerald fronds wafted in a still breeze. Red squirrels chittered overhead, leaping from one gnarled branch to another, rustling the broad leaf canopy.

Colm—the copper-haired Celt who had promised me forever. His fingertips leaving mine were the last thing I remembered.

The sky shivered, and thunderbolts had struck the sea. Ice pellets shot down, and balls of hail battered the sand, striking everything in its path.

I turned away from Colm's anguish, from his love. A greater force had called to me, and I was helpless against it. No, that was a lie. I wanted to know. I needed to know. Who I was. What I was.

The haar wrapped me in warmth and swallowed me whole, the whorling sea giving me up to the sky. The needle bounced out of the groove and, everywhere, became elsewhere. One moment I was grounded—the next, I found myself thrown into a sparkling abyss, like a fly caught on a gust of wind. I had fallen from the sky, landing in superhero fashion—crouched on my heels, fists flailing. How far I had traveled, I could not say—this place was that and so much more. The aroma hit me first—damp earth touched by a faraway sea.

I stood, taking stock of my current condition, running my hands over my bones and finding none broken. My leggings had ripped at the knees. I gazed at my bare feet, toes curling into the soft earth. The oversized caramel-colored work shirt had held up. My silver link bracelet—still dangling from my wrist, not a single sapphire out of place from the dangling horseshoe. But where were my shoes? I ran my fingers through my hair, trying to tame the Kraken, realizing I had lost my hair scrunchie, leaving me no choice but to let my hair fall naturally, untamed in all its snake-like glory.

When I was young, I would chase the wind, leaping into the air and relishing the sensation of flight. Arms outstretched, I would soar high above the tall grass, unafraid of where I might land. I would lie on my back, lost in the rolling skies, at one with the universe. The earth would whisper, and I would listen.

What happened on the strand in Ardara brought back those same sensations.

My gaze followed the moving shadows and the stray sunbeam illuminating a man in its path. Dressed in soft leathers, with an archer's bow slung over his broad shoulders, stood a man—Finvarra, the King of the Faeries.

I rubbed my eyes and looked again. He was the man from Ériu's vision—my biological mother, the Princess of the Dead. The thought of opening that door filled me with dread.

I held my head high, anticipating the moment our paths would cross. This meeting was inevitable. Orlaith had confirmed the impossible —this immortal being was my natural father. Was it only yesterday that the older woman served tea to Colm and me in her sister's flat in Dublin and, in no uncertain terms, revealed the truth? I had sisters. I was the progeny of a Faerie King.

He stood taller than any mortal man, thick-limbed and broad-shouldered. His nose was straight, and his lips were full. But his eyes— nothing could prepare me for those. Shimmering silver streams circled dark pupils of a crushed velvet hue. Banded in smoke and framed by long lashes, those lustrous orbs held me captive.

His jet-black hair swept away from his face with a leather thong, revealing the sharp, chiseled features of a respected king. A golden diadem adorned with blood-red rubies rested upon his regal head.

I folded my arms across my chest and swallowed the rock lodged in my throat.

"Rioghain, may I have a word?" He called me by my middle name, Ree-an, his golden voice piercing the silence. Even the squirrels listened—they sat at attention, twitching their tufted ears, awaiting his royal command. Leaving the footpath, he joined me among the ferns and, with a slight bow, presented himself. He seemed ageless.

I found myself caught in his silver-eyed gaze. I wanted to laugh and cry at the same time. He should be dead if he ever existed at all: myth, legend, the Faerie Folk. This Other Crowd, this Otherworld the Irish whispered of, existed. I recalled the words of a believer—what is faith but belief in the unseen?

Thank you for following Calla and Colm on their journey into the faerie realm in The Scald Crow, the first book in the Beyond the Faerie Rath Series.

If you enjoyed exploring the magic, mystery, and danger of Ireland's hidden worlds, I'd love to hear your thoughts!

Your review helps other readers find their way to The Scald Crow and means the world to me as I continue crafting the series. Whether a few words or a full reflection, your voice makes a difference.

Thank you for being part of this adventure!

Hanna

ABOUT THE AUTHOR

Awards:

Mary Christmas, a Steamy Small-town Romance.

N.N. Light's Book Heaven 2024 Book Awards
First Place for Best Holiday Romance

Unwrapped in Roros

Passionate Ink - 2023 Passionate Plume - Finalist

Finding Tiegan

American Book Fest Awards 2023
Winner - Romance Erotica.
Paranormal Romance Guild
Second Place 2022 Reviewer &
Reader Choice Award
Contemporary Romance Writers
Stiletto Contest Winner 2022
N.N. Lights Book Award 2021.
Best Erotic Romance

Sorrento Seduction

Passionate Ink - 2022 Passionate Plume - Finalist

N.N. Lights Book Award 2022 - Finalist

Hanna's Story:

I began my writing career in the pre-dawn of a winter morning while my husband snored like a train. We could call my husband the catalyst. If not for him, I would never have gone to the kitchen to make coffee, feed the cat, and sit on the loveseat in front of the fire. In those moments of wondrous quiet, it was there that I did something I had never thought possible. I opened my laptop, and while the coffee went cold, I wrote a story. My husband had no idea that these sojourns to the loveseat in front of the fire would become a daily occurrence, that writing would become an obsession, but the cat knew. She knows everything.

I write stories that make you laugh, make you cry, and make you love. Thank you, friends, for reading!

In the beginning, there was an empty page.

I am a writer who lives in Muskoka, Canada, with a husband who snores, a hungry cat, and an almost perfect canine––he's an adorable little shit.

Visit Hanna Park at
https://www.hannapark.ca

facebook.com/hannaparkwrites
instagram.com/hannaparkwrites

ALSO BY HANNA PARK

Novels

Finding Tiegan

Novellas

Mary Christmas

Sorrento Seduction

Unwrapped in Roros

ACKNOWLEDGMENTS

My heartfelt gratitude goes to my family, who support my writing obsession with humor and grace, and to my editor, Judi Mobley, who whips my words into shape.

Hanna's Awards
    2024 N.N. Light's Book Heaven - Winner
    2024 Heart's Award - Finalist
    2024 Passionate Plume - Finalist
    2023 American Fiction Awards - Winner
    2023 Passionate Plume - Finalist
    2022 Stiletto Contest - Winner
    2022 Paranormal Romance Writers Guild
    2021 NN Light Book Award -Winner